THE VIDEO TAPE

BRIAN O'SULLIVAN

This is a work of fiction. Names, characters, places, and incidents either are the product of the author's imagination or are used in a fictitious manner. Any resemblance to actual persons, living or dead, events, or locales is merely coincidental.

THE VIDEO TAPE

Copyright @2025 **Brian O'Sullivan**

All rights reserved.

ISBN: 9798289780201

Published by **Big B Publishing**

San Francisco, CA

No parts of this publication may be reproduced, stored in a retrieval system, or transmitted in any form or by any means, electronic, mechanical, photocopying, recording, or otherwise, without the prior written permission to the copyright owner.

This book is sold subject to the condition that it shall not, by way of trade or otherwise, be lent, resold, hired out, or otherwise circulated without the publisher's prior consent in any form of binding or cover other than that in which it is published and without a similar condition including this condition being imposed on the subsequent purchaser. Under no circumstances may any part of the book be photocopied for resale.

❀ Created with Vellum

DEDICATION

*Rule #1 of **Dedication Club** is that you can't do the same dedication twice. Screw that!*

*This book is dedicated to the **Psychological Thriller Readers** Facebook group —again.*

You guys—and mostly gals—have changed my life!

TRIGGER WARNING:

*If you like good thrillers, you might be up all night reading THE VIDEO TAPE,
and lack of sleep may cause irritability :)*

You've been warned!

❧ I ❧

BOBBY MCGOWAN

I watched the videotape for a fifth successive time.

Ten minutes earlier, I'd been ready to walk out the door, but now I was transfixed by what I was looking at, despite not knowing exactly what it was.

Was it a low-quality B-movie? A snuff film? A bad joke?

The not knowing kept me rewinding it repeatedly, and prompted me to want to take the case. I'd done the world's quickest one-eighty.

"I'm intrigued," I said. "But you do know that I'm not a cop or a private investigator, right?"

"That's exactly why I wanted to hire you, Bobby," the man said. "Dozens of cops and several PIs have looked at this video and none have ever come close to solving this riddle, this case, this enigma—whatever you want to call it. So the fact that you're an outsider is actually a good thing. And don't play coy with me. I know you found your mother's killer by initially looking at a photo album. You're well equipped to handle a case like this."

My argument that I wasn't a cop or a PI had fallen on deaf ears.

"So, when would I start?" I asked.

"You already have."

And just like that, I was working a new case.

"Do you want to talk about compensation?" Ernest Riley looked to be in his early eighties, but gave off the vibe of someone a few decades younger. His silver hair was combed from left to right, and there was a discernible part that the comb left. I'd bet Ernest had been parting his hair like this for a long time. There was a certain panache in which it was parted that told me he'd perfected it over the years.

"Sure, we can do that," I said.

"But it's not going to change your mind one way or the other?"

"Something like that."

"This is easier than I expected," Ernest said.

"You were either going to get a hard no or a hard yes. There wasn't going to be much waffling on my end."

Which wasn't exactly the truth. I had gone from a *no* to a *yes* in minutes, after all.

"When I was doing my research, I'd heard that about you. It's surprising because you seem like such a nice guy in person."

"I don't think those two are incompatible. I am a nice guy. It's just if I have something in my sights, I go after it."

"Like your mother's killer?" he asked.

"Yes."

"And the Annie Ryan case?"

"Yes."

"Both impressive feats."

"Thank you."

"Okay, let's get a few things out of the way. I can give you a copy of the videotape that we just watched, but the original is still in the possession of the Los Angeles Police Department."

"That's fine."

"I also have an old-school VCR I'll give to you. I'm assuming you don't have one."

"I do not."

"I'll give you a DVD of it as well."

"Great."

"And there's one more thing I will give you: your space. If you want to report something back, great. If not, I'll kind of let you do your thing."

"I work better that way."

"Good, because the LAPD probably aren't going to help you out much."

"Not that I really care, but why is that?"

"Because this videotape has been in their possession since 1995 and has

THE VIDEO TAPE

never led anywhere. They've never even definitively told me whether the video contains a real murder or not."

"Can I ask how you came into possession of the videotape?"

"It was the summer of 1995, and I hosted a garage sale. Well, our entire block was hosting one. I lived on Collier Court here in Los Angeles, and ten families were living there at the time. We held a block garage sale. It was packed with people. Probably a few hundred people came through throughout the day. It may be hard to believe now, but garage sales were all the rage back in the nineties. When we finally closed up shop at dusk that evening, there was this videotape that was not one I'd put out there. It wasn't labeled, and all of mine were labeled. I'm a very organized person. You'll learn that about me. Intrigued by the videotape, I put it in my VCR at home and was shocked at what I saw. I hand-delivered it to the LAPD that next morning."

"And you're sure it didn't come from your house."

"Bobby, in 1995, I was a widower and my lone child was living in Italy. I can promise you there were no videotapes like this in my house. I had about thirty VHS tapes, all classics like *Jaws*, *The Godfather*, and *Chinatown*. Movies like that. Not this filth." He pointed toward the old-school VCR that had played the videotape.

"Okay. Had your child been back visiting?"

"No. And by the way, my lone child is a daughter. If you think a woman could have done this, maybe you're not the right man for the job."

"I wasn't suggesting anything about your daughter, and I agree, this was almost certainly a man who did this. The way they move and use the knife makes me think it's a male."

I told myself not to bring up Ernest's daughter again. He was pretty touchy about it.

"I'm sorry. It's just that when I first turned in the videotape to the LAPD, they had a million questions about me and my daughter and it pissed me off."

"I don't blame you. Is there anything else you can tell me about the video?"

"No, but I have someone I'd like you to meet. I'm eighty-two and my memory isn't what it once was."

"You seem to be doing pretty good to me."

"Thank you. I'm doing well enough, but I forget details about the case."

"After thirty years, that would happen to anyone, but okay. Who would you like me to meet?"

"His name is Noble Dunn, and he is a retired LAPD police officer. I've written down his address and he's expecting you today."

He handed me a piece of paper.

"Today?"

"Don't worry, he lives close. I'm not sending you on a wild goose chase through Los Angeles."

I smiled. "Good. Did Mr. Dunn work the case?"

"Yes. It sometimes felt like he was the only one in the entire Los Angeles Police Department who gave a shit."

"Sounds like a stand-up guy."

"He is. However, I should warn you about something before you meet him because it can be pretty alarming."

"What is it?"

"He and some psychopath had a life-or-death struggle, and Noble has a nasty knife wound down the whole left side of his face. It goes from his forehead to the bottom of his neck. It's jarring, so I'll let you know beforehand."

"Okay. Thanks, Ernest. You said it was a fight to the death?"

"It was. Luckily, Noble is still around to talk about it."

I MET NOBLE DUNN LESS THAN TEN MINUTES LATER.

Ernest Riley had been right, and Noble lived a mere five minutes from him, which came as a pleasant surprise. Although I hadn't lived in Los Angeles that long, I'd already had numerous examples of people telling me something was fifteen minutes away. Then, thirty minutes later, I'm still stuck in traffic on the 405 or the 10 freeways, cursing them from my car.

And yes, I'd already become accustomed to the Los Angeles tradition of putting "the" before the name of the freeways.

Ernest had been right about another thing as well. Noble Dunn's scar was shocking to see in person. I'd have been subtle about it if I hadn't been forewarned, but I'm glad I had been.

"You must be Bobby McGowan. I'm Noble Dunn."

"Nice to meet you, Mr. Dunn."

He escorted me into the house, and we sat at a kitchen table mere feet from the front door.

"Call me Noble. No need for last names."

"I feel the same way. Call me Bobby."

THE VIDEO TAPE

Noble was a black man in his mid-fifties with a bit of a gut. He had salt-and-pepper hair and wire-rimmed glasses.

He escorted me to a kitchen table, and we took seats across from each other.

"How did you get along with Ernest?" he asked.

"I liked him. He said he forgets some things, but seemed sharp as a tack to me."

"Don't let old Ernest fool you. He's all there. He's sharper than your average tack."

"I'll keep that in mind. He told me how he came upon the videotape. Do you believe him?"

"I do. I believe everything that Ernest has told me over the years. I've been dealing with him off and on for three decades, and he's never lied to me. At least, not that I know of."

"So you think someone really came to a garage sale, and just left a videotape of someone being killed?"

"First off, we don't 100% know that someone was killed. The LAPD had many experts look at it, and most people thought it was likely the real thing, but there were differing viewpoints."

"Some people thought it was a fake?"

"Yes."

"What do you think?"

"I'm convinced it's real. And as for the garage sale, I know it sounds like a wild story, but yes, I believe Ernest."

"How could a woman just go missing? I mean, you do see her eyes and a part of her face in the video."

"Remember, this is 1995. There isn't much of an internet. Not many cell phones to speak of. It's not like we could get her picture out to the masses. And honestly, maybe this is the LAPD's fault, but when the internet started to become big ten years later, that case wasn't exactly on our radar anymore. And yes, you see her eyes, but that would be a tough ID to make unless you knew her well. The killer did that intentionally, I'm sure."

"No question. However, I still think a parent or a good friend would recognize her."

"Maybe, but if this was a runaway or someone living on the streets, then maybe their parents were no longer looking for her. Maybe she was from the Midwest and came to Hollywood years ago, only to get swallowed up by it."

"So I'm to assume it's not someone born here."

"If a girl had gone missing from a local high school or college, we'd have known about it and tried to match the eyes. This wasn't a girl who was missed by many. That's sad, but I'm pretty sure it's true."

I wasn't sure if I said "Ugh" or just thought it.

"This isn't going to be some fun case, Bobby. You won't cross the finish line and triumphantly throw your hands in the air. You might not pass the finish line at all."

"It's a good thing I already agreed to take this case."

Noble let out a slight smirk. "Sorry. Just telling you what's in store for you."

"I get it. Now, back to the actual case. Ernest told me he was a widower and lived alone."

"That's right. His wife died of ovarian cancer in her forties. And his daughter Lily was studying abroad in Italy in 1995. Trust me, it would have been easier for us if Ernest Riley had somehow been involved, but I can assure you he wasn't. I believe that with every bone in my body."

"I know I'm brand new to this case, but I felt he was also candid with me."

"Ernest being earnest," Noble said.

I laughed. "Good one. Have you used it before?"

He smiled. "Once or twice. Good catch, Bobby. Maybe they were right about you."

"They?"

"When Ernest came to me, telling me he wanted to hire another private investigator, I asked around. And your name came up a few times. I was surprised to find out you weren't a licensed private investigator, but what does that matter? You have accomplished things, including catching your mother's killer. Achievements will always matter more to me than a piece of paper."

"Thanks."

"I just call it like I see it."

"Is the LAPD still actively working this case?"

"When I retired from the LAPD a few years back, I knew they were pretty much done investigating the videotape. That's what everyone called it—just the videotape. Our higher-ups didn't like us calling it a snuff film because they'd never officially confirmed that it was one. Plus, the phrase 'snuff film' brings a lot of unwanted attention. So we always just referred to it as the videotape. It was one of the few cases I couldn't put behind me when I retired. It still nagged at me. So when Ernest called a few weeks back and said he'd like to give it one last try, I said I'd help him. And that's

THE VIDEO TAPE

when I did my own research, and after a week or so, I told him I'd recommend giving you a chance."

"One last chance," I said.

"You don't miss out on much, do you?"

"I try not to."

"I'm guessing Ernest didn't tell you, but he is dying. He has stage four cancer."

"How long does he have?"

"If he makes it six months, that would be a surprise."

"That's terrible."

"He's a great guy, and I'll miss him dearly when he goes."

"If the LAPD didn't solve this in thirty years, what possible chance do I have to solve this in six months?"

"How long did the Santa Barbara PD have your mother's case? You solved that."

"You weren't lying. You did do your research."

"I wasn't going to have Ernest hire some knucklehead."

"Well, I'm honored you two have decided to go with me. I'll give it everything I can."

"I believe you will. Do you have any other questions while you've got me here?"

"When Ernest first came to the LAPD with the videotape, were his neighbors checked out? He said that most of them attended and had their respective garage sales."

"If you'd made a snuff film, why would you leave it at a neighbor's garage sale? Why not just destroy it?"

"I get your point, but I was thinking along a different line."

"Like what?"

"What if the videotape had come into someone else's hands—someone not involved in the actual killing? Maybe they didn't want to turn it into the police themselves. If they intentionally left it at a garage sale, they'd have to assume it would find its way to the cops, and they wouldn't have to answer any questions of how it came into their possession."

"Interesting. It's not a bad theory. And to answer your earlier question, they interviewed all the neighbors."

"Do you have that information?"

"I did you one better. I've printed up two police reports about the videotape. I have the original and a more recent one from a few years ago. Sadly, they aren't much different, since we never even had so much as a suspect."

BRIAN O'SULLIVAN

Noble handed me the police reports.

"But maybe you'll find something we missed," he added.

"Let's hope."

Noble stood, so I did as well.

"Good luck, Bobby."

"Thanks for everything."

"If you need any help, I'm only a phone call away. Maybe you're the guy we've needed all these years."

"No pressure, right?"

Noble smiled, and we said our goodbyes.

෴

I ARRIVED HOME AND WATCHED THE VIDEOTAPE FOUR MORE TIMES.

Ernest had given me an old-school Panasonic VCR from the 1990s. It's what I was probably watching my very first few movies with—maybe *Toy Story*, *The Wizard of Oz*, *E.T.*, movies like that.

This was not that type of movie. Not by a long shot.

It was the most brutal—and mysterious—thing I'd ever watched. I felt like a fever dream. I knew what I was watching had taken place, but it felt otherworldly. That's the only way I can describe it.

It begins with a woman in a white dress standing in the middle of an octagon-shaped room. No, more like an atrium.

She flips her long, blond, straight hair over her shoulder. The shot is very cinematic.

She is wearing a purple scarf that covers most of her face, but you can see her eyes. That's about it.

We focus on her standing there for approximately ten seconds. You don't yet know that the woman will soon be in duress, but it's still very ominous.

The woman is white and has translucent skin, as if she hadn't seen the sun in weeks.

She turns around and looks behind her, and then we see someone else for the first time. They are much bigger than the woman, and they're wearing an armored mask, something seen in medieval times. None of the face is visible, but I assume it's a male. He approaches her, carrying a three-foot-long, samurai-type sword.

The man circles the woman a few times, making it excruciating to watch. The woman, still covered in the scarf, appears to raise her

THE VIDEO TAPE

eyebrows. It's almost like this is something new—something has gone off script.

I wonder if she was brought to this room under false pretenses. Maybe she thought they were filming a movie, and now she realizes it may be the worst kind of movie of all.

Yes, I was completely guessing.

She looks like she's about to scream when the man, in a shockingly quick move, darts toward her and stabs her through the chest. The woman falls to the ground, and the dress immediately fills with blood.

If this is somehow a fake, it's a damn convincing one. Everything about it looks real.

Her scarf still covers her face, but her eyes begin to water. She reaches for her chest, but you can tell she's under duress and struggling to move. The blood starts to overtake more of her dress.

She looks up, and the man has made his way over and is now standing above her. He raises the sword over his head.

He stays in that pose for several seconds, making it almost unbearable to watch.

Finally, the man brings the sword down toward the woman's neck.

Right before the sword is sure to decapitate her, the video shuts off.

❧

COULD THE VIDEO BE A WELL-EDITED SCENE FROM A STUDENT FILM?

Maybe.

Could the video just be a prank, someone hoping to get a reaction from people like me?

Maybe.

But something told me it was neither of these things.

Everything in my wherewithal was telling me this was real.

It also told me to run as far away from this case as possible.

Tell Ernest Riley thanks, but no thanks, and be on my merry way.

But that wasn't going to happen.

I'd seen that woman's eyes, and it's not something I would soon forget.

I wasn't going anywhere.

꧁ 2 ꧂

I noticed something on the twentieth viewing of the videotape—give or take.

When the sword is swung down toward her head, the woman ever so slightly swivels her hips, and for a split second, you can see the tag of her dress. I was staring at the videotape, and even though I paused it, I still couldn't be sure. The tag I thought I was seeing was white, and so was the dress, and maybe it was just part of the dress. I couldn't be sure.

But maybe an expert could.

⁂

An hour later, I was at a business in Santa Monica called Swish's Photo and Video.

I'd done a quick Google search, and they had excellent reviews and seemed to specialize in what I was looking for—or at least, the general ballpark. It's not like I could just google "what's the best business at reviewing a videotape to judge if it might be a snuff film."

I was greeted by Swish himself, a man around fifty with a large tattoo on his right forearm. I recognized it as a Marine Corps tattoo.

"How can I help you? I'm Swish, and yes, this is my place."

I wondered if that's how he greeted everyone who entered his store—probably a good strategy. People would assume they were in good hands if they were talking to the owner.

THE VIDEO TAPE

"Is Swish your given name?"

"No, it's Michael, but everyone knew about seven Michaels when I was growing up, so my nickname became Swish."

"I thought maybe you were just good at basketball."

His look told me he'd heard that joke one too many times over the years.

"I've never heard that one before," he said, proving my inclination correct.

"My bad. Well, it's nice to meet you, Swish. I'm Bobby."

"How can I help you, Bobby?"

"I've got an odd request."

"I specialize in odd requests."

"Okay, good. I have an old picture of a woman in a dress, and I'm trying to figure out what clothing line her dress came from."

"You're right, that is a very peculiar request. I assume you have a picture of it."

I'd decided not to bring the whole video. I couldn't risk having him see the woman being stabbed, so I'd taken a picture with my phone. I showed it to him.

"Is this a picture of a picture?"

"Sort of. It's a picture of an old VHS videotape. Actually, it's a picture of a DVD that's a copy of an old VHS tape."

He moved his fingers to try to focus on the dress's label.

"I can tell you right now, this will be impossible."

"I guess I shouldn't be surprised."

"The pixels become too blurry as I focus on the label."

"There's nothing you can do?"

"Not with a picture of a picture. And certainly not with a picture of a DVD of a copy of an old VHS tape. If you brought the original videotape in, that might be a different story. I have some pretty cool software that could go to work on the original. We'd at least have a chance, unlike with this."

He handed me my phone back. I'd kind of expected an answer like this, but still hadn't decided what to do.

"Okay. I have to talk to the person who has the original and see if that can be arranged."

"Your request is getting weirder by the minute."

"What if I have a recording of the original?"

"In what form?"

"I have both a VHS tape and a DVD."

"But it's originally a VHS tape."

"Yes."

"I'd want the videotape. DVDs are clearer than VHS tapes, but I'd still want to go with the original. We'd certainly have a better chance than you would with this screenshot."

"Okay. I'll have to come back later with the videotape."

"This must be some dress," he said, and I gave him a nervous laugh. "And this request is even odder, considering you probably weren't even alive when this video was recorded."

"Can you tell from my picture what year the video was made?"

"It wasn't from the last ten to fifteen years. My guess would be sometime from the late eighties to the mid-nineties, and I'd lean more so that it was the nineties."

Swish was good. Since Ernest Riley turned the videotape over to the LAPD in 1995, it most likely was from that decade. There was the chance it had been lying around since the 1980s, but that seemed unlikely.

"I'll be back in twenty minutes with the videotape," I said.

I DIDN'T LIKE THE IDEA OF SHOWING SWISH THE VIDEO, BUT IT WAS MY best chance at getting an early lead on the case.

I'd stand next to him and make sure he didn't fast-forward or rewind past the part with the woman's label on the dress.

I entered my apartment, grabbed the videotape, and cursed myself for not having brought it in the first place.

I walked back a half hour later, and was again the only customer.

"I wasn't sure I'd see you again," he said.

"I'm back, and I have another request to make."

"Let's hear it."

"I don't want you fast-forwarding or rewinding from the moment I've paused on the tape."

"Okay, if you say so."

"I mean it," I said adamantly.

"What is it, a snuff film?" he asked.

I laughed, probably too much. I wouldn't have made a very good actor.

"It wouldn't be the first one I've looked at," Swish said, likely reading my reaction. "Well, it wouldn't be the first one a customer thought was a snuff film. I'm pretty sure the couple I've looked at were fake."

THE VIDEO TAPE

I realized then that Swish, the Marine Corps vet, didn't need to be handled with kid gloves. He'd seen it all, I'm sure.

"How can you tell?" I asked.

"Almost thirty years in the video business gives you sharp eyes. I can see when people make quick edits that might not be obvious to the average person. I can line up two pictures and see if the blood stains are in the same position. With my computer programs, I can focus infinitely more than the human eye, and see if a knife is actually puncturing skin. Things like that."

That settled it. I was going to show Swish the videotape.

"Do you have some sort of doctor or lawyer oath where you can't discuss what a client or customer shows you? Or at the very least, can I swear you to secrecy?"

"No, on the former. Yes on the latter."

He looked at me and could tell I remained skeptical.

"I've seen a lot in my years doing this," he said. "Nothing will surprise me, and I know how to keep my mouth shut. Plus, I'm sure it's not a snuff film."

"Okay, I'm going to trust you."

"Here, let's ensure no one walks while you show me this."

Swish walked over to the front door, lowered the blinds, and turned the sign from "We're Open" to "We're Closed."

"Here, let's go in the back," he said.

He led me to the back of the office, where two large TVs sat beside each other.

"Let me see the videotape," he said.

I gave it to him, he put it in a VCR, and he took two plugs and connected them to one of the TVs.

"Are you a cop?" he asked.

"No."

"A private investigator?"

"More or less."

"Well, Bobby, it's time to find out if you've got a snuff film on your hands. When you're ready, I'll let you press the play button."

There was no turning back now. I pressed play from the beginning.

He watched with unwavering interest.

"May I watch it again?"

I pressed play a second time.

He remained silent for several seconds after it finished.

"Well, what do you think?" I asked.

"It doesn't have any of the usual trappings of the obvious fakes I've seen. Ones where I can immediately eliminate the possibility of it being a snuff film."

"So you think it could be the real thing?"

"Yes, it's possible. And I would have considered that extremely unlikely just ten minutes ago. If it's not real, this is an elaborate fake. But I will need about twenty-four hours to examine the videotape in depth before I give you my final answer."

"Would I need to leave the videotape?"

"You could send me the file if you'd prefer."

"Do you promise not to make a duplicate of the videotape?"

"I promise."

"Then I'll leave it with you."

"Okay. Would you like to know how much I'm going to charge?"

"You can tell me tomorrow. I'm sure it will be worth it."

"I'll see you in the morning. How about ten?"

"I'll be here."

❈ 3 ❈

I returned the following morning, and I could instantly tell that Swish had found something.

His smile was beaming.

"This may be my greatest work," he said. "Follow me to the back."

I returned to the two massive TV screens. On the TV to my left was the label, blown up to probably a thousand times its original size. On the other TV, it looked like asphalt. I couldn't tell what I was looking at.

"What did you discover?"

"I'm sure you realize what is pictured on the left."

"The label of the women's dress."

"Exactly. And as you can see, I've blown it up a thousandth of its original size."

God, I'm good. "Even then, it's still hard to make it out," I said.

"Very true. Here, use this magnifying glass."

We'd blown something up one thousand times, and I still had to use a magnifying glass.

I could make out the words "Made in the USA." It was apparent this was the back of the tag, but even with the magnifying glass, I couldn't see the scrambled letters on the other side of the tag, where I was hoping to see who had made the dress.

"You said this was your best work," I said.

"It is."

"Well, then, how were you able to see the other side of the tag?"

BRIAN O'SULLIVAN

"I wasn't."

"I don't understand."

"Despite spending hours and hours, I couldn't make out what was on the front of the tag. Maybe the tag was so thick, you couldn't see the other side, or maybe the camera angle didn't allow it."

"I know there's a but coming," I said.

"But I don't give up easily, which brings us to the picture on the second TV. Do you know what it is?"

"It's the ground where she fell."

"That's correct. The concrete is the ground of the atrium. Now, take this magnifying glass one more time."

He handed it to me and told me where to look on the TV. After a few seconds, I saw what he was referring to. I couldn't believe my eyes. The light from the atrium had hit the tag at a certain angle and reflected it down to the concrete below it. It looked like a shadow on the original videotape, but some letters appeared when you magnified it a thousand times.

I could make out the smallest of lettering on the asphalt. It said Halo, and below that, 100% cotton. Halo had to be the name of the company.

"You're a genius," I said.

"Usually I'd say you were crazy, but for what I accomplished here, I tend to agree."

"How did you know to look at the concrete?"

"I didn't at first. After more time than I'd care to admit, I finally considered the possibility that the light from the atrium might reflect the tag."

"And end up on the concrete below?"

"Yes. The light or sun must have hit the tag at a certain angle, sending the letters on the front to the concrete below."

"I'm assuming no human eye could have seen this."

"A human wouldn't have a chance in the world. Shit, an eagle wouldn't have a chance. Remember, this is blown up a thousand times, and then you're using a magnifying glass to focus in even more."

"Truly amazing work, Swish."

"I agree." He smiled.

There was the other big question I hadn't broached yet, and it was now the elephant in the room.

"Have you come to a conclusion on the other thing?"

"On whether it's a real-life snuff film?"

"Yes."

THE VIDEO TAPE

"If not, it's the best fake I've ever seen. If I were a betting man, I'd put the odds at 90/10 that it's real. I can't believe I'm saying that."

"What makes you so sure?"

"Like I said yesterday, I've done this long enough to tell when someone splices in another video. This is not done once in this video. It's one continuous take. I closely looked at and rewound the scenes where the sword enters her body. I'm pretty darn sure it's real."

"Holy shit."

My words hung in the air for several seconds.

"Yeah, holy shit," he said. "Now what? You go to the police?"

"They've had their crack at this. It's mine now."

I couldn't believe how forthright I was with Swish and continued trusting the man. He'd accomplished way more than I ever could have expected.

"Understood. I'm not trying to tell you how to do your job."

"I had a couple more questions if you don't mind."

"Shoot."

"Can you tell what type of camera this was filmed on?"

"I thought you'd never ask."

Swish leaned over and grabbed a piece of paper from the desk.

"I was able to narrow it down to a few brands, models, and prospective years. It appears to be from the early to mid-nineties."

I looked down at the sheet of paper, which listed the possibilities.

"You deserve a raise."

"Well, I'm the owner, so a raise is unnecessary. Plus, you haven't seen the bill yet."

I should have negotiated more with Ernest Riley. I hadn't planned on spending money this early into the investigation.

"Whatever it is, it's worth it," I said.

He extended his hand and I shook it.

"Let's return to the front and I'll give you the bill."

"Thanks for all of this."

"Good luck, Bobby. Be careful. If the people who made this film are still alive, I'm sure they would do anything in their power to stop you."

"I'll be fine."

His look told me he wasn't so sure.

4

"Nice to meet you, Bobby. I'm Jaycee Mullen."

The woman in front of me was dressed immaculately. She was about a decade older than me, but gave off a youthful vibe on first impression.

We were at Cafe Zella on Wilshire Ave., a local coffee shop specializing in pastries, or at least that's what the internet said.

Jaycee had suggested the spot, and I'd quickly googled it.

"I'm sorry about your mother," I said.

"Thank you."

Jaycee Mullen was the daughter of Edith Mae Mullen, who had started Halo, the clothing line that made the dress that Jane Doe—that's how I now thought of her—was wearing. On our phone call that morning, Jaycee told me that her mother had just died two months ago.

"You must be curious why someone wants to show you a dress from decades ago."

"Yeah, you could say that. Let's get a coffee first, and then we can talk business."

We walked to the front of the line, and I ordered an Americano and a bear claw. Jaycee got a cappuccino and a lemon bar of some sort. I paid for both. This was the furthest thing from a date, but she'd agreed to meet me. It's the least I could do.

We sat, and they delivered our coffee and pastries a few minutes later.

"So, what is it about this dress that's so important?"

THE VIDEO TAPE

I took a sip of my coffee, which was just a way of delaying my answer. I'd been debating how much to tell her. I couldn't tell the truth, and even the still picture of Jane Doe would have looked suspicious. She wasn't in any sort of natural position to model a dress.

So, I'd cropped the woman out as much as I could.

"A friend of mine is making a movie set in the mid-nineties and found this dress in an old movie. He thought it would fit his main character."

"Bullshit," she said.

I wasn't expecting that. I looked at Jaycee with my mouth agape.

"Yours was such an odd request that I did my own little research. You said on the phone your name was Bobby McGowan, so I googled the name."

My lie had blown up in my face. Spectacularly.

And it's not like I could deny who I was. She'd seen my picture online.

I still hadn't responded when she continued. "You better watch what you say next. If it's another lie, I'm out of here, and I'm taking my free coffee and lemon bar with me."

It was time to be more forthcoming, but I wasn't ready to use the phrase "snuff film."

"The woman who was wearing the dress was murdered. And I'm trying to narrow down a time frame on when this dress was made."

"There you go. Was that so hard?"

I gave her a brief, nervous smile.

"And I'm sorry about your mother," Jaycee said. "I kind of did a deep dive on it last night."

"Thanks, but how did you originally know it was me? You hadn't seen my face yet?"

"I saw an interview you did after you caught the killer."

I did more than *catch* the killer, but didn't go there.

"And you recognized my voice?"

"Exactly."

"You'd make a pretty good PI yourself," I said.

She laughed and took a bite of her lemon bar.

"So, are you ready to show me the picture?"

I grabbed my laptop and scrolled to the clearest picture I had. I'd downloaded the DVD to my laptop and taken many screenshots. I was no longer underprepared, as I had been with Swish.

"It's not anything from this millennium," Jaycee said. "I'm sure of that. I'd have to go through some of my mother's old catalogues and see if it's listed. She was pretty good about indexing all the clothes she made, so there's a decent chance I might find it."

"Great. Thank you."

"Do you know anything else about the dress?"

"No. Just that Halo made it, and it said 100% cotton and was made in the USA."

"Well, all of my mother's clothes were made right here in LA, so that doesn't help. But the fact that it was 100% cotton helps narrow it down."

"Okay, good. And the dress was made in 1995 or before."

"That helps too. Can I see the picture again?"

I showed it to her.

"How were you able to see that the dress was from Halo and 100% cotton?"

"An expert on videos was able to focus in on the picture. A set of human eyes wouldn't have stood a chance."

I didn't want to discuss how I'd come upon my information. Two days into the investigation, I was already spending too much time explaining myself. I was the one who should have been asking the questions.

"Who shopped at Halo?" I asked. "Was it a high-end place?"

"It wasn't cheap. My mother became pretty well known, and as her popularity grew, the prices only went up. I remember being a little girl and asking her how she could sell a dress for two hundred dollars. And I was saying this in the mid-nineties. They only got more expensive."

"How many stores did she have?"

"Only one. It was a boutique store. She probably could have gone to Nordstrom's or Macy's, but that was never her goal. She liked knowing how singular her dresses were."

"And the shop was located in West Hollywood, correct?"

"That's right."

"When did it close?"

"When my mother retired about ten years ago."

"If it was lucrative, I'm surprised it didn't continue."

"I'm her only child and decided to pursue a different career path. She also thought it had run its course. She was almost happy that it wouldn't continue after her death. It made her feel like Halo was very much a clothing line of its time and place."

"She sounds like quite a woman."

"She was. As I'm sure yours was."

"Thanks. Yes, she was. I've got a question, but this may sound crazy."

"I'll be the judge of that."

THE VIDEO TAPE

"You said your mother kept a great inventory of things. Is there any way she'd have an old listing of everyone who bought this dress?"

Jaycee considered my question. "Doubtful, but not impossible. I'll have to take a deep dive on all her old sales receipts and things like that."

"Would you mind?"

"You seem like a nice kid. Sure, I'll check them out."

"Kid? We're probably around the same age."

"I'm in my late forties. You?"

"Thirty-four. Well, you look like my age."

"Flattery will get you everywhere, Bobby."

"My plan worked."

She laughed.

"Should we meet up for another coffee sometime next week. That would give me enough time."

"That would be great. Do you want some money for your work?" I asked.

"No. Looking through old dresses will be a nice way to spend time remembering my mother."

"Thanks, Jaycee."

"I'll be in touch."

5

I was only fifteen minutes from Noble Dunn, so I decided to pay him a visit.

I'd learned a little more about him since our first visit.

Noble had been a famous Los Angeles police detective, and several articles about him were on the good old internet.

His near-death fight had occurred with someone named Roger Theus, a criminal who committed several murders. He'd also successfully orchestrated a plan to have a district attorney intentionally throw his murder case. This was one bad guy.

Theus had ambushed Noble outside of his home and tried to take a knife to his throat. Noble had sensed him just in time and slid his arm in front of his throat.

That was the good news.

The bad news is that Theus sliced Noble's forearm, and then continued upward, slashing Noble deeply along his throat and then across his cheek, before coming within a few millimeters of taking out his eye.

At the last second, Noble knocked the knife out of Theus's hand, saving his eye in the process. The knife landed about ten feet away, equidistant between them. Knowing he was severely injured and that if Theus got the knife again, he'd be a dead man, Noble sprinted toward the knife and dove the final few feet.

Theus did the same, but was just a split second later than Noble. That made the difference between life and death. Noble gripped the knife, and

THE VIDEO TAPE

seeing Theus lunging toward him, he held it in place. Theus was in the air, and gravity had already taken over. He tried to swivel his body to avoid the knife, but it was too late. The knife punctured his right side, which might not have been fatal on its own, but Noble still feared for his life and took the handle of the blade and stuck it in even farther. It punctured Theus's liver, and he bled out before 911 got there.

If I had been Noble, I would have waited a few minutes until I made that call. Roger Theus didn't deserve to go on living.

Noble Dunn was a nice guy, and it was hard to imagine him stabbing a man to death.

I had to remind myself that he had been an LAPD detective for twenty-plus years. Maybe he was a nice guy, but he certainly wasn't a pushover.

"Hello, Bobby. I didn't expect to see you this soon."

"I was in the neighborhood."

"Working on the case?"

"But of course."

He led me into his house, and we sat in the same seats as the day we'd met.

"I miss working a case," he said. "It's better than sitting at home all day and growing old. I'm just pitter-pattering around most of the time."

It sounded like an outdated phrase my father might use. I needed to visit my old man. Now that I was based out of Los Angeles, I didn't get to see him as much. I'd make a trip to Santa Barbara the first chance I had.

"Can I get a little personal, Noble?"

He looked surprised. "We've only known each other for a few days, so I don't know how personal you can get, but sure, what do you got?"

"I did a little research after first meeting you, and I just wanted to say I'm sorry for what you went through with Roger Theus. He sounds like a real scumbag."

"He was, and the world is a better place without him. Now, let's talk about the case at hand. Have you learned anything substantial about the videotape?"

The nice guy had laid down the law. Roger Theus would not be a talking point.

"I have," I said.

"You're kidding." He was genuinely surprised.

"I'm not. After viewing the video over and over, I finally noticed something. The label from the woman's dress flashed for a split second."

"The police noticed that."

"And ..."

"And once they noticed it, they blew the picture up. The problem was that only the back of the label had flashed, and they couldn't get anything of use out of it. We couldn't see the front of the label."

I just nodded.

"Don't tell me you found something more than that."

"You seem like a straight shooter, Noble."

"I like to think so. Why do you ask?"

"I took this case because I want to investigate it on my own. I don't want the police looking over my shoulder, and I certainly don't want to update them every time I make a discovery."

"I have no problem with that."

"So if I told you that I did discover something about the label, you're not going to run to the LAPD?"

"No, this is your case. Now, if you find the killer, I'd suggest bringing in their help, and not trying to do it alone."

I wryly smiled. He was alluding to my ignoring the police and going after Conrad Drury—my mother's killer—all by myself.

"I promise I'll let you know if I ever discover the killer's identity."

"You can tell the LAPD. I'm just an old, retired detective and probably can't help you much anymore."

"Stop selling yourself short. I know your accomplishments."

He nodded briefly, but Noble Dunn wasn't one for compliments. "So, what did you find, Bobby?"

"I found Swish, and Swish did the heavy lifting."

"Who is Swish?"

"He's a video expert, and originally he'd come to the same conclusion as the LAPD."

"Originally ..."

"Yeah. He then worked his magic and found that the light from the atrium was hitting the back of the label, which caused the front of the label to reflect onto the concrete below. He then blew it up a thousand times and used a magnifying glass after that."

"Jeez. Sounds extreme."

"But it worked. I was able to find out the company that made the dress."

"You're kidding."

"I'm not."

"What was the name?"

"And you're not going to take this to the LAPD, right?"

"If I say something once, that is my word."

"Okay. Fair enough. The clothing company was called Halo."

"I've never heard of it."

"It was a small boutique shop based in West Hollywood. It closed several years ago, and the original owner recently died. But I was able to get in touch with the owner's daughter, and she's going to run through her mother's old stuff and see if she can identify the dress."

"I'm speechless," Noble said, and then didn't say anything for several seconds, as if to confirm it.

"You've accomplished more in two days than anyone has in ten years," he said.

"What happened to being speechless?"

He laughed. "I can tell having you on this case is going to be *interesting*."

"Never a dull moment," I said.

"So, what's next?"

"Keep hitting the pavement. Keep asking questions until I ask the right one. I might check out the seedy part of Los Angeles—the place where, if snuff films are really a thing, you might find one."

"You're mother's killer never had a chance," Noble said. "You're a regular old Pit Bull."

"I hope you mean the dog and not the rapper."

He looked at me quizzically, and I realized a man of Noble's age probably had no idea who Pitbull was.

"Don't worry, you're not missing much," I said.

"Why don't we meet once a week or so. You don't have to update me every few days. It's become readily apparent that you're damn good at this."

"Thanks. I'll hit you up next week."

We shook hands, and I left his house seconds later.

I found a local library and read the police reports that Noble had given me.

Not once, not twice, but three times.

I made notes and tried to memorize as much as possible. It wasn't a huge file, and I thought I had a pretty good grasp of everything.

Reading them a fourth time would have caused diminishing returns.

BRIAN O'SULLIVAN

WHEN I RETURNED TO MY PLACE, IT WAS SEVEN P.M., AND I WAS TIRED and hungry.

My apartment complex—The Mighty Wilshire—was located on Wilshire Boulevard, but it was far from mighty.

It was livable; I'd give it that. And it was affordable for LA standards. I'd give it that, too. But mighty? Far, far from it.

There were twelve one-bedroom apartments, six on the bottom and six directly above them. A crescent pool and a hot tub were in the middle of the complex. I'd yet to use either.

I was in apartment 1-A on the bottom left. There were only twelve apartments, so I'm not exactly sure why they had to put A after the 1, but, oh well.

Welcome to our twelve-unit complex. You'll be in apartment Alpha Beta Gamma-1857292-316 of Subset C.

As I approached, I saw a piece of paper neatly folded in half and taped to my front door. I'd only moved in two weeks ago and already paid rent for June, so I knew I wasn't getting evicted. Maybe it was a welcome letter from management.

I unlocked my door, grabbed the letter, and took it inside. I locked the door behind me and opened the piece of paper.

It was brief, to the point, and left me gasping for air.

SEEN ANY GOOD MOVIES LATELY?

❧ 6 ❧

The logical response would have been to go to the cops.

But I didn't want to.

If I told them about the note, I'd have to disclose my conversations, and suddenly the case would no longer be mine. They'd know about Halo, and they'd know an expert on videos thought it was a snuff film.

Several officers would be back on the case, taking fingerprints of the front door of my apartment. I'd be done with the case before I'd gotten started.

Was I being selfish?

You're damn right I was, but I had reason to be. The cops had spent twenty years not doing shit about my mother's murder and I was able to accomplish the impossible. The same was true of the Annie Ryan case.

And they'd had the videotape in question for three decades.

So, excuse me if I prefer working without people constantly looking over my shoulder.

I decided not to contact the police.

Which meant I'd be in charge of watching my own ass. There was someone out there. Someone who knew I was now working this case. And someone who knew where I lived.

I should have been scared—and part of me was—but a part of me also saw this as a good thing.

Now that they knew I was looking into Jane Doe's murder, they were

BRIAN O'SULLIVAN

more likely to make a mistake. Shit, maybe they'd already made one by leaving the note.

I'd be sure to get the note dusted for prints, not by the LAPD, but by an old friend from Santa Barbara—Officer Mark Patchett.

He'd been my nemesis in the years while my mother's murder went unsolved, but I now considered him a friend. He'd run the note for me.

And I wouldn't tell anyone else about it.

༺❧༻

I WOKE UP THE NEXT MORNING AND DECIDED TO HEAD TO MY LOCAL Home Depot.

I would pick up a video camera and install it above my apartment. If this asshole came again, I'd know.

After Home Depot, I'd mail the note to Detective Patchett. I grabbed it only at the ends and slid it into a Ziploc bag.

༺❧༻

I'D DEBATED TELLING NOBLE DUNN ABOUT THE NOTE, BUT DECIDED against it. He'd been candid with me, and I believed he wouldn't say anything about what I'd discovered thus far. A note left by a potential killer was a different story, however. He might feel that it necessitated notifying the LAPD.

For what seemed like the umpteenth time, I reminded myself I wanted to go this alone.

A half hour later, I was about to enter the Home Depot on Santa Monica Boulevard when something hit me, and I walked to the side of the front entrance.

I called Noble, who answered on the third ring.

"For someone who said he doesn't want any help, you sure like contacting me," he said.

I laughed. "Sorry, this will be quick."

"Give it to me."

"Ernest said he originally delivered the videotape to the LAPD in a manila envelope."

"That's right."

"Is that envelope still in the property of the LAPD?"

He considered it for a few seconds. "Honestly, I don't know. It's never come up. If they watched the videotape soon after opening the package,

28

THE VIDEO TAPE

they'd have known the importance of the envelope and kept it. Then again, it's been thirty years, and things do get lost. That's a long way of saying I'm not sure."

"Can you find out, and if they have it, send me a picture of the envelope? I don't need to see the original. A picture of it is fine."

"Dare I ask why?"

"It's probably nothing."

"I don't believe that, but I'll give you the benefit of the doubt this time. I'll call you when I get an answer."

I wanted to see if the note on my door and the manila envelope had the same handwriting. I didn't think Ernest Riley had anything to do with the girl's murder, but he was in possession of the videotape after all.

If by some chance the handwriting matched, I'd have to ask Ernest some very uncomfortable questions.

"Thanks, Noble."

I hung up, grabbed a cart, and entered Home Depot.

After purchasing what I wanted, I spent the next hour and a half installing a camera outside my apartment.

I'd caught two killers, but something about this case was different. The fact that the man had killed a woman on camera—I had no doubts about that anymore—made him a special type of sadist.

And for that reason, I was more on edge than usual.

I finished installing the camera around one p.m. It was far from subtle, hanging right above the front door.

That was intentional.

I figured I could have gone one of two ways. One, I could have hidden the camera in hopes that they would return, and I'd be able to see them on video. Or two, I could have made the camera so obvious that they wouldn't even approach my door again.

I'd chosen the safer option for one of the rare times in my life.

◈

I ENTERED MY APARTMENT, SLIGHTLY MORE AT EASE, AND TRIED TO think of a way to attack the case.

With my mother's case, I had a starting point. I interviewed people who knew the man in the photo album. With Annie Ryan, there were fifty family members I could interview.

With this case, I didn't know who the victim was or anyone involved in the crime. Swish had been a great help, and Jaycee would get back to me within the week, but what could I do now?

Several minutes later, I'd come up with a solid, albeit grungy idea.

I'd considered it, and now was the right time. I would hit up some of the sex shops and more disreputable businesses in Hollywood. If you were going to find places that might carry snuff films, you might as well start there.

Hollywood was famous for making films.

Let's see what type of movies the Hollywood underground made.

7

BLISSFUL—yes, the sign was in all caps!—was an adult-themed store on Hollywood Boulevard.

It was my third stop of the day, but the first one in which I made any headway.

It was in Hollywood's grimy, run-down area, but the store was surprisingly pristine.

A woman approached me with a pierced nose and bright, shoulder-length red hair. She had a pretty face, and it almost felt like the nose piercing and the hair were trying to hide it.

I couldn't help myself. I was already being judgmental of this woman, not because of her look, but because of her workplace.

She wore jeans and a Pink Floyd shirt with the renowned prism from *The Dark Side of the Moon.*

Her nametag included both her first and last names and said Paige Turner. I enjoyed the play on words. Maybe the employees at BLISSFUL deserved some slack from me.

"How can I help you?" she asked.

"Is Paige Turner your real name?"

"Would you use your real name if you worked here?"

"Probably not," I conceded. "I was hoping you could help me."

"I can help you find something. We don't actually *help* our customers."

I was getting off on the wrong foot with *Paige Turner*. It would be the

31

only *getting off* that would be occurring. She'd made that clear. Not that I was here for that. Far from it.

"That's not what I meant," I said.

"I know," she said. "I'm just giving you shit."

I smiled, realizing I must have looked like the biggest square in the world. Granted, BLISSFUL wasn't my scene, but I didn't want to look like Ned Flanders. I told myself to loosen up a bit.

"So, here's my question, and you don't have to tell me it's peculiar, because I already know it is."

She looked intrigued. "Okay. I'm listening."

I knew I couldn't just say I was looking to rent a snuff film, so I had to come up with something. My lie hadn't worked with Jaycee Mullen, but she'd had the advantage of knowing who I was. This attractive woman with the bright red hair didn't know me from Adam.

"I'm a graduate student at USC film school, and I'm writing a paper on snuff films," I said.

"I wasn't expecting to hear that. Maybe I was wrong about you."

"Did you think I was a square?"

Paige smiled. "Something in that vein. A stick-in-the-mud. Fuddy-duddy. A traditionalist."

"Fuddy-duddy? I haven't heard that one in a while."

"Yeah, well, I like keeping the classics alive."

I hated to admit it, but I was coming around on Paige Turner. Ah, who was I kidding? Despite not loving the nose ring—and being neutral on the red hair—I'd found her attractive almost immediately. There was definitely something about her.

"So, as to my question," I said.

"You never actually asked a question. You just said you're writing a paper on snuff films."

"You're pretty quick-witted."

"For someone who works in a porn shop?"

"That's not what I was going to say."

"But you were thinking it."

"Maybe. And maybe I was being a judgmental prick," I said.

"You seem all right. Now ask your question."

"I've got a few. Would you, or any similar shops in Hollywood, carry snuff films? And if not now, do you think maybe they did back in the early to mid-nineties?"

"I was born in 1998, so I'm not sure what the protocol was in the 1990s

THE VIDEO TAPE

for selling videos of women being killed on camera, but I can assure you we don't sell them now."

It was a brutal response.

"Ouch. I can assure you, I get no satisfaction in asking these questions. I'm just trying to get a better understanding of snuff films."

"A store like ours would never sell them. We'd be shut down in the blink of an eye. Plus, believe it or not, we are a classy business with a classy owner who would never allow filth like that into her store. Now, if we're talking Hollywood Boulevard in 1993, is it possible that some seedy adult stores sold some nasty ass videos? Sure. But snuff films? If so, I doubt it's something they advertised. And I can assure you that BLISSFUL never knowingly rented or sold a snuff film."

She was offended that I'd gone there.

"I'm sorry. Let's take snuff films off the table for now. Have you ever sold videos of men violently hurting women in videos?"

"Define violent."

"I don't know. Choking a woman."

"Yes, we have videos of men choking women, but not in the way that you're thinking. We also have videos of men spanking women, and even some with women being whipped by men. But these are all videos in which the woman knowingly signed on for what she was doing. So if you consider that violent, then yes, we have violent videos. If you mean violent, as in the man is hurting the woman against her wishes, then no, we don't carry shit like that. And fuck anybody who does."

Paige Turner was a firebrand, and damn if I didn't like it.

"I get it. Your owner and the store itself would never sell a video of a woman being hurt against her will."

"That's right. She never would."

She'd mentioned earlier the owner was a she, but I'd been slow in picking up on it. I was surprised.

"Your owner is a woman?"

"Yes. And she's a badass."

"Okay, let me change course. If it were socially acceptable, do you think any of your clients would rent a snuff film?"

"This may be hard for your square-ass to understand, but not everyone who likes kinky sex wants to see a woman murdered on film."

"Whoa whoa whoa. That's not what I'm saying."

She stared at me, but didn't say anything.

"I'm not here to argue with you. I promise. I'm just trying to understand who on earth would ever want to watch a snuff film," I said.

33

"You tell me. You're the one who seems so interested in them. Maybe you're the creep you're pretending to inquire about."

This woman could certainly give it back as easily as she took it.

"Trust me, I'm not a creep."

"Okay, maybe I was a little hard on you. As you can tell, I'm pretty loyal. To my owner and our customers. Now, do we get some crazies in here sometimes? Someone who looks like they wouldn't pass up a snuff film. Sure, I've seen a few of them, but I promise they aren't our regulars. They are good people."

"I apologize for being so confrontational. I respect your loyalty."

"Will you look at this? The fuddy-duddy has a soft spot for old Paige. I accept your apology."

"Thanks. What's your real name?" I asked.

She paused for a good five seconds, debating whether to tell me.

"What's yours?"

"Bobby McGowan."

She paused for another few seconds.

"I'm Nori Bridgewater."

I extended my hand and she shook it.

"It's a beautiful name," I said.

"Thanks. If you tell anyone here, we won't have another one of these conversations."

"Your secret is safe with me."

She extended her pinky finger. "Pinky swear."

I touched my pinky to hers.

"You have to say it," she said.

"Pinky swear," I said.

"Now that I've answered one of your questions, you have to answer a few of mine."

"Go."

"Are you really a film student at USC?"

"No."

"Are you a private investigator?"

"For all intents and purposes, yes."

"Are you researching a real-life snuff film?"

"Yes. Investigating is more like it."

We sat there and stared at each other for a solid ten seconds. Some of life's best moments are random interactions between strangers, and this was one of the most memorable I'd had in a long time. It didn't hurt that I was captivated by the woman in front of me.

34

THE VIDEO TAPE

"I have someone you should talk to," Nori said.

But I want to talk to you. "Who is that?"

"Darian Hague. She's the owner I've mentioned. Owned this place for over thirty years."

"I'd love to meet her. I'd said earlier that I was surprised a woman owns this. Is that sexist on my part?"

"No. I was surprised too. This is a business usually dominated by men. As I said earlier, she's a tough woman. She had to be to make it in this business."

"I bet."

"She likes me, and if I ask her to meet with you, I bet she will."

"I accept. Thanks, Nori."

She leaned in toward me. "You're only allowed to say that name when I'm the only one you're talking to."

"I understand. Sorry."

"Darian already left for the day and won't be in tomorrow. Can you stop back in on Friday?"

"I'll be here. What time?"

"We open at nine, but she'll be here at eight to set up. You'll get better answers than you would once the customers show up."

"I'll come at eight. Will you be here?"

"I'll be here, Bobby."

"Promise." I extended my pinky one more time.

She extended it to mine, and they touched.

We shared a laugh, and then I turned to go.

There was no denying it.

I was already smitten.

8

"Bobby, this is Heather Wolfe."

Jaycee Mullen got back to me the following morning, way quicker than I'd expected. I drove to Hollywood to meet her. I was only a few miles from BLISSFUL, but I'd have to wait a day to meet the owner.

"Nice to meet you, Heather."

Jaycee leaned forward. "Heather worked with my mother for the last ten years of the store, and even though she didn't work for her when this dress was made, she knows as much about the business as anyone now that my mother is gone."

"Okay, let's get down to it then," Heather said. She was no-nonsense.

"Great," I said.

Jaycee sat back and watched as Heather did her thing.

"The dress you inquired about was made in 1994. I studied it intently, right down to the lace ruffles. We've had similar dresses, but I'm 99% sure this is the one."

I didn't question Heather Wolfe. She radiated competence. "Would you have any guess on how many of these dresses you sold?"

"Less than twenty," she said. "We were a boutique shop, and Edith—Jaycee's mother—never made more than twenty of any dress. Chances are more likely it was between five and ten."

"Is there any chance there was only one sold?"

"Highly unlikely. Edith only made a singular dress when someone

36

wanted a dress or an outfit made specifically for them. It's cost-inefficient and time-inefficient to only make one dress to sell. But like I said, she was also boutique, and making more than twenty of any one outfit made her feel like a factory. That's not what Edith wanted."

"Is there any way to find out the woman who bought that dress?"

"No, I'm sorry. Edith didn't keep records back then. And don't be so sure a woman bought it. Just as often, it was a man buying a dress for his wife or girlfriend."

It made me wonder. Was the dress itself significant? Did the killer specifically have Jane Doe wear that dress, or was it just random that she had it on that day?

"What was Edith's clientele like back in the nineties?"

"Her dresses weren't cheap. That's kind of the point of being a boutique clothing line. If she sold them for the same prices as Target or Ross, she'd never have made it as a businesswoman."

"So they tended to be bought by people with a little money?"

"I'd say that's a fair assessment."

"Who tended to buy Edith's clothes? White people? People of color?"

"That's an odd question."

"I know. I'm just trying to narrow down who might have bought this dress."

Heather turned to Jaycee, seemingly perturbed.

"What is this all about, Jaycee? I agreed to do you this favor, but this man is asking some obscure questions."

"A woman is dead," I said. "And this dress is all I have to go on."

My statement seemed to placate Heather Wolfe.

"Oh. I didn't realize that's what we were doing here." She shot a glance at Jaycee.

"If I could find out who was likely to have bought the dress, that could help narrow down my suspects," I said.

Heather seemed intrigued now. Nothing like a decades-old murder to get someone's attention.

"No certain race or ethnicity bought Edith's clothes more than another. This section of Hollywood in the eighties and nineties was very diverse. It was just as likely that a native Angelo bought this as an immigrant cabbie from Calcutta."

I'm unsure why the Calcutta immigrant had to be a cabbie, and my expression told her so. She seemed to realize her mistake.

"I'm sorry," she said. "I wish I could help more. But there's no way to know who bought this specific dress. And like I said, there might be up to twenty out there."

"I understand."

I tried to think of any other important questions, but I couldn't come up with anything, so I ended the conversation soon thereafter.

🙛🙙

I CALLED MY FATHER THAT NIGHT AND TOLD HIM ABOUT MY NEW CASE.

He seemed fascinated by it.

I told him I'd get up to Santa Barbara when I could, but the case was too new, and I had to stay in LA.

"How about I come see you instead?"

"Really?"

"Yup. How about Saturday?"

"Great. See you then."

❧ 9 ❧

On Friday morning, I went back to BLISSFUL.
I was looking forward to meeting Darian, and I was *really* looking forward to seeing Nori again.

On the way there, I got a call from Detective Patchett. No fingerprints on the note. Damn.

I knocked on the back door, and Nori opened it, quickly whisking me in.

"We're closed for another hour, so I can't have people thinking we're open."

"No problem. I can't imagine the type of people who are waiting at the back entrance at eight a.m."

"Are you badmouthing my clientele again?"

"Only the ones who are here at eight a.m."

Nori laughed.

She was wearing a Ramones T-shirt and some white pants. The band's name was in bright red, and her hair complemented it perfectly.

Was the guy who knew nothing about dresses the day before now a fashion expert?

My inner voice was giving me a little shit.

"Darian is making sure all of the shelves are stocked. She'll be here soon."

"You'd think she'd have you or another fellow employee doing that type of work."

"I asked the same thing when I first started. Darian said when she first worked here, well before she bought it, that she was assigned to stock the shelves, and she's enjoyed doing it ever since. Even once she bought the place."

Just then, a woman appeared from the back of the store. She wore a flowery dress and a white headband, giving off a youthful vibe, even though she was probably around sixty.

"Darian, this is the guy I told you about."

I extended my hand. "Bobby McGowan."

"Darian Hague. Nice to meet you."

We shook hands.

"You're lucky I like our mutual friend Nori here," she said. "When she told me what you're investigating, I can't say I was too impressed."

I wondered if she called Nori by her real name during business hours.

"I realize how sordid it sounds. It's not like I chose the case."

"But you did choose to take the case, right?"

Darian was tough, but she was charming in how she did it.

"You're right. I could have turned it down."

She tapped me on the shoulder.

"Hey, I've owned a sex shop for over thirty years. Who am I to judge?"

"Is that the proper nomenclature? I was thinking adult bookstore or something like that."

"We have a few books, but we're much more than that. Some people used to call it an adult store, and then about ten years ago, I started hearing it called an adult entertainment store. I quite like that one."

"Anything to anesthetize it."

"Well said, Bobby. They want to anesthetize my shop. It's called BLISSFUL for Christ's sake. I think everyone knows what's going on in here."

I looked at Nori, whose face said, *I told you you'd like Darian.*

"Well, I think this place has a lot of charm."

"Thank you. We try. Okay, enough small talk. Nori told me you've seen a snuff film. Or, at least think you have. I've heard about those things for decades, and have never seen the real thing. We've certainly never had one at the store."

"How can you be sure?"

She thought about it for a moment. "I guess I can't be sure. But I've been shown some pretty nasty videos over the years, and I've even had some people claim they had the real thing. They both ended up being cheesy, obvious fakes."

THE VIDEO TAPE

"Why would people show them to you?"

"Because they wanted to put them on our shelves to sell or rent."

"Would you put the fake ones on your shelves?"

"No. We're a sex store. We specialize in weird, kinky stuff. But we don't specialize in violence."

"I understand. So nothing ever approaching a snuff film that you know of?"

"As I said, the only two videos that were even suggested as being snuff films were so obviously fake as to be comical. I remember watching the videos and laughing. You'd see a knife coming down near a woman's arm, and in the next shot, there would be a lone papier-mâché arm just sitting there by itself. I'm talking in the eighties and nineties when they didn't have CGI and shit like that."

"And nothing ever looked more real than that?"

"How many different ways are you going to ask me? If I thought it might have been the real thing, I'd have called the cops in a New York minute."

Darian was wildly convinced of everything she said. She wasn't a woman who beat around the bush.

"Okay. Thanks. And don't think that just because you're a sex shop, I assumed you sampled in dirtier things."

"It's not an outrageous assumption. There are shadier sex shops that I wouldn't put it past."

"Could I get the names of those before I go?"

"Sure, but most of them closed long ago. The sex industry is a lot cleaner than it used to be in my heyday." Darian laughed.

"You miss the good old days, don't you?" I asked.

Nori was standing beside us, but hadn't said a word. Darian turned to her.

"You're right, Nori. I do like Bobby."

"I thought you might."

Darian turned back toward me.

"And yes, Bobby, I do miss the good old days. But I'm still in business more than three decades later. Not many people in any business can say that, and even fewer who work in this business."

"You should be proud of all you've accomplished."

"She is. Can't you tell?" Nori said, and Darian laughed again.

"That's why I love this one." She grabbed Nori.

Darian was touchy, but in a fun, feminine way. With a guy, it might be creepy, but not with her.

41

"Ah, I love you, too," Nori said.

"Don't you screw this one over, Bobby."

"Darian!" Nori exclaimed. "I literally just met the guy two days ago."

"I love getting a rise out of her. Anyway, let's get back to why you're here. How can you be so sure that you're in possession of a snuff film?"

"I can't be sure, but I had a reputable expert examine it, and he said it was the real thing."

"Can I see it?"

"Are you serious?"

"Yes. I've seen some crazy things in my career. I'm a big girl. I can take it."

I'd known it was possible she'd ask to see it, but it still took me a bit by surprise.

"I'm sure you have, but you did admit you'd never seen a snuff film."

"True. But I've answered all your questions, and I'm going to give you a list of some of the seedier sex shops. The least you can do is show me the videotape."

"That's fair."

"How about you, Nori?" Darian asked.

"You don't have to watch it," I said. "You probably shouldn't."

"Being a protective boyfriend," Darian said. "Good for you."

"We're not ..." Nori started.

"We're not dating. We just met two days ago. Blah blah blah. I know. I'm just jerking your chain."

Nori couldn't help but laugh.

"How graphic is it?" she asked.

"You see a woman stabbed in the chest. It's graphic and not pleasant, Nori. I'd advise against it. If there is a silver lining, the video cuts off before you see the most gruesome part."

That convinced her to do the exact opposite of what I suggested.

"I want to see it."

When I took this job four days ago, I hadn't planned to show anyone the videotape. Now, this was going to be the second and third person to have seen it. No wonder I was getting notes left on my apartment.

"Are you sure?"

"I'm sure."

"Darian, do you guys have VCRs? If not, I can just show you on my laptop?"

"We have a few old VCRs, but they are boxed up, and it would take me a few minutes."

"I'll grab my laptop," I said.

"Perfect. We've got some huge televisions in the back, and we can just plug your laptop into them."

"Okay. See you in a minute."

WHEN I RETURNED, DARIAN LED US TO THE BACK CORNER OF THE store.

"Can I ask you a serious question?"

"Of course, Bobby."

"Why, when there is so much porn out there nowadays, would someone come to a place like this to watch a dirty movie?"

"These TVs aren't for watching dirty movies. We have always been more about sex toys, and if you wanted to rent a videotape, we'd prefer that you watch it off-site. We had a few personal TVs when I first bought the place, but it was gross, and I got rid of them quickly."

I nodded as we arrived at one of the televisions.

"Find the video on your laptop, and when you're ready, you can plug the laptop into the cord right here."

"Are you sure you want to watch this, Nori?"

I was trying to give her one last chance to get out of it. I didn't bother asking Darian. She wasn't going to take no for an answer.

"Yes."

"Okay." I then stuck the cord into my laptop and pressed play.

I had one eye on the videotape and one eye on Nori. She continued to fascinate me, and I wanted to see how she reacted to the video.

As it turned out, not well.

She got through the first fifteen seconds, but shrieked when the woman was stabbed. And when the samurai sword started coming down toward Jane Doe's neck, she yelled, "Turn it off!"

A split second later, the video turned off.

"Wait, was that you?" Nori asked.

"No. That's where the video ends."

"Play it again," Darian said.

The look in her eye told me she might have noticed something.

"Did you see something?"

"Just play it again."

"Nori?"

"You can play it again, but I'll turn my back."

I played it three times in total and then waited for Darian's response.

"There's something familiar about it," she said. "But I can't place my finger on it."

"What could possibly feel familiar about something like this?"

I'd come off as more disagreeable than planned, but she didn't seem to notice.

"I don't know how to describe it. It's like I've seen the setup for this before."

"As if you'd seen a longer movie that contained this scene."

"No. I'd remember that. But something just strikes me as, and I hate to keep using this word, familiar."

I glanced at Nori. She looked like she'd seen a ghost. I should have insisted that she didn't watch it. I gave her a quick smile, but she didn't respond. It's like she was in a daze.

"I know they are, for the most part, hidden, but does the woman or the killer remind you of anything or anyone?" I asked Darian.

"No, it's just the overall vibe. Nothing that specific."

"Does her dress look familiar?"

"No. Should it?"

It was worth the chance.

"Have you heard of a clothing line called Halo?"

"Yeah. Wasn't that located here in Hollywood?"

"It was. Did you ever shop there?"

"I think I might have been in one or two times. Years ago. But I don't remember much about it, and I'm pretty sure I never bought anything from there."

"Okay. How about the atrium? Any chance you know the location?"

"I was wondering if maybe that's what struck a chord, but I don't think it's that. Who knows, though? You said this is thirty years old."

Nori interrupted. "I think I'm going to go use the bathroom."

She stormed off, and Darian turned to me. "Maybe you shouldn't have let her watch the videotape."

"No shit," I said, a bit perturbed. "I tried to dissuade her."

"Why don't you go check on her?"

I STOOD OUTSIDE THE BATHROOM, FEARING I'D HEAR NORI THROWING up. Instead, I heard tears.

"I'm outside if you need a shoulder to cry on," I said.

THE VIDEO TAPE

I wasn't sure how she was going to take that, but she came out of the bathroom and did precisely what I'd offered; put her head on my shoulders and continued to cry quietly.

"I've never watched anything like that," she said.

"I should have put my foot down. I'm sorry."

"You tried. It's not your fault."

Darian had walked over and was standing behind us.

"Like I said, he's a keeper."

I liked Darian, but this was a bit much.

"I don't think this is the time," I said.

"You're right, Bobby. I never did learn the right times to hold my tongue."

Nori pulled her head off my shoulder and wiped her eyes.

"Hey, Nori, I've got things under control for the next few hours. Why don't you and Bobby go out and grab some breakfast?"

I glanced at Darian, and she shot me a quick wink. Darian Hague was a sixty-year-old rabble-rouser.

"Are you sure?" Nori asked.

"You've known me long enough. If I say something, I mean it."

"I'll be back by nine-thirty."

"Give yourself till ten."

"Thanks."

"Check out Breakfast Sammies. Best breakfast sandwiches and breakfast burritos in town. Tell them Darian sent you."

"Will do," I said.

Nori hugged Darian, who then opened the front door for us.

45

❧ 10 ❧

I drove us to Breakfast Sammies. Was the owner named Sammie, or was it just a take-off of sandwiches?

It was only half a mile down the road, and still a lousy area of Hollywood, but just knowing Darian Hague ran a business around here made things seem brighter. She was a breath of fresh air, even if that air came from a woman who sold sex toys to the general public.

We were seated, and I ordered a breakfast burrito. Nori ordered their signature sandwich with egg, ham, avocado, and a chipotle crema. As soon as I heard her order, I was jealous.

We sat, and I reminded myself to avoid talking about the videotape.

"Who brought you that videotape?" Nori asked.

So much for that.

"Are you sure you want to talk about it?"

"I'm okay now. It was just that initial shock of seeing it."

"All right. If you say so."

She smiled at me. "I say so."

"An older man brought it to me. He'd originally brought it to the LAPD over thirty years ago. They had the tape this entire time and never made any progress. It doesn't even sound like they were ever convinced it's a snuff film."

"Are you?"

"Yes. I think it is the real thing."

"It's so horrible. The expression in that young woman's eyes."

THE VIDEO TAPE

"I know. It's hard to watch."

"I probably should have heeded your advice."

"You didn't know how you would react to it."

"Not well, apparently."

Our orders arrived a few minutes later, and we both took a bite.

"It's excellent."

"Darian knows all the good restaurants on this side of town," Nori said.

"I'm not sure what expectations I had about meeting your boss, but she's exceeded them all."

"She's quite a woman. And she looks out for all of her employees."

"You especially."

She reached over and grabbed my hand. "She liked you. And I do too for different reasons."

This was all so unexpected, but I wasn't complaining. Nori was captivating. The fact that I'd seen her sensitive side this morning only made me gravitate to her more.

There was no denying it. I liked the woman in front of me.

"So, where do you live, Bobby? This shady side of town?"

"No. A place that's a little more staid. And boring."

"Boring sounds kind of nice if we're being honest. And I'll bet you can safely walk at night in your neighborhood."

"So you're not a big fan of this section of Hollywood?"

"It has its moments, but most are during the light of day. I wouldn't want to be eating here alone at eleven p.m."

"Plus, who wants a breakfast sandwich that close to midnight?"

Nori laughed.

"Cheesy," she said. "But funny."

"I try."

Her hand made its way back to mine.

"We should meet outside of BLISSFUL some time."

"Aren't we outside of BLISSFUL right now?" I said jokingly.

"Don't be a sarcastic doofus."

She was right.

This is your chance, Bobby! Stop making jokes.

"My father is coming to town tomorrow night," I said. "Would you like to join us for dinner?"

I quickly realized how weird it sounded.

"It's not like it sounds," I backtracked. "This isn't some plan to have you meet my father. He's chill, and I thought having you meet him would be fun."

"Well, I usually don't like first dates to include their parents, but if we count this breakfast as a date, then I guess it's technically the second date."

This time, I grabbed her hand. "Thanks for making it easy. And it won't be both parents. Just my father."

"No problem. Are your parents still together?"

"There's something I should tell you," I said.

I told Nori about my mother's murder, the photo album, and the investigation that led me to Conrad Drury.

She sat and listened intently, almost choking up a few times.

"I'm so sorry, Bobby."

"Don't be. I'm just glad you know now. But no more talk of death."

"Good. It's not even ten a.m. and I'm already exhausted."

The waiter came over and I paid for both of us despite Nori's protests. It was our first date, after all.

☙❧

I DROPPED HER OFF AT BLISSFUL AND TOLD DARIAN HOW MUCH WE enjoyed the restaurant.

"I hope you two used the time to get to know each other," she said.

"Subtlety is not your specialty," I replied.

"Look at what business I'm in. Not a lot of subtlety in it." As she said this, she was holding a leather mask. The timing was perfect.

"Listen, I have to run. Thanks for everything, Darian. Can I get that list of the shadier sex shops?"

"Of course."

"And let me know if you remember why that video seemed familiar."

"I will. It was nice meeting you, Bobby."

"Likewise, Darian."

I turned to go.

"I'll see you tomorrow night," Nori said.

"What's tomorrow night?" Darian asked.

"I'm meeting his father."

"Jeez. This progressed fast. Do you want to bring your father by the shop, Bobby?"

I smiled. "You guys have been great, but this is my cue to go."

They laughed as I headed toward the exit.

MY HIGH DIDN'T LAST VERY LONG.

When I arrived at the parking lot in the back of BLISSFUL, I had an unwavering feeling that someone was watching me. I glanced around, and there was no one else in the lot. I looked at the apartments overlooking the lot; no one was peering down.

And yet I couldn't shake the feeling.

With my mother's and Annie Ryan's case now under my belt, I knew when to trust my instincts. And they were telling me that I was being watched.

But with no one visible, there's not exactly anything I could do, so I got in my car and headed back to my apartment.

This time I had a co-passenger.

It was a big fat pit in my stomach, telling me I had just been watched.

11

I woke early and was instantly fixated on the dinner that night. Inviting a girl I'd just met to have dinner with my father was crazy enough. The fact that she had bright red hair, her nose pierced, and worked in a sex shop made me seem downright nuts. My father was an accepting man, but it was hard to imagine he'd have much in common with Nori Bridgewater.

What were you thinking, Bobby?

TO TAKE MY MIND OFF THE DINNER, I DECIDED TO FOCUS ON THE CASE at hand.

I'd accomplished quite a bit in less than a week on the job. I'd met with Ernest, Noble, Swish, Jaycee, Heather, Nori, and Darian. I'd become convinced that the videotape was, in fact, a snuff film. I'd even discovered where Jane Doe's dress was made. The LAPD hadn't accomplished half of that in thirty years of having the videotape.

That was the good news.

The bad news was that I'd brought attention to myself, first, with the note left on my door, and second, with being watched outside of BLISSFUL.

Even after a night to sleep on it, I still believed I had been watched. I couldn't shake the feeling. It's not like it was some wild theory. He had left a note on my apartment, after all.

What if the guy was following me?

And that simple question led me to another one of my crazy ideas.

"What did you say this was for?"

I was back at Home Depot. The employee didn't comprehend my question, so I tried explaining it a third time.

"I want to put a camera on my car to see behind me."

"A camera on your car? I'm not sure I've ever heard of anything like that. Sounds pretty silly to me. No offense."

If the guy were just having difficulty understanding, I'd have let it go, but he was also condescending. And his face belonged on the Mt. Rushmore of smug faces—definitely top four all-time.

"You've never heard of a police car with cameras on it?"

"Are you a cop?"

"That doesn't matter."

"Yeah, it does. John Q Public isn't allowed to put cameras on their cars."

"Are you sure about that? You must be the cop."

"Just a concerned citizen," he said, his smug face in full effect.

"Let's call your manager over and ask him."

That slowed him down, but only a bit. "I'd need to know why you want to install a camera on your car."

"Is that protocol for Home Depot employees? To know the motivation of all of its customers?" I asked, with a slight hint of sarcasm. And by slight, I mean the size of the Grand Canyon.

"I think I've figured it out," the guy said. "You're an asshole so people are out there following you all the time. That's why you need the cameras. Now I understand. Thanks for helping me see the light."

This would have been comedic if the guy weren't being such a jerk. Two could play at that game.

"Congrats on seeing the light. You probably haven't had many of those lightbulb above-the-head moments."

"I've had more of those moments than you'd ever know."

"Now that I think about it, you're probably right. When you don't understand things at first, you have a lot more opportunities for those types of moments."

BRIAN O'SULLIVAN

He moved closer to me, and I thought he might take a swing. I was 6'2" and two hundred pounds, so I was a pretty big guy, but this behemoth still dwarfed me.

I didn't care. I wasn't going to take a step backward.

"You got everything under control here, Tripp?"

A manager approached out of nowhere. He hadn't heard anything, but probably saw us squaring off.

Tripp—that would be his name!—was a complete jerk, but I didn't want the guy to lose his job. I wasn't that petty.

"Tripp was just answering a few questions for me," I said. "He's been very helpful."

I'm unsure if the manager believed it, but he grunted and then meandered down one of the expansive Home Depot aisles.

"Thanks," Tripp said, surprising me.

"I'm not here to get you fired. But you're not getting my business."

And with that, I walked out of the store.

I returned to my place and watched the videotape for the 50th and 51st time. Approximately.

Nothing new stood out this time. Not that I expected anything after so many viewings.

☙❧

AT THREE P.M., I GOT A TEXT FROM MY FATHER SAYING HE'D CHECKED into his hotel.

When we first set this up, I invited him to stay at my apartment, but he vehemently declined my offer.

I called him, and after saying our pleasantries, asked if I could bring a friend to dinner.

"A male or female friend?" he asked.

"A female."

"I knew it by the way you said friend."

"You're insufferable, Dad."

"I can't wait to meet her, but do you think bringing a woman to meet a parent this early on is advisable?"

"That's what she said."

This was a rare example of this phrase not being said tongue-in-cheek.

"Well, she's right."

"You know what? I think you two are going to get along famously.

Probably at my expense, but I can live with that. Screw it, I'm bringing her."

"Perfect. Then I'll be happy to meet her. You're still picking me up, right?"

"Yeah. I'll be there at five. We can hang out for a bit before we head to dinner."

"Be good to see you, Bobby. I can't wait to hear more about the new case."

"It's a wild one."

I had no plans to tell my father about the note left on my door. There was no reason to scare him. But he would relentlessly try to learn everything he could about the case.

"Great. See you at five."

I called Nori and offered to pick her up along the way, but she said she'd prefer to drive herself.

Not exactly ideal. I was used to picking up the girl on a first date—I still didn't count Breakfast Sammie's as a date—but I guess this wasn't your typical first date.

And I only had myself to blame.

❧ 12 ❧

I parked in the hotel parking lot and walked to my father's room.
He opened the door with a big smile and led me into the clean
but relatively small hotel room.

"It's great to see you, Bobby."

"You too, Dad."

I asked if he wanted to have a drink at the hotel bar.

He declined and said he'd wait to have wine with dinner.

"So, tell me about this girl," he said.

"She's not like most girls that I've brought home over the years."

"How is that?"

We might as well get it out of the way before they meet.

"Well, first off, she has bright red hair."

"I have no problem with that. Kids are wild these days."

"Her nose is pierced."

"See my previous answer."

So far, so good.

"What does she do for work?" my father asked.

"This is where you might have a problem."

He looked at me.

"How bad could it be?"

"She works at an adult store."

It took my father a second to say anything. He was choosing his words
carefully.

54

THE VIDEO TAPE

"Like an adult bookstore?"

"Yeah, they have books."

"Amongst other things?"

"Yes."

"Like what?"

"Use your imagination, Dad."

"In this particular case, I think I'd rather not."

I laughed.

"I met the owner. She's a darn fun lady, and the store isn't as bad as you're probably thinking."

"I'll be the judge of that."

"Wait. What?"

"If I like this girl tonight, I want to see where she works tomorrow."

I was not expecting that.

"Okay. Why the hell not?"

My father looked rather excited.

"I can't wait. What's her name, by the way?"

"The store owner or the girl you are meeting tonight?"

"Your date."

"Nori Bridgewater."

"Wow, what a beautiful name."

"On that, we agree."

"Well, let's get this show on the road. I can't wait to meet red-haired, nose-pierced Nori."

I just shook my head.

⚜

WE HEADED DOWN TO MY CAR AND MADE OUR WAY TO THE restaurant.

I'd decided on a place in Santa Monica mere feet from its world-famous pier. The restaurant's name was The Surfing Fox, and the reviews online had been quite good.

As my father and I approached the front of the restaurant, my mind was racing.

Was my father going to like Nori? Was Nori going to like my father? Would her job turn him off? Would she be turned off by having my father at dinner?

"Bobby!"

Nori snapped me out of my thoughts as she crossed the street behind us. I turned around and couldn't believe how great she looked. At work, she'd been casual, wearing T-shirts of old bands. Not on this night. She wore a sexy, green dress. Her hair and the green dress gave me Christmas vibes. Not that I'd ever mention it.

"Nori, I'd like you to meet my father, Robert McGowan senior."

She shook his hand, and I tried to judge my father's reaction. He smiled and quickly shot me a glance, which meant he approved. I'd have just as easily known if he disapproved. I could read my father like a book.

"I didn't know you were a junior," she told me. "He must be a good man if he raised you."

Nori was laying it on pretty thick, but my father enjoyed it.

"Let's see if you feel the same way after dinner," he joked.

We entered the restaurant and I gave my name. We were quickly seated, and our waiter, a man in his thirties, asked if we'd like to order a drink.

"I'd like a glass of Sauvignon Blanc," my father said.

I said I'd wait until dinner to have a glass. Nori did the same. I'd long ago made a rule that if I drove to a dinner, I'd limit myself to one glass of wine. I wasn't even a big wine drinker, but I preferred it to having a cocktail at a restaurant. Meanwhile, I'd never order wine at a bar. Go figure.

"Did Bobby tell you the good news?" my father asked Nori.

"I don't think so. What is it?"

"I'm going to come by and see your work tomorrow."

"You do know where I work, correct?"

"Yes, he told me."

"And you still want to come?"

"Curiosity killed the cat."

"I guess I'd better make a good impression tonight. You may not be as impressed tomorrow."

My father laughed.

"I'm sure it will be fine, Nori."

I took it as a good sign that my father was using her first name this early in the night. They had a good camaraderie for having known each other for all of five minutes.

"So, Bobby, how did you end up at Nori's work? I know it's for this new case you're working, but how did you end up at her place specifically?"

"Luck of the draw," I said. "I was hoping to see some of the more *interesting* stores in Hollywood, and Nori's happened to be one of the first ones I walked into."

"Well, if this works out between you two, I'd say that was quite the fortuitous choice."

THE VIDEO TAPE

"C'mon, Dad."

Nori just laughed.

The shoe was now on the other foot. My father had replaced Darian, and now I was the punching bag.

"Nori, what did you think of my son when he walked in?"

"I initially thought he hadn't been to too many places like ours."

"Indeed," my father said. "He's such a square."

Nori laughed.

"That's the word I used."

"I'm sitting right here, you two," I said, and they both laughed.

"Honestly, we had a rough first few minutes. But after that, we took a liking to each other," Nori said. "We were talking about a somber subject, but we had a nice little banter right off the bat. Kind of like you and I are having right now."

My father was impressed by Nori. It was obvious.

"Are you ready for a few tough questions?" he asked.

"Shoot."

"You seem like a nice young lady. You're obviously smart. How did you end up working at an adult store—not that there's anything wrong with that."

He was doing a variation of an old *Seinfeld* joke, but it went over Nori's head. She was too young. Shit, I was only old enough because my father had the show on constantly when I was a kid.

"I have a graduate degree in creative writing from the University of Missouri. I had been working for a publisher in Missouri, but that's not exactly where the literary heavyweights are located. So I decided to make the jump to Los Angeles at twenty-six years of age. I got here, and within the first week, I'd applied to five different publishing companies. I got three rejection letters, and the other two didn't respond. I knew when I moved out here that it wasn't the ideal time in the publishing world, so I decided to apply for something in the service industry to pay the bills in the meantime. A server or a bartender. Something like that. I was dropping my résumé off at a restaurant across from BLISSFUL one day, and my future boss, Darian, happened to be there, waiting to be seated. She quickly gave me a business card and asked me to check out her place. She must have liked my overall vibe, which probably means the hair and the nose ring. So, I took her up on her offer and went by her work the next day; the rest is history. I will get back to applying to publishers soon, but to be way too honest, I like Darian, my co-workers, and I've even come to love BLISSFUL. This world fascinates me."

57

When she finished, Nori blushed. "Sorry, I talked for so long."

"You were great," I said. "I learned a lot."

"A graduate degree in creative writing," my father said. "Impressive. I'm sure you'll put it to good use. And don't worry about people judging you for your job. I had a pretty thankless job before I met Bobby's mother."

"Which job?" I asked. "Not sure you told me about this."

"Well, I wasn't that proud of it."

"What was it?"

"I worked as a server at a drive-in movie theater. We had to wear this ridiculous tuxedo-like thing, and walk around to each car and ask if they wanted any food or drinks. Half the cars had people making out. It was beyond humiliating."

Nori laughed. "Our generation missed out on the drive-in theater experience."

"It was all the rage back in the day."

"You're probably around Darian's age," Nori said. "I bet you guys will get along just fine."

Was she secretly trying to set them up? It sure sounded that way.

"I guess we'll find out tomorrow." My father smiled slyly. "So, Bobby, any updates on your new case?"

"Nothing substantial." I chose to be vague. "I'm still investigating, but it's a decades-old videotape. I'm not sure how much I can do."

"He's bullshitting, Nori. Bobby wouldn't take the case if he didn't think there was a chance he could solve it. He was always like that. As a kid, he'd start these jigsaw puzzles with like a thousand pieces. His mother and I would shake our heads, knowing there was no chance he'd ever finish it. But we'd be proven wrong, and sure enough, a few weeks later, he'd have finished the darn thing. Bobby comes off as a nice guy, but you'll see, he's very dogged."

"He must be," Nori said. "He convinced me to come out on a first date with his father present."

They shared a laugh.

"You two are too much," I said. "Well, I guess I shouldn't have worried about how you would get along."

"Fast friends," my father said.

"For sure. And by the way, I kind of like your son."

Nori grabbed my hand, and we held each other's gaze.

This was progressing faster than I ever could have imagined.

THE VIDEO TAPE

⚛

THE REST OF THE DINNER FOLLOWED SUIT.

We all had a great time, and there was never a dull moment—or an awkward silence.

I ordered a lobster roll, my father got a hanger steak, and Nori ordered fish tacos. The food was solid, but that was almost secondary.

The company was what mattered.

I tried to pick up the check, but my father beat me to it as always.

He'd probably have to be ninety years old and in an old folks home before he let me pick up a tab.

"So Nori, are we still on for tomorrow at your work?" my father asked as we walked outside.

"Of course. What time were you thinking?"

"How late are you open till?"

"Seven p.m."

"And your boss will be there around seven?"

"She'll be there. She loves to both open and close her place. She's crazy like that."

"Perfect. Bobby and I will swing by at 6:45. I can get a full day in LA, end it at your work, and then drive back to Santa Barbara after that."

"Are you sure you want to drive home at seven p.m., Dad?"

"I'm sixty-two, not ninety-two. I'll be fine."

Nori looked at me, and I just shook my head.

"The old man is going to do what he wants," I said.

"Old man, my ass," my father said.

I kissed Nori on the cheek and told her I'd see her tomorrow. My father hugged her and said the same.

As we approached my car a minute later, he turned to me. "She's a fantastic woman. I loved her."

"I thought you would."

"Bullshit. You were nervous."

"Those aren't mutually exclusive. I thought you'd like her, and I was still a bit nervous, hoping I'd be right."

"Well, you were right. She's great. That red hair even grew on me."

"I know, right? Now I can't imagine her without it."

"The nose piercing might take a little longer for me to get used to."

I laughed. "Baby steps."

"I hope it works out for you two. She's a keeper."

The night couldn't have worked out any better.

59

13

I picked up my father the next day at noon as he was checking out of his hotel. I told him to leave his car there, and we could pick it up before meeting Nori and Darian.

We spent most of the day at the Getty Museum, something he'd long wanted to see. The last time he'd visited, I stayed at the Beverly Hilton Hotel, and we'd seen Hollywood and Beverly Hills. So this time, we stuck to the west side of Los Angeles, and I showed him Santa Monica and Malibu. We drove along the PCH and up into the Pacific Palisades. My father couldn't believe all the damage the January fires had caused.

We had a nice early dinner on the Santa Monica Pier, almost a stone's throw from The Surfing Fox. My father was only in town a little over twenty-four hours, but I felt we were getting a lot of quality father/son time.

I dropped him back off at his hotel parking lot at 6:15, and suggested he follow me to BLISSFUL.

"I'll see you there. I do know how to use GPS."

It seemed like half of my father's jokes these days were about how he was just a young whipper snapper.

I PULLED UP TO BLISSFUL AT 6:40, AND MY FATHER ARRIVED MINUTES later.

THE VIDEO TAPE

We both parked in the back, and I tried not to think about the feeling I'd had the day before. I certainly wasn't going to tell my father. I tended to leave out anything that might make him worry about my cases. I'd already omitted the letter left on my apartment door.

"Are you ready for this?" I asked.

"Ready for it? I'm looking forward to it!"

I opened the door and immediately received a wave from Nori. My father waved back as if she were waving to him. He realized his mistake and laughed.

Seconds later, Darian walked toward us.

"How are you, Bobby?"

"Nice to see you, Darian. This is my father, Robert."

My father shook her hand, and they exchanged pleasantries.

"All right, Darian," he said. "I want the full tour. I'll let my son talk to your second in charge, while you show me the ropes of owning an adult-themed store."

Darian laughed and whisked my father away.

I walked up to Nori, and she gave me a quick peck on the lips.

"I wasn't expecting that."

"I couldn't exactly do it in front of your father last night."

I smiled and kissed her back as quickly as she'd kissed me.

"Do you want to come back to my place tonight?" I asked.

"Yes," she said with certainty.

"I was going to say I could cook for you."

"Great. It was going to be a yes regardless."

"Perfect."

I'd expected a yes, but I wasn't expecting her to do it with such aplomb. It's like she expected it.

"It looks like your father and Darian are getting along."

Nori pointed to the other side of the store, and I saw my father watching Darian as she showed him God knows what.

"Since my mother died so young, I always wanted my father to end up with a second wife. He's had some girlfriends, but nothing has ever lasted too long. But I'm still holding out hope. That said, he and Darian would be the all-time odd couple."

"Never say never. It's not exactly like you and I were likely to become friends."

"Is that all we are?"

"I'll tell you after tonight." She winked.

A far-away voice interrupted our moment.

61

BRIAN O'SULLIVAN

"And here's where we keep our strap-ons," Darian said.

Calling this moment surreal would have been one hell of an understatement. Having an adult toy store owner show my father the strap-on section was not on my bingo card—not tonight, not ever.

"They are cute," Nori said.

"Stop."

"Maybe we should go on a double date with them."

"Please stop."

"Your dad can move to LA, date Darian, and start working here with us."

"Please, please, please stop."

Nori laughed quite loudly, and they looked in our direction.

"What are you kids laughing at?" Darian asked.

"Nothing," Nori said.

I saw my father look suspiciously in our direction, so I gave him a thumbs-up. He did look happy—I had to admit it.

Ten minutes later, the tour was done, and they returned to the front.

"Darian is a great host."

"Your father is a good listener. He seemed genuinely interested."

"I've had quite a few days," my father said. "You're a delight, Darian. And I loved our dinner last night, Nori. This just gives me an excuse to come down and visit Bobby again in a few weeks."

"I'd love to have you back," Darian said. "I wasn't able to give you the full tour."

I didn't even want to consider what that meant.

"I think that's a great idea," Nori said. "Can't wait to see you in a few weeks, Robert."

They exchanged hugs, and then Darian hugged my father. It was a freaking hug-fest.

Not to be outdone, I gave my father a parting hug.

"Let me walk you to your car," I said.

"I think I can handle that, but thanks, Bobby."

"You don't have a choice. Your son is walking you to your car."

"Okay, then."

My father said one more final goodbye, and Darian opened the back door for us.

"It sure seems like you and Darian got along well."

"She's a fascinating woman. I'm in Santa Barbara, and she's down here, so I'm not expecting anything. I'd like to see her again the next time I visit you, though."

THE VIDEO TAPE

My father was happy, and I, in turn, was delighted for him.

"Thanks for coming down, Dad. Drive safely. The sun is going to set in an hour or so."

"By that point, I'll only be thirty minutes from home. I'll be fine."

"Love you, Dad."

"I love you, too, son."

❧

MY FATHER GOT INTO HIS CAR AND HEADED ON HIS WAY. I WENT BACK inside and out of Darian's earshot, gave Nori my address. I had offered to drive her and then take her home whenever she wanted, but she insisted she'd rather have her own car. I understood.

"How much longer do you have to clean up?"

"Probably twenty minutes. And then I'll take a quick shower at my place, so I'll see you in about an hour, maybe a little more. Sound good?"

"Sounds great."

14

Nori and I had sex that night.

I'd like to claim I was Don Juan the first time, but we were still trying to figure each other's bodies out, and it probably wasn't my all-time best performance.

I definitely improved the second time, a few hours later.

And by the time we had sex a third time the following morning, I had her eating out of my hands. Okay, that might be a slight—big!—exaggeration, but we certainly were enjoying each other's company.

She was a beautiful, sensuous woman.

Along with being intelligent, fun, kind, open-minded, and all the other qualities.

Slow down, Bobby. You've known her for all of a week.

I hated my inner voice sometimes.

"CAN I MAKE YOU SOME BREAKFAST?" I ASKED.

"You're pulling out all the stops, aren't you? I'd love some."

"Eggs Benedict fan?"

"Who isn't?"

"Probably be about fifteen minutes. Want a coffee as well?"

"I'm the guest. I don't want to lounge in bed all day. I'll get up and make the coffee."

THE VIDEO TAPE

"Great."

For the next twenty minutes, we talked as we cooked together. It felt natural and something a couple of thirty years might do.

"Does this feel like it's moving too quickly?" I asked when I finished making the Hollandaise sauce in the blender.

"Usually, I'd say yes. I rarely sleep with someone until at least the third date."

"This is basically our third date."

"How is that?"

"The breakfast at Breakfast Sammie's could be considered a date. The dinner with my father definitely was. And then my inviting you over last night also constituted a date."

We'd gone back and forth on what was considered a date.

"If you count jumping into bed as a date."

"I do. At least for the sake of winning this argument."

Nori smiled. "Fine, you win." She poured each of us a coffee.

"You can set them on the dining room table," I said.

Calling it a dining room table was a stretch. It was a little nook in the corner of the kitchen. That's about as close to a dining room table as you'd get in a one-bedroom apartment in Los Angeles. Spacious, they were not.

Five minutes later, we were eating, and she complimented me on my cooking.

"You're a pretty good cook."

"I have my moments. Or to be more precise, I have about five things I can make well. Eggs Benedict just happens to be one of them. If you'd wanted Corn Flakes instead, I was screwed."

"I've heard those pesky Corn Flakes trip up all the prominent chefs. Flay. Ramsay. Zakarian."

"Anthony Bourdain barely finished culinary school after failing the Corn Flakes challenge."

"I miss that guy," Nori said.

"Me too."

She looked like she wanted to say something, but couldn't pull the trigger.

"What is it?" I asked.

"I like you."

"I like you, too."

And that was it. The only L word muttered was like—not the more aggressive, relationship-changing one. Like felt more appropriate.

We didn't say anything more until we finished breakfast.

65

"I should get going. I have to work in an hour, and need a shower after last night."

"And this morning," I said.

She smiled.

"Yeah, that too."

"I'll give you a call tomorrow. Let's plan on meeting up later this week."

"I'm already looking forward to it."

Ten minutes later, we kissed goodbye, and Nori drove away.

AFTER A TWENTY-MINUTE SHOWER, I DECIDED I COULDN'T LET TODAY be wasted.

It was only ten a.m., and just because I might be falling for Nori didn't mean I could just waste away the day.

I glanced at the list I'd made. I'd accomplished more than I could have expected. That didn't mean I should rest on my laurels.

I looked it over one more time and knew what I would do.

IF BLISSFUL FELT FOREIGN TO ME, THEN BANGERS WAS LIKE A whole new planet.

There was a classiness to the former. The latter was hell on earth.

It didn't help that the name of the business was tacky as fuck.

The sign to BANGERS was also in all caps, which made it even worse.

When you walk in, the first thing you see is a blow-up doll of a woman. Nothing wrong with that in and of itself. The problem was that this blow-up doll was gagged with a ball gag. Making it worse, her hands were tied behind her back.

I wanted to get the hell out of BANGERS, but this was one of the businesses that Darian had told me to check out, so I shouldn't just leave without getting the lay of the land.

I approached a man who sat behind an elevated desk. He looked to be in charge. Not that that was anything to be proud of in a dump like this. He was in his forties, had a huge gut, and wore huge Coke-bottle glasses.

"Can I help you?" he asked. It was accusatory. Maybe he knew all his regulars, and a new face aroused suspicion.

"Do you guys sell videotapes?"

"Yes."

THE VIDEO TAPE

"What type of movies do you have?"

He looked perturbed by my question.

"We've got our Oscar winners on that wall, and all the Disney films on the other. What the fuck kind of movies do you think we carry?"

"What if I'm looking for something even more *interesting* than your common bondage film?"

"What do you mean exactly?"

"Something where people are put through a lot."

"You're going to have to be more specific."

I felt dirty even though I was just playing a role.

"I have a client who is interested in finding out if snuff films are for real."

"What year is this?"

"It's 2025."

"We don't just have snuff films hanging from the walls."

He was yelling, but the only other customer didn't turn around.

"Let's say it's 1995. Would you have then?"

"Are you a cop?"

"No."

"A fed?"

"No."

"What are you?"

"I'm just trying to find out how someone might have purchased a snuff film back in the nineties."

"So you don't have a client trying to rent one right now?"

"No."

"Well, I'll tell you what. Even though I wasn't working here back in the nineties, I can tell you for sure that this place never rented no snuff films."

"So you did rent them?"

My double-negative joke went right over his head.

"Do you have anything you want to purchase here in 2025. If not, I'd suggest you get the hell out of here." He leaned over his shoulder and yelled, "Hey Artie, he thinks this is Hard Hank's back in the day."

Artie, the lone customer, laughed and said, "That place was different. That's for damn sure."

"What was Hard Hank's?" I asked.

"Don't worry. Hank died decades ago. Nothing for you there."

I told myself to remember the name Hard Hank's, not like that would be tough.

"Is there anything else you need? I've got a business to run."

67

The guy was a jerk, and the business was disgusting, and on some days, I'd have left him with some sarcastic parting shot.

On this day, I just walked out. I went by another business that Darian had suggested, and told myself I was due for an extra-long shower that night.

When you think of Hollywood, you think of all the stars it's produced over the years. Bogart. Bacall. Newman. Hepburn. Nicholson. Streep. People don't realize Hollywood also has a seedy side, and I'd been immersed in it for the last week.

Honestly, I was getting sick of it.

I went home that night and took another twenty-minute shower.

My day had been bookended by long showers.

For entirely different reasons.

15

Of the next six days, I spent five of them with Nori.
We were getting very close, and even though it had only been about two weeks, we were basically a couple. We may not have called each other boyfriend and girlfriend, but we were certainly behaving like it.

I don't want to say my investigation took a back seat, but I definitely looked forward more to seeing her than hitting another one of the shadier sex stores that Darian had suggested.

I'd now visited ten of them, and despite them all being of dubious character, none would acknowledge ever having carried snuff films. They were probably telling the truth, and it's not like they would admit to having carried them even if they had. I began asking all of them about Hard Hank's, and while most of them had heard of the place, no one had any "hard" evidence that they'd carried snuff films. And no one knew anyone who used to work there.

I guess I shouldn't have been surprised. From what I could ascertain, they closed sometime in the late nineties.

I wasn't getting much out of these excursions, unless you count feelings of disillusionment.

It was time to take a different route.

BRIAN O'SULLIVAN

The next morning, Nori called me and said she was planning our date for that morning.

She asked if I could meet her at eight a.m., and I agreed.

She gave me an address, and I met her at the predetermined spot.

I was surprised to see it was a park, and she was sitting on a little bench.

I approached and kissed her. "This is cute."

"Oh, I forgot to tell you one thing."

"What?"

"We're not having a date today."

"You've lost me."

"Mr. Weaver."

A man appeared from behind a concrete bathroom ten feet from the bench.

What's going on?

The man looked to be in his seventies and had a gray goatee that needed to be trimmed.

"Alfred Weaver at your service."

At your service?

Who introduced themselves that way, and more importantly, who the hell was this guy?

"What is going on here, Nori?"

"That's for you to find out, Bobby."

And with that, she walked away.

Alfred Weaver's hand was extended, so I shook it, even though I had zero idea what was happening.

"What is this?" I asked.

"Nori reached out to me and wanted us to meet. It probably has something to do with this."

From behind his back, he produced a paperback book. He handed it to me, and when I looked at the title, I knew what Nori had up her sleeve.

Snuff Films: Fact or Fiction?

Alfred Weaver was listed as the author.

"Your girlfriend told me you might have some questions for me."

"Yes. Yes, I do. I'm sorry I was a little standoffish. I had no idea what was going on."

Alfred Weaver sat on the bench, and I joined him. Not exactly what I'd imagined when I first saw Nori sitting here.

"No problem, Bobby. Can I call you Bobby?"

"Of course."

70

THE VIDEO TAPE

"So, where would you like to begin?" Weaver asked.

"How about with the title of your book. Are snuff films just fiction, or are they made?"

"There's no doubt that snuff films are real. Now, that doesn't mean you can buy them at any corner store—or any disreputable store for that matter. But they absolutely have been made before."

"Have you viewed any yourself?"

"Of course," he said. "I spent over a year researching this book. If you're going to write a book on snuff films, you sure as hell better view a few of them yourself."

"How did you get ahold of them?"

"I'm afraid I can't divulge the names of the people who gave them to me."

"I'm not asking for names. I'm asking how."

"By asking questions. I became a nuisance. Finally, when people realized I was a writer interested in this stuff, they'd have a friend willing to show me one."

"Would you meet these friends?"

"Only once. The other times they hid behind their friends and would only give me the snuff film to watch, but I'd have to return it right after."

"Why would people be willing to show you them?"

"Because I'd promise to pay them if the snuff film was legit."

"How could you tell?"

"I could never be completely sure, but I saw enough of them to know that at least a few were real."

"You saw some fake ones?"

"Several. That's kind of the point of the title. While it's a fact that there are snuff films out there, usually it's fiction and someone has edited the film to make it look real."

"Did Nori tell you why she wanted you to meet with me?"

"She only said you had a great interest in snuff films."

That was enough for now. I'd tell him about my videotape if I felt he could help.

"What cities did you see these snuff films in?" I asked.

"I went wherever the leads took me. I once went to Des Moines, Iowa, just to see an alleged snuff film. That was a waste. An obvious fake."

"Did you spend much time here in Los Angeles?"

"But of course. This is Hollywood, after all."

"True, but they aren't known for making that type of movie."

"Hollywood has produced every type of movie over the years."

BRIAN O'SULLIVAN

He was probably right about that.

"Were any of your real snuff films from Los Angeles?"

"I don't want to give away my entire book, Bobby, but yes, Los Angeles was the location of a few real ones."

I told myself not to get my hopes up.

"Where would they sell these?"

"Like I said earlier, not at any shops you'd expect."

"How about a seedy sex store catering to porn."

I almost wanted him to say yes. It would make my recent visits to these places less of a waste of time.

"Still very unlikely. The owners of these businesses know that snuff films are like touching the third rail. If you sell those things, the LAPD would be on your ass before you knew it. The feds, too."

"Then where? Were they sold to individual buyers?"

"Now you're catching on. The business of snuff films is not really a business. It's knowing an individual who would pay for one."

"Sickening," I said.

"Indeed."

"How would someone go about finding a buyer who was interested?"

"Well, they wouldn't exactly advertise in the yellow pages." Weaver thought this was the funniest thing ever, and laughed loudly at his own joke.

"That was a good one," I said, primarily to get into his good graces, although it wasn't the worst joke I'd ever heard.

"The truth is, there was no one way. If you ran in the wrong crowd and knew some truly deranged people, then you might just hear of someone looking for a real snuff film."

"Would people ever be hired to make one?"

"I've heard rumors of that. Yes."

"Did you ever find an actual example of that happening?"

"It wouldn't have stood up in a court of law. Hearsay three times removed."

"But you had evidence of someone paying for a snuff film."

"Yes, I think so."

"Could you tell me who it was?"

"I'm sorry. I can't elaborate on that."

"How about a hint?"

"Sorry, no."

This guy was a tough nut to crack.

THE VIDEO TAPE

"What a sordid book this must have been to write. Impressive stuff," I said, trying to build him up.

"It was. But also fascinating. Low life scumbags are much more fun to write about than upstanding citizens."

"I'm sure that is true. It doesn't mean I wouldn't find them revolting."

"Of course. I mean, this is a book on snuff films. If you're not revolted, you've got some issues."

I flipped the book over and saw the picture of the man sitting across the bench from me.

"When did you publish this book?"

"It will be twenty years later this year."

"Did you find any snuff films on VHS? Possibly from the early to mid-nineties?"

"Of course."

"What does that mean?"

"I viewed snuff films—or alleged ones—from the 1940s, 50s, 60s, 70s, 80s, 90s, and 2000s. You name it."

"Jesus."

"You'd have a tough time believing in the son of God if you saw some of what I saw."

"Was this strictly the United States?"

"No, no, no. The majority of the confirmed snuff films were from foreign countries. I only mentioned Des Moines and Los Angeles because it's two Americans talking."

"What other countries did you research this in?"

"How much time do you have? Brazil, Colombia, South Africa, Russia, and even supposedly neutral Switzerland. And those are just a few off the top of my head."

"Sounds like this could have been dangerous."

"There were times when I was worried."

"Did you get any threats after you wrote the book?"

"No. I never mentioned the real names of anyone I interviewed."

"Did the cops ever come and ask you questions?"

"No."

"I'm surprised."

"Sadly, my book was not the best seller I'd hoped it would be. It kind of got lost in time. So no, the cops weren't exactly beating down my door. They probably hadn't even heard of my book."

How did Nori find this guy?

"What would you have done if the police had approached you?"

BRIAN O'SULLIVAN

"I would have told them I can't give up my sources."

"But we are talking about murder."

"You forgot what I told you."

"Remind me."

"It was always a friend of a friend. I never met face-to-face with the person who had the snuff film. And never with the sick individual who made the film."

"They don't deserve to be called films," I said, disgusted by the whole thing.

"I don't disagree. If you come up with something better, let me know."

Should I tell Weaver that I was in possession of one?

"You said you wrote this twenty years ago. Did you keep in touch with any of your contacts from the book?"

"It's hardly a group of people you want to keep in touch with."

"That's not a no."

"No, I haven't kept in touch with them. Could I find a few of them again? Now that's a different question."

"Understood."

"Bobby, I've been very forthcoming with you. I haven't pried as to why your friend Nori reached out to me. I haven't pried by asking why you're so clearly infatuated by snuff films."

"But ..."

"But now I need to know why I was invited here today. I think you owe me that."

To tell or not to tell?

Fuck it, I'd shown half of Los Angeles at this point.

"I have a videotape."

"I kind of figured that's where this was headed. And what exactly do you want? You want me to look at it?"

"Yes, I could show it to you. But I'd also like to talk to someone you interviewed in your book. Someone from Los Angeles, preferably someone who might be knowledgeable about snuff films in the early nineties."

"How about this? You show me the videotape, and if I think it's real, I'll reach out and see if any of my old contacts would be willing to meet with you."

"I'm agreeable with that."

"Where shall we watch it?"

My mind immediately went to BLISSFUL. I hadn't brought my laptop, and even though I had the file saved on my phone, it was just too small to view on a cell phone.

74

THE VIDEO TAPE

"Do you have a free fifteen minutes?"

"Do you mean another fifteen minutes?" he asked sarcastically.

Alfred Weaver was not a very likable man.

"Yes, I've got another fifteen minutes for you," he said when I didn't answer.

I called Nori. She was already back at work, setting up for the day. I asked if Weaver and I could head to BLISSFUL and watch the video.

"Of course. That's what I was hoping for."

"I'll see you in a bit."

⊗⊰⊗

ALFRED WEAVER FOLLOWED ME THE FIVE BLOCKS TO BLISSFUL, AND Darian greeted us when we entered.

After introducing the two, she walked us back to the TVs and whispered, "When is your father coming back to visit?"

I couldn't help but laugh.

"Hopefully never," I joked.

"Bobby, don't make me tell Nori you're being a bad boy."

"Me? A bad boy? Never."

"You put in a good word with your father, and I'll put in a good word with Nori. He is a handsome man."

"I'd rather rewatch the snuff film than continue this conversation."

We both shared a morbid laugh. Gallows humor at its best/worst.

Darian turned on the TV, and I felt instantly guilty. My joke, even though very much in jest, now hung in the air as I was about to watch Jane Doe being killed again. Just because I'd viewed it dozens of times didn't detract from the sheer horror of it all.

I decided to watch Alfred Weaver's reaction instead of the video itself. He cringed a few times and covered his eyes as well. It was reminiscent of George C. Scott in *Hardcore* and Nicholas Cage in *8MM*.

But something felt like it hit home with him. I couldn't put my finger on it.

When it ended, I couldn't help but ask him. "You've seen several of these. Why did you react so intensely to this one?"

"I've reacted this intensely to every one I've ever seen."

It was a fair and honest answer, and I sounded like a schmuck for asking the question. This hadn't been the best five minutes of my career.

And yet, something told me he recognized the video.

75

"Maybe you think it gets easier, Mr. McGowan, but I assure you it doesn't."

I was definitely on my back heel now.

"I didn't mean it that way. I apologize."

"That's not how Bobby meant it," Nori said.

I could handle this myself, but I still appreciated her standing up for me.

"I know," Weaver said. "I just get a little tense when I see these things."

"So you think it's real?"

"I do."

"Now that I've shown it to you, can you put me in touch with one of the people you interviewed for the book?"

"Are you sure you want to do this? It's nasty business. You're going to feel grimy after work every day."

"I already do. At least this way I'd have a better chance of solving it."

"Okay. I'll make a few phone calls and get back to you."

We exchanged numbers.

"Thank you for everything today, Mr. Weaver."

"You're welcome. Now, where is the exit?"

Something had spooked him about the videotape. I didn't buy his excuse that they all affected him this way.

"I'll walk you out," Darian said, and grabbed his arm.

Nori gave me a quizzical look. "That was weird, wasn't it?"

"Yeah. He did not take that well. Not that anyone should."

"Are you happy I set it up?"

I'd forgotten to thank her.

"Thank you so much, Nori. It was very thoughtful. How did you come up with it?"

"I went on Amazon, and there are like five books written on snuff films. I reached out to all five authors. Two got back to me. My plan was for a Zoom meeting until I found out that Alfred Weaver lived here in Los Angeles. He was initially reluctant to meet you, so I bribed him."

I laughed. "How much did that set you back?"

"Don't worry about it. It was my treat. Let's just say, I'll let you buy dinner next time we go out."

"It's a deal. Thanks again for setting me up with an expert on snuff films."

"I can safely say that sentence has never been uttered in the history of mankind."

THE VIDEO TAPE

I smiled. "Yeah, you're probably right. So, dinner tonight?"

"You know what, I don't want you to buy me dinner. I want you to cook me dinner."

"You liked the Eggs Benedict?"

"I did. Now I want to see what you can do for a full dinner."

"Challenge accepted. Tonight?"

Nori grinned. "I thought you'd never ask."

"When are you off?"

"At five. I'll be up at your place by six."

"And you work tomorrow, right?"

"Yeah. I'm opening."

"You and Darian work entirely too much."

"You're not wrong."

"Why don't you let me drive you to my place tonight. I have some more investigating to do today anyway. And I'll drop you back here in the morning."

"That'll work. I'll see you at five."

"See you then. I will make you the best meal you've ever had."

"I'll be the judge of that."

"I'm going to knock your socks off."

"The rest of my clothes, too?"

And that's when I heard Darian yell, "Get a room!" from her office a few feet away.

"Bye, Darian."

"Bye, Bobby. Invite your dad back to LA."

I laughed as I walked toward the exit.

16

I woke up the next morning in the arms of a woman I was falling for.
I'd be lying to myself if I said any differently.
I'd made chicken parmesan for dinner, and she seemed to love it. Within minutes of finishing dinner, she kissed me despite the copious amounts of garlic I'd put in the sauce. Maybe we've been wrong all these years, and garlic was actually an aphrodisiac. Maybe not.

We made love once and fell asleep in each other's arms, which is where I woke up.

"I need to take a quick shower," Nori said.

She'd had me pick up a change of clothes at her place on the way over last night.

"Okay. Do you want company?"

"Raincheck. I don't want to be late today."

A LITTLE LESS THAN AN HOUR LATER, I PULLED INTO THE BACK OF BLISSFUL.

As had become customary, I looked around after I parked. I neither saw nor heard anything suspicious. Maybe I'd been wrong about that day.

"Thanks for driving me back," Nori said. "I'll call you after work."

"Great. But you're not done with me. I'm making sure you get into work safely."

"It's not even nine a.m. I'll be fine."

"Sorry. I'm a creature of habit. Just want to wait until you're safely inside."

We walked from the car to the back entrance. Nori put in a key to open the regular lock and a second key to open the dead bolt. I'm sure Darian had thousands of products, so I couldn't blame her for making it challenging to get in.

Nori opened the door but turned to face me before walking inside.

"Okay, I'm safe. Thanks for looking out for me."

I leaned in to kiss her goodbye when I saw something about twenty feet behind her. It took me a second to realize what I was looking at.

"Oh my God," I yelled.

Darian Hague was on the ground, and she wasn't moving.

Nori turned around and screamed at the top of her lungs.

I stepped in front of her, trying to block her view.

"Give me one second," I said. "Don't look."

I took a few steps toward Darian, and my fears were confirmed. Without question, she was dead.

She was on her back, and her eyes were bug-eyed and looking straight up. Her formerly white blouse, which she'd been wearing when I last saw her yesterday, was now a dark red, overtaken by blood.

The similarities to the woman in the videotape were undeniable.

Walking a few steps closer, I saw several tears in her dress. I assumed a knife of some sort had done this.

Maybe a sword.

I intentionally kept my body between Nori and Darian.

"You don't need to see this," I said. "Why don't you call 911?"

Nori began to cry, and I could hear her inching closer.

"Trust me, you don't want to see this. You can call them from outside. I'll be right out."

"Okay," she said through tears.

The videotape had affected Nori greatly. This was much, much worse. It was a real-life body, and someone who happened to be a good friend of hers.

"She's dead, right?" Nori asked.

"Yes."

She continued to cry as I watched her head toward the door.

I took a final step toward Darian and was now standing over her. I hoped something would jump out before the police arrived and escorted me outside.

"I'm so sorry, Darian."

I noticed that right around her navel, her blouse had been opened slightly. There looked to be dozens of stab wounds in that little area.

As I moved my gaze closer, I discovered that it wasn't just stab wounds. The killer had used his knife to carve something into her abdomen.

When I realized what it said, I fell to the ground.

On her flesh, the killer had carved five letters.

B-O-B-B-Y.

❧ 17 ❧

The police arrived about five minutes later.

I was a shell of myself, and couldn't believe what I'd just seen.

I'd walked outside to be with Nori. I couldn't stand to be near the body any longer. I figured it was better she find out from me, so I told her what I saw on Darian's abdomen. She stared at me in disbelief.

When the police arrived, they separated Nori and me and assigned two officers to ask us questions. I'm sure it was just protocol in case two guilty people wanted to conspire to keep their stories straight.

But in that moment, I just wanted to hug and console Nori. Instead, she had a member of the LAPD peppering her with questions.

The officer asking me questions was probably around fifty with a goatee that looked too dark for a man his age.

"How did you happen upon the deceased?"

I told him everything, and when I was just about done, I added the part about seeing the letters of my name carved into her abdomen.

"Holy shit," he said. "Wait here."

He disappeared inside for a minute and returned with someone in plain clothes, likely the lead detective. They had a quick little conversation out of my earshot.

He looked hardened like a detective who had been on the job too long. He walked in my direction.

"Are you Bobby McGowan?"

"I am."

BRIAN O'SULLIVAN

"I'm Detective Heald."

"Nice to meet you," I said. Considering what I'd just seen, it sounded trivial, but my parents had ingrained politeness at a young age. Some things never leave you.

"You just told a colleague of mine that the killer carved Bobby into her chest because of you. How can you be sure of that?"

In that moment, I realized this was no longer my case. The LAPD had taken over. It's not like I could lie and claim this hadn't all started with the videotape I'd been hired to investigate. Once they heard that, they were going to take over.

I told myself I was being selfish. Catching Darian's killer was all that mattered.

"Almost three weeks ago, I got a phone call," I said and proceeded to tell him everything that had happened, starting with my meetings with Ernest and Noble, followed by my visit to Swish the very next day. I even included the part where the killer—I assumed—left a letter on my apartment door.

When I was finished, Detective Heald looked at me like a disapproving father would look at his son.

"You should have come to us long before this."

"The LAPD has been in possession of this videotape for three decades."

"Well, things changed when someone left a note on your door. We could have run that for fingerprints."

I didn't tell him I already had, and none had been found. I didn't want to risk getting Officer Patchett in trouble.

"I guess I'm more of a lone wolf," I said.

"What the fuck does that mean? Are you even a PI?"

"Not exactly."

"What the fuck does not exactly mean?"

He was beyond agitated.

I told him the story of my mother, and then proceeded to tell him about the Annie Ryan case.

His anger softened ever so slightly.

"Ah, you're that guy. You've accomplished a lot, but that doesn't mean you can just go lone wolf on the LAPD. As I said, you should have come to us."

"I'm sorry."

"Funny, you don't seem that sorry."

I had to watch myself. I was close to making a new enemy.

82

THE VIDEO TAPE

"Listen, Detective Heald. I've told you everything I know. All I want is for you to catch the guy who did this. I haven't known Darian long, but she was a great woman. And my girlfriend, who is being interrogated right now as well, was extremely close to her. I'm not trying to be a jerk. I want you guys to catch this psychopath."

He looked me over, judging if I was being forthright.

"Okay, I believe you. Now, what more can you tell me about Darian Hague?"

Before I could answer, I heard Nori crying uncontrollably. I looked over and my heart broke for her.

"Can I go be with my girlfriend for one minute?" Whether she was technically my girlfriend was up for debate, but I didn't feel like getting into semantics with Detective Heald. "I'm not going anywhere. I'll answer your questions when I'm done talking to her."

"You can go talk to her for one minute. And one minute only."

Heald managed to be a jerk even when he was being somewhat magnanimous.

I walked over to Nori, whose eyes were red and puffy. Who could blame her? Darian had not only been her boss but also a motherly figure to her.

It wasn't fair that Darian was gone. And I imagine that—like me—Nori couldn't stop thinking about the way she went.

The detective saw me approaching. He glanced toward Detective Heald and then stepped aside. He would give me a little time before resuming his questioning of her.

"I'm so sorry, Nori," I said.

She leaned her head onto my chest and sobbed and sobbed. Several officers watched us, but I couldn't have cared less.

"She was such a great woman. She didn't deserve this," Nori said.

"She was amazing. And you're right, she didn't deserve this."

Nori removed her face from my chest and looked me in the eyes. "I don't care what you do, but you must catch this guy. He needs to be punished for what he did."

I'd already conceded that the LAPD would take over the investigation, but I wouldn't tell Nori.

"I'll do everything I can."

"Good."

She raised her eyes to mine again.

"Your father is going to be really sad as well."

I'd been so focused on Darian's death—rightfully so—that I'd

BRIAN O'SULLIVAN

forgotten that she and my father had a moment. They genuinely seemed to like each other's company.

The last thing Darian told me was to invite my father back to LA.

As if things couldn't have gotten any worse, I'd have to call my father later that day and tell him the devastating news.

"They had a nice little back and forth that day, didn't they?"

Through her tears, Nori managed a small smile. "I think they kind of liked each other."

I looked over at Heald, who was not so patiently waiting. "I have to answer a few more questions from the detective, Nori. If you finish before me, don't leave. We should talk."

"I'll wait here until you're done."

I gave her a final hug and walked back over to Detective Heald.

"Thanks for that," I said. "Where were we?"

"I was asking if there's anything else you can tell me about Darian."

"I know she's owned this place for decades. I could tell she was tough, but she was also a sweetheart. I liked everything about her."

"Did you meet her through your girlfriend?"

"Yes and no."

"What do you mean?"

"I came to this business to ask about snuff films, and that's when I met Nori." I pointed at her. "I didn't meet Darian until Nori introduced me to her."

"And then you asked her about snuff films?"

"Yes."

"And did you show her your video?"

"Yes."

"And you think she was killed because of your investigation? Because of you?"

It was a logical question, but I hated how he'd added the *"Because of you"* at the end.

"That's a pretty good guess, considering my name is etched into her stomach."

"Don't be a fucking smartass," Detective Heald said, and several officers looked in our direction.

I never seemed to get along with the police, and this time would be no different.

"Can I go?" I asked.

"No. I think we are going to take you down to the station."

"Why? Because of my comment?"

84

THE VIDEO TAPE

"No, that's not it."

"I can't just answer your questions here?"

"That ship has sailed. I can play hardball, too."

"I wasn't playing hardball."

"Well, I felt you were. And that's all that matters. So I'll take you down to the station where you can finish up with my questions."

"Can I at least drive myself to the station?"

He considered it. "If you're even ten minutes late, I'll put out an arrest warrant for a missing witness."

I could have asked if that was even a thing, but what was the point? I'd just be digging myself a deeper grave.

"I won't be late. Which precinct?"

He gave me the address.

"I'll see you there," I said.

Detective Heald walked away without giving me the courtesy of a reply. I walked over to Nori, who'd just finished answering her detective's questions.

"I'm sorry, but I must go to their Hollywood station."

"What? Why?"

"This detective has it in for me."

"Do you want me to come down with you?"

"No, then he would just give you shit, too."

"Okay. I'll meet you somewhere after. Your place?"

The note on my door sprang to mind. And I instantly felt a wave of desperation. This guy—I still assumed the killer was a male—knew where Darian worked. He knew where I lived. And I had to believe he knew who Nori was.

Fuck. Fuck. Fuck.

"Did you hear me, Bobby? Should we meet at your place?"

"No. Is there a restaurant around here that you like? Somewhere that has a lot of people?"

"There's plenty."

"Well, pick one. And stay there until I get back here."

"You're scaring me, Bobby."

"Well shit, it is a scary situation." I didn't mean to say shit so loud. "I'm sorry."

"You don't think he'd come after me or you?"

"I don't know what to think, Nori, but we should start having our heads on a swivel."

85

"This is so screwed up. Just yesterday, we were all hanging out together. Now, Darian is gone, and who knows what will happen to us."

"Don't say that. We'll get through this."

"With a madman after us? That doesn't sound too appealing."

I hated hearing that, but she wasn't wrong. Things had changed.

"Listen, I hate doing this, but I must get to the police station. Pick a restaurant. I expect I'll be back this way pretty soon."

"Okay. I'll text you where I end up," Nori said.

"Do you want me to have one of these officers escort you there? I could ask."

"The sun is out, and it's the middle of the morning. I'll be fine."

"It's not like killers can't strike during the day."

"This is a lot of fun, Bobby. Jeez."

"I'm sorry. Just worried about you."

"You better go answer your questions."

"Okay. I'll see you later."

❦ 18 ❦

The LAPD kept me for nearly an hour, and I had to answer some of their questions two, three, and four times.

It was Detective Heald and some other detective who barely said a word. It was apparent that Heald had the seniority.

I was annoyed because I just wanted to go back and see Nori, but I can't blame the LAPD. They had a gruesome murder on their hands and wanted to get any information they could.

Unfortunately, I didn't have much to give them.

I kept telling them the secret to finding her killer was to reopen the case of the videotape. Heald seemed skeptical. Maybe because then he'd be admitting that the LAPD had dropped the ball regarding the thirty-year-old case.

I insinuated that if they'd ever found the killer, this never would have happened.

"We can't be sure this woman's murder is related to your investigation into the videotape."

I was going to repeat what I said earlier, but tried to say it as non-threatening as possible.

"I'm not trying to be a jerk, but why would someone carve my name into her body if it wasn't?"

Heald had no comeback to that.

He tried to suggest that Bobby might be the name of Darian's ex-boyfriend, but his heart wasn't in that theory.

87

BRIAN O'SULLIVAN

Finally, after about fifty minutes, the interview neared its end. We were combative for most of it, but Detective Heald softened.

"Okay, Bobby, you can go now. Thanks for answering all of our questions. This is my interview style. I try to keep the interviewee off balance. I hope you understand. If it matters to you, I believe you've been telling us the truth."

It was hard to say thanks after how Detective Heald treated me. But I didn't want to be a jerk since we might have to deal with each other down the line.

"No hard feelings," I said.

We shook hands and ended on a relatively high note.

It wouldn't last.

◦✦◦

I DROVE TO SEE NORI, WHO HAD BEEN SADDLED UP AT OUR OLD SPOT: Breakfast Sammie's.

She was sitting in the back, and only had a coffee in front of her.

"I came as soon as I could," I said.

"You're fine. I needed the time to send some texts and make a few calls."

"Fellow employees?"

"Yes. And my parents."

"What did they say?"

"My mother wants me to move home."

My first inclination was to laugh it off, but from her parents' point of view, it would be a logical next step. It was the first time I realized I might lose Nori as well.

"What did you tell them?"

"I said it's not just as simple as moving home. I might have to help plan a funeral. I now have you in my life."

"So you told them you're staying?"

"At least for now."

This would be just my luck. The first woman in a while I'd grown to like, and she moves back to Missouri.

Could be worse, Bobby. Look at Darian.

I had to remind myself that whatever I was going through, Darian had endured a thousand times worse.

"Speaking of family," Nori said. "Have you called your father yet?"

"No. I will later today, though. What time is it?"

88

THE VIDEO TAPE

"It's 11:45."

"This is officially the longest day ever, and it's not even noon."

She grabbed my hand. "I can't believe Darian is gone."

"I know. It's horrible."

"Do you think the guy in the videotape is the one who killed her?"

"What else am I supposed to think?"

"So the guy killed in the mid-nineties and again in 2025. That's thirty years apart. Do you think those are the only two people he ever killed?"

"When you put it that way, probably not."

"So we could have a serial killer on our hands?"

"It's possible."

"And he likely knows who we are."

I had never told Nori about the letter left on my door. I didn't feel like burdening her with it now.

"Yeah, I'd say that's a safe assumption."

"Maybe my parents are right, and I should go home."

Darian's death was brutal enough. If this killer somehow got to Nori, I'd never be the same. I could never let that happen. Even if that meant losing the woman I'd fallen for in record time.

"If you feel like that's the right thing to do, I won't stop you."

She put her head in her hands.

"Fuck all of this," she muttered.

We were getting some stray glances at this point. While I didn't care what they thought, this wasn't the place to have the conversation we were having.

"Let's get out of here, Nori."

She picked her head up from her hands.

"Okay."

19

We spent that first night in a hotel.

It couldn't last, but I felt safer not returning to my place for at least twenty-four hours.

Nori got a lot done and contacted several of her co-workers. Most had already heard. News travels fast these days, especially when it's a woman murdered in her place of employment. Or, in Darian's case, in the business you own.

Nori also contacted Darian's lone child, a daughter named Mira.

I contacted Ernest and Noble and set up times to meet them the following day. The hotel was going to be a one-day thing. We had to get back to the real world, even if a killer was out there.

I turned on the TV before we went to bed, and Darian's murder was the lead story on KTLA, the most watched of the Los Angeles television stations.

They did not mention the videotape, snuff films, Nori, or me. They did release Darian's name and said she was a pioneer in the adult bookstore world. BLISSFUL was far more than a bookstore, but maybe that sounded better than sex store.

"Can you turn this off?" Nori asked, and I obliged.

We were both asleep within ten minutes.

It had been a horrible day.

THE VIDEO TAPE

I WOKE UP THE NEXT MORNING AND ASKED NORI IF SHE HAD A FRIEND'S house where she could stay.

"Yeah. I have two different friends named Grace. Either one would put me up."

"Which one lives farther away?"

"Grace Kildare lives a good forty miles south."

"I'd say the farther the better, so I'd stay there."

"I'll call her, but I already know she'll say yes."

"Okay, good. I have things I must do today, and we both know we can't stay in this hotel forever."

"I get it."

"What's going to happen with BLISSFUL? You won't reopen it any time soon, will you?"

"I'm not sure. I will discuss it with Darian's daughter, who said we could talk more today. I don't even know if I'd want to reopen or work there again. I have a lot of thinking to do."

"Sounds like we both have a busy day. Listen, I'm just a phone call away. If anything is out of the ordinary, call me. Actually, call the cops first. And call me when you get down to your friend Grace's."

"I will. And I'll worry about you, too, so keep in touch."

"Okay, let's get out of here. I'll drive you back to BLISSFUL so you can get your car."

"I can't believe it was only yesterday morning that we found her body."

"It's been a long freaking twenty-four hours."

"And I've got some more bad news."

"What?"

"Darian didn't have any cameras inside or outside the business."

"Why?"

"Because she thought people going into an adult store didn't want to be seen on camera."

I hated to admit it, but it made sense. Darian's logical decision was now going to make it much tougher for the LAPD to catch her killer.

I DROVE NORI TO HER APARTMENT FIRST SO SHE COULD GRAB SOME clothes. On the way over, I'd convinced her she could make all her phone calls at her friend Grace's house, and she agreed to head down there this morning. It was a load off my mind. I didn't want her roaming around Los Angeles by herself.

BRIAN O'SULLIVAN

After she grabbed her clothes, I drove her to BLISSFUL.

We said goodbye, and I didn't feel safe until she was in her car, heading on to Hollywood Boulevard.

I did my cursory look at the apartments above but saw nothing suspicious.

I glanced back at BLISSFUL and said one final prayer for Darian Hague.

⚜

AFTER RETURNING TO MY PLACE, I GRABBED MY PHONE AND MADE THE call I dreaded.

"Hello, Bobby."

"Hi, Dad. I've got some terrible news."

Usually, my father would make a joke at that point, assuming I was exaggerating, or calling with good news. I'd used that trick before. This time, he seemed to sense the dread in my voice.

"What is it, son?"

"You remember Darian, the owner of BLISSFUL."

"Of course. How could I forget her?"

"She was murdered."

"Tell me you're kidding."

"Sorry, Dad. I'm not."

"Oh my God. How horrible. When? How?"

"Either yesterday morning or the night before. Probably the night before, when she closed up the store. And the killer used a knife."

I didn't want to give more specifics than that, and I was not going to tell him what the killer had carved into her abdomen. If he found out about it from the news or through a friend and got mad at me, I could truthfully tell him I was just looking out for him.

"I'm afraid to ask, but does this have something to do with the case you took on?"

"Yes. I'm pretty sure."

"Jeez, Bobby. You should drop this case. This guy is going around killing people. Killing people you know. You could be next on his list for all we know."

Everything he'd said was true.

"You're not wrong, but I'm also not dropping this case."

"Bobby."

My father often tried to make his point by sternly saying my name. It

92

worked numerous times throughout my childhood. However, I was a grown man, and he wouldn't change my mind.

"I'm sorry, Dad. I'm staying on. I'm staying on for the woman killed in the videotape. And I'm staying on for Darian. I can't just drop the case now. The killer would win."

"I don't care about winning and losing, Bobby. I care about you staying alive. And what about Nori? What if that beautiful young lady is next?"

"Don't say that, Dad."

"Don't pretend like it hasn't crossed your mind. You've thought about it."

"Yes, I have. And so has she. And right now, we want to put all our energy into catching this killer."

If you can feel someone shaking their head from the other end of a phone, I felt it at that moment.

"I'm going to be safe, Dad. I've installed a camera outside my apartment. Nori is staying at her friend's house outside of LA."

"This guy just killed a woman at her place of work. I don't think a camera or a drive out of Los Angeles will deter him."

My father was just looking out for me, but we began talking in circles.

"You've been a great father and have taught me well. I will use that brain you gave me, and I'll be smart going forward. And you know what? I'm going to catch this mother effer, and have him pay for what he did to Darian."

I heard my father exhale, which always meant he was done arguing. "Darian was a sweet lady."

"She was. And she liked you."

"I liked her, too. I was already planning my next Los Angeles visit. I was going to ask her to lunch."

This was becoming really tough. "I'm so sorry, Dad. I don't know what to say."

"There isn't anything to say. We'll never know if me and her would have had more than just a moment."

I couldn't take much more of this. I hated hearing my father so sad. "I'm going to hang up in a second. This is so unsettling."

"I know it is, Bobby. I'm so sorry. Tell Nori I'm thinking about her, too."

"I will."

"And one last thing."

"What is it?"

"Go fucking catch this guy, Bobby."

My father, who hardly ever cried, could be heard softly sobbing on the other end.

"I will, Dad."

"And be safe."

With that, my father hung up, and seconds later, he wasn't the only McGowan man crying.

20

I woke up the next morning and felt hungover, despite not having had a sip of alcohol.

All the sadness of the last two days was weighing on me, and I felt listless.

When I'm actually hungover, I try to go for a run. It settles me down and helps my mind get back to normal.

I decided it might be just what I needed.

I jogged about three miles, ending up along the bluffs of Santa Monica, looking out at the Pacific Ocean. I ran past the world-famous Santa Monica Pier and down into the equally well-known Venice Beach.

I took in all the people smiling and having a great time during the early days of summer in Los Angeles. I took in all the palm trees, and constantly looked out onto the vast ocean next to me.

I needed it.

The last few days were dark, and the seedy side of Hollywood was far different than the bluffs of Santa Monica.

At one point, a couple walked by me as I looked out on those bluffs. They were in their thirties and both wearing colorful workout gear.

"I can't believe Todd and Emma's wedding in Italy is only a few weeks away," the woman said.

"I can't wait. We'll be drinking some Italian wine I can't pronounce and eating some gnocchi in a pesto sauce," he said.

And just like that, they'd walked by me.

But I couldn't get their brief conversation out of my mind. I wanted to crash Todd and Emma's wedding, be in Italy, and be carefree as I drank wine and ate gnocchi.

Instead, I was mired in a brutal murder investigation.

I told myself I was going on a much-needed vacation when this was over.

I RETURNED TO MY APARTMENT OUT OF BREATH, BUT FEELING relatively good. It's not like I had forgotten all that had happened—how could I?—but I'd managed to look at the bright side of life for an hour or so.

I knew with all that stood before me, it wasn't all going to be palm trees and ocean views, so I enjoyed the moment.

I CALLED NORI, WHO HAD ENJOYED A NICE QUIET NIGHT AT HER friend's house.

It's just what I needed to hear. I wanted to see and spend time with her, but more than anything, I wanted her to be safe. I suggested, very unobtrusively, that she stay there one more night.

She agreed but said she'd be back in LA on Thursday because she was meeting with Darian's daughter, who wanted to plan a memorial at BLISSFUL.

"She wants to have the memorial in the spot where her mother was killed?" I asked.

"That's what I asked, but she was adamant that's where Darian would have wanted it. That was her life, and she was proud of all she'd accomplished there."

"I don't like it. Not from her daughter's end. I understand that. But the killer is familiar with BLISSFUL. What if he makes an appearance there or sees you walking into the event?"

"Not to be rude, Bobby, but I think it's time we stop pretending he doesn't know who I am. I've thought about that a lot lately. I was Darian's

THE VIDEO TAPE

right-hand woman, and I'm your girlfriend. If he's watching us at all, which I think we can both admit he is, then surely he knows who I am."

"You're probably right." I hated to admit it.

"Plus, in the end, it's not my choice. She's Darian's daughter and will make the final call."

"Did she say when she wants to do it?"

"Soon. Possibly as early as Saturday."

"That's only three days away."

"She doesn't live in LA, and has to get back to her family by Monday. That's why she's leaning toward Saturday. Anyway, I'll find out all that stuff when I meet with her tomorrow."

"Okay. Call me after you talk to her. I'm just glad you're safe with your friend."

We were early in our relationship and had never used the word love, so I was surprised by what I heard next.

"Love ya, Bobby."

It wasn't an "I love you," which is much more committal. I liked the way she had done it.

"Love ya, too, Nori."

"We'll talk tomorrow."

"Bye."

The following two days went by in a flash.

I had another interview with the LAPD on Thursday morning. When we finished, Detective Heald said he had more questions for Nori.

I told him she was staying at a friend's house outside of LA, and asked if he could interview over the phone. He agreed to that.

❧

NORI MET WITH DARIAN'S DAUGHTER MIRA, WHO STUCK TO HER GUNS.

The memorial was going to be held on Saturday at BLISSFUL. Nori said she couldn't be talked out of it.

It was obvious where Mira got her stubbornness from—her mother.

I missed Darian.

21

Darian Hague's memorial was a raucous affair.

I know that sounds odd, considering that she died in such a brutal fashion, and we were ostensibly there to mourn her death. But it felt more like a party.

People truly celebrated her life. There was a podium where people could come and speak about Darian, and boy, did they ever. Twenty people must have spoken.

It was bizarre to have the memorial in the spot where she died, but it somehow ended up working. It almost made it feel like she was there with us in spirit.

The people who spoke covered her whole life. Her sister talked about growing up in Louisiana and how she always wanted to move to California, and did so the week after graduating high school, choosing San Francisco first. The year was 1981.

Some old friends talked about her time as an eighteen-year-old in San Francisco and mentioned that her hair went down below her butt. They said Darian was a hippy at heart, but this was the early eighties, and the vibe in San Francisco was changing. This was no longer the summer of love.

So, after a few years in the City by the Bay, she moved to LA. She was only twenty-one years old at the time.

There were too many Los Angeles stories to absorb. At least five people came up and spoke about her early days in LA, and how she was one of the prettiest and most motivated women living in Hollywood in the mid-eighties.

Every guy wanted to date her, and she dated more than her fair share, but Darian was more interested in becoming a businesswoman.

Sure, her chosen business wasn't one that most women would think—much less want—to open, but Darian moved to the beat of a different drum.

In 1990, at the ripe old age of twenty-seven, she opened BLISSFUL. She had taken a small loan from her parents to help launch the place and promised to pay them back within three years.

She paid them back in less than two. Darian was a woman of her word, which repeatedly appeared in the speeches.

Many people mentioned how proud Darian was of owning BLISSFUL. It's not easy to own any business, much less an adult-themed one, for thirty-five years.

Nori did not speak, but some of Darian's employees talked about how great a boss she had been.

She did seem to have a 100% approval rating.

Her daughter Mira said that despite being a tough-minded business-woman, she'd been a fantastic mother.

She closed by saying, "I love you, Mom," and you could hear people yelling "Hear, Hear," or "Cheers." This summed up the liveliness of the memorial.

Not once was her cause of death mentioned.

That's not why we were all there.

I don't know if Darian had any Irish heritage, but this felt more like an Irish wake than a funeral.

❧

EVERYONE SEEMED TO BE ON A HIGH WHEN IT ENDED.

"I think that went well," Nori said as we cleaned up.

"That's an understatement."

"It was a pretty darn nice affair, wasn't it?"

"It was the most celebratory memorial I've ever been to."

"Good. That's what Darian would have wanted."

Just because I enjoyed the event doesn't mean I wasn't keeping tabs on all the attendees.

I took a mental snapshot of everyone I came across.

Attending the memorial or funeral of the person you killed is not unheard of, and I paid my due diligence to everyone I met. No one jumped out as a potential suspect. Not that I should have been surprised. They'd have been on their best behavior if they were somehow there.

Darian's daughter had hired someone to videotape the memorial, so if something came up later, I'd have that in my back pocket.

Two hours after the memorial had ended, we were finally close to finishing cleaning.

At that point, it was just me, Nori, Darian's sister and daughter, and their husbands.

Darian's daughter, Mira, approached me and Nori. "Thank you very much for helping set this up, Nori. You were a true friend to Darian."

"It's the least I could do."

They hugged, and then Mira turned toward me. Her expression was no longer exuberant. "And thanks for your help, Bobby."

More was coming, and I wasn't sure I would like it.

"I don't know why my mother was murdered. Neither do the police yet. But if it has something to do with your investigation, I want you to find the scumbag who did this. Do you understand?"

"Yes, I do."

"Good. Well, I'm glad we got that part over with."

And just like that, she returned to being the vivacious woman she'd been all day.

"And Nori, you guys can go whenever you want. We are pretty much done."

"You sure?"

"I'm sure. You two have been great."

"Thanks for everything, Mira."

"You're welcome. And let's talk in the next few days. I need to decide once and for all if we will keep BLISSFUL open. Whether you want to take over my mother's duties. Things like that. We have a lot to talk about."

"Great. I'll reach out soon."

They hugged, and Nori grabbed my hand, leading me toward the back door. We said our goodbyes to the people remaining and exited BLISSFUL.

"Do you want to stay over tonight?" I asked.

She'd told me Grace was having people over that night, and she didn't want to overstay her welcome.

"Yeah, but I'll drive myself."

"Okay. See you soon."

THE VIDEO TAPE

❦

I ARRIVED AT MY APARTMENT, PARKED MY CAR, AND RETURNED TO THE street where Nori always parked. She arrived a few minutes later.

"I'm so happy that went well," she said.

"It was perfect."

"Darian would have loved it. She would have been making her rounds. Having a drink. Regaling people with stories."

"I knew she was quite a woman from the moment I met her, but I didn't realize how many lives she'd touched. And my gosh, that hair from the early eighties."

Nori laughed.

"I know. That must have been a wild time to be alive."

"She lived an extraordinary life. That doesn't mean it wasn't cut way too short. It was. But she accomplished a lot in her time on earth."

As we approached my apartment, I saw another letter taped to my door. My heart sank.

"What is that?" Nori asked.

I played dumb. "Probably an alert to pay rent."

"Your landlord has to tell you when to pay rent?"

"Or maybe they're doing a fumigation or something."

Nori wasn't buying it, so she arrived at the door first, grabbing the paper. "Well, let's open it up and see."

"Nori, don't."

"Why?"

"Let's talk inside."

I grabbed the note from her hand and opened the door.

Nori scowled as we entered. "That's pretty rude, just grabbing that from my hand."

"Would you mind sitting down?"

"You're being weird. What is going on?"

"Don't you want to sit down?"

"I can take this standing up. Whatever 'this' is."

It was too late to lie. Nori wasn't going to budge until she saw what the letter said. Maybe my fears were misguided, and it was something from my landlord. Unfortunately, I didn't think so.

"A few days after I first saw the videotape, I came back here, and there was a letter just like this one waiting for me."

"What did it say?"

"It said, 'Seen any good movies lately?'"

BRIAN O'SULLIVAN

She hadn't been expecting that and seemed muddled for a brief moment.

"That's very scary, Bobby."

"Yeah, it was. And I'm afraid this might be the same kind of letter."

"Maybe it is and maybe it isn't. One thing is for sure, though. We're both going to see what it says. It's not like you can just put that in your room and I'm suddenly going to forget about it. So we might as well get this over with."

I didn't have any options. "Okay."

"I'm sure it's not that bad," Nori said.

But her expression told me she was having doubts herself.

I slowly tore the tape off and fully opened the letter.

Nori came and stood next to me, and we both read it.

It was worse than I expected. Way worse.

Written in the same big bold writing as the last one was the following:

DARIAN'S FUNERAL WAS QUITE THE PARTY. LET'S HOPE WE CAN DO THE SAME WHEN IT'S NORI'S TURN.

22

I didn't know what to say. I didn't know what to do.

How do you come back after seeing/reading something like that?

I tried to say all the right things. Or, at least, what I thought was right at the moment.

He's just trying to scare us. We could hire a bodyguard. He's after me, not you.

Nothing seemed to help, and maybe there's nothing that can help in such a situation.

So I just shut up and let Nori cry on my shoulder.

WHEN WE WOKE UP THE FOLLOWING MORNING, WE HAD THE "TALK."

"I want your honest answer. Do you think I should move back to Missouri for a bit?" Nori asked.

Selfishly, I wanted her to stay. I loved dating her. I loved how we were getting closer every single day.

But if she was truly in harm's way, I couldn't in good conscience tell her that she should stay.

"If you moved home, you could always come back when this case is solved."

"No offense, Bobby, but the police have had this case for thirty years and never solved it."

BRIAN O'SULLIVAN

"That doesn't mean I won't. Plus, they will now be looking at it with new eyes. I think we have a great chance of catching him."

My words landed flat.

"You don't sound that confident," Nori said.

I shrugged. "I love being with you, but I can't guarantee I can always protect you."

"If I decided to move, would you want to have a long-distance relationship?"

"It's not ideal, but I want to be with you, Nori, and I think you want to be with me."

"Of course I do, but how long will this last? What if this goes on for six months? A year? Three years?"

"I don't know what you want me to say. I want to stay together. Hopefully, this doesn't last three years. Shit, I hope this doesn't last three more days."

"I like you a lot, too, Bobby. But I'm not sure I can handle looking over my shoulder every day. That's no way to live."

"Then I think you should move home. And trust me, that takes a lot for me to say."

We decided to leave it at that.

Ten minutes later, Nori was getting ready to leave, and I walked her out to her car.

"You sure you don't want me to come with you?"

"Don't take this the wrong way, Bobby, but maybe I'm safer without you around."

That hit like a ton of bricks.

"I mean, I'm sorry," she continued. "But this person obviously has it in for you. Knows where you live. Etc. Etc. And maybe it's just better if we break ties for the next few days."

I hated hearing it, but there was a lot of truth to it.

"Maybe you're right, but please stay out in public during the day," I said. "And I'd feel much better if you returned to Grace's."

"I can't just stay there forever."

"If you must stay at your place, go home before it gets dark. If you change your mind and want to come back here, just call me."

Nori gave me a long hug.

"Like I said, I don't think that's a good idea, but I'll be in touch later today."

There wasn't even a "Love ya" to finish.

104

THE VIDEO TAPE

❧

I HAD A JOB TO DO.

I could have sat around all day worrying about what would happen to Nori and me, but that wouldn't have accomplished anything. If she was going to move, then the best way to get her back to Los Angeles was to catch this psychopath.

So it was time to get down to business.

"Hey, Bobby."

"Noble, were you able to find out if the LAPD kept the package that the initial videotape was sent in?"

"Shit, I'm sorry. I called when you first asked, but didn't hear back."

"Can you follow up and text me back as soon as you find out?"

"Sure."

"Thanks."

Next, I called Alfred Weaver.

"Hello."

"Mr. Weaver, this is Bobby McGowan. We met about five days ago."

"Yes, Mr. McGowan. I heard about the tragedy that befell the owner of BLISSFUL. That's not related to the videotape you showed me, is it?"

If there was a time for a lie, this was the time.

"I don't think so."

"Well, I'm sorry for your loss, regardless."

"Thank you. Were you able to talk with any of your connections? I'd still love to meet with one of them."

"I did. And he finally got back to me earlier this morning. I was going to reach out to you later today."

"What did he say?"

"He'd be willing to meet with you if you promise not to mention his name to anyone."

"I'm fine with that."

"That includes the police, whoever hired you, or your girlfriend."

I didn't like the way he'd thrown in Nori. It sounded dismissive. To be honest, I didn't like much about Alfred Weaver. He was a grade-A douchebag.

But I needed to meet with this guy, so I said nothing.

"I won't tell anyone," I said. "So, how do I get in touch with him?"

"Can I give him your phone number?"

"Sure."

"All right, I'll tell him to contact you."

"What's his name?"

"He likes to call himself Mr. Z."

"Okay. Thanks."

I hung up, and was already tired of "Mr. Z" even though I'd never met him.

This wasn't Watergate. I wanted to ask him a few questions about snuff films. Going by Mr. Z sounded beyond pretentious.

Turned out I was mistaken.

Mr. Z had every reason to want to keep his anonymity.

23

It was four p.m. when I saw an incoming call from Nori.

"Is everything okay?"

"You may want to come down to my apartment."

"Why? Did something happen?"

"Just come down."

"You're all right, though?"

"Yes, Bobby."

I RAN TO MY CAR AND SPED TOWARD HOLLYWOOD.

She'd said she was okay, but I was still anxious. Something was up.

When I arrived, I noticed a police car out front, and my anxiety ratcheted up.

Nori stood outside her apartment, looking in my direction. As I approached her, I saw that the police officer was sitting in his car, filling out some paperwork.

"What happened?"

She took out her phone. "This was waiting on the door to my apartment."

In the now recognizable handwriting, "BE SEEING YOU SOON, NORI."

"I'm so sorry," I said.

BRIAN O'SULLIVAN

"It's probably a good thing."

"How could that possibly be a good thing?"

"I was on the phone to my mother when I approached my apartment. When I saw the note, she heard me tense up. I'd seen the note at your place and figured this was the same thing. When I opened it and read it, I told my mother what it said. She broke down in tears. And guess what she did a few seconds later?"

"I don't know. Called the cops for you?"

"No, I called the cops. She booked a flight out here. She arrives later tonight, and we will fly back to Missouri tomorrow morning."

"You're moving home?"

"I don't really have a choice anymore," she said, tearing up.

I leaned in for a hug, even though I was getting tired of giving freaking hugs. I wanted to catch this animal.

It dawned on me that I hadn't looked at my camera from the night before. I'd been so busy trying to console Nori that it almost seemed secondary. Hopefully, it got a good look at the person who left the note.

"I'm sorry it's come to this, Nori. When I first walked into BLISSFUL, I'd never considered the possibility that you'd be drawn into this."

"It's not your fault, Bobby."

I appreciated her response, but the fact is that it was my fault. If she'd never met me, she'd still be working at BLISSFUL, and Darian would still be alive. I hadn't expected this, nor done it maliciously, but Nori was moving home because she met me. That was just a fact.

"When does your mother land?"

"Not until later tonight."

"You're not leaving my sight until she gets here."

"Okay. Thanks, Bobby."

A second later, I saw a familiar face stepping out of a car. But just because it was a familiar face didn't mean it was someone I wanted to see.

"Hello, Bobby."

"Hi, Detective Heald."

"I need to talk with you. Nori told me you received a note at your apartment as well."

"I did. And I have a video of whoever left it."

"You do?" Heald asked.

"I forgot to check it last night. There was so much going on. What is your email? An app on my phone connects to the camera, and I can send you the last twenty-four hours."

108

THE VIDEO TAPE

Heald gave me his email address. "And there are no cameras at this apartment complex, so yours will be vital."

"Happy to help."

"We will need to ask you a few questions, though."

"I'm going to spend the rest of the day with Nori. Can I come in tomorrow morning?"

He looked us over. "Sure. Can you come in at nine?"

"I'll be there."

His eyes moved from me to Nori's.

"Thanks for your help, Ms. Bridgewater. I hope we can leave you out of this investigation from here on in, but if we have to give you a call, I hope you'll be willing to answer a few questions."

Nori must have told Heald that this was all too much for her and she was moving home.

"That would be fine," she said.

"Thanks. I'll be going now." He walked down to his car before turning around. "Hey, Bobby."

"Yeah?"

"Why don't you bring that note to the station tomorrow? And try to avoid handling it in the meantime."

"Understood."

"I'll see you tomorrow," Heald said. "Safe travels, Nori."

❧ 24 ❧

ori and I spent the rest of the day together.

We stayed in and ordered a pizza.

We tried—for the most part successfully—to keep things light. We'd said pretty much all we could about Darian's murder and the two letters left on our respective apartment doors.

An hour before her mother was set to arrive, she initiated sex. We both knew it would be our last time or the last for a long time. It was bittersweet.

After we finished, Nori took a quick shower.

When she reappeared, I asked her a question I'd avoided all day.

"Do you want me to be here when your mother gets here? I could just sit by my car."

"Are you asking if she's going to hate you?"

"I guess so, in my own weird way."

"I told her that none of this is your fault. I've also told her how close we've become, and that I genuinely care about you."

"She doesn't think this all happened too quickly?"

"My parents married after knowing each other for all of two weeks. To them, we are moving at glacier-like speed."

I laughed, and it felt good. "If I'd known that, I'd have asked you out that first day."

"I'd probably have turned you down. Your timing was perfect."

"Until now," I said. "The timing on this sucks."

THE VIDEO TAPE

"Yes, it does."

"How about tomorrow morning? Do you need help?"

"Nope. We're staying at a hotel tonight and meeting my friend Amber in the morning. She's going to pick up my big stuff. I only have a bed, a small couch, and a dresser. She's going to store them at her house for now. I'll pack my small, personal stuff and they'll come back to Missouri with me."

"What about all your clothes?"

"I'll take as much as I can. Maybe I'll have Amber send some later on if needed. You've seen how I dress. I have a few dresses, pants, and many of my favorite band T-shirts. It's not like I'm Anna Wintour."

I had no idea who Anna Wintour was, but it hardly seemed important.

"I get it. Just thought I'd offer. And I assume you don't want me to stay at the hotel with you guys."

"Sorry, Bobby. My mother wouldn't like that."

Nori's phone buzzed. Her mother was two minutes away.

"I have one favor to ask, Nori."

"What is it?"

"Don't get too comfortable at home. I'm going to catch this asshole, and I want you back in my life. So don't get back to Missouri and sign a year lease or something crazy like that."

"You don't have to worry about that. I don't think my mother will let me leave her house for at least the first several weeks."

"See, I knew I'd like your mother."

Nori managed a slight smile. "You'd like her under different circumstances. And by the way, say goodbye to your father for me. That night seems so long ago."

"It does. I'll say goodbye for you. He liked you a lot."

"I'm getting sad now."

"Because of my father?"

She laughed and leaned in and kissed me. "This might be our final kiss for a while. Please be safe, Bobby. Give me a reason to come back to LA."

"I'll be here. I'm going to get the bad guy, not vice versa."

Just then, some lights hit Nori's apartment door.

"That's probably her."

"I'm so sorry it's come to this, Nori."

"Stop saying that. I'm so glad I met you. As you know, I love ya."

She smiled as she said it.

"Love ya, too."

A split-second later, there was a knock at the door. Nori went to answer, and I took a few steps back, so they could have a moment without me loitering around.

They were crying before her mother had shut the front door behind her. And not just a few whimpers. Full-on bawling.

This lasted several seconds before Nori finally swiveled them around to face me. They both wiped their eyes in unison. Nori was the spitting image of her mother. The old maxim that it could have been her older sister applied here.

"Mom, this is Bobby. Bobby, this is my mother."

I went to shake hands with her, but she leaned in for the hug. Yes, I'd gotten sick of hugs, but this one was warranted, and I was just happy that she accepted me. If the roles had been reversed and someone was putting my daughter in harm's way, I'm not sure I'd have been as receptive.

"You've made my daughter very happy these last several weeks."

"Thank you. I'm sorry that it's ending like this."

"It's not."

"What do you mean?"

"Look in my eyes, Bobby."

I did as she said.

"I want you to catch this guy. My daughter loves LA, and I want to be able to send her back. But not like this. Can you understand that?"

"Of course. I told her it was probably for the best."

"Thank you for that. You seem like a good man."

I don't know what I expected from her mother, but it certainly wasn't this.

"It's been a pleasure to meet you, Mrs. Bridgewater. I think it's time I go and give you guys some time alone."

"Remember what I told you."

"I will."

Nori grabbed my hand and walked me out of the apartment, shutting the door behind her.

"Please be safe, Bobby," she said, repeating her earlier plea.

"Text me tomorrow morning."

"Okay."

"And then text me when you arrive back home safely."

"Will you get out of here before I get emotional again?"

It was time for one last kiss. I leaned in and gave her a long, passionate one.

"This isn't goodbye. This is 'till next time.'"

"Stop making this a sappy romantic comedy and get the hell out of here."

"Bye, Nori."

"Bye, Bobby."

I headed toward my car, my emotions getting the best of me. That had been happening too much lately.

"Love ya," I heard her say.

"Love ya," I yelled back.

And just like that, Nori was gone from my life.

25

I woke up the following morning with a hollow feeling.

I was going to miss Nori greatly. Sure, we'd keep in touch and probably talk quite regularly. But it wouldn't be the same. Not even close.

Anyone who's gone through a breakup—and for all intents and purposes, this was—will tell you to throw yourself into your work.

So that's what I did.

"I'm Bobby McGowan. Are you Mr. Z?"

I felt silly just saying it.

"I am. Listen, I don't feel safe talking in public. There's a little basketball court about a hundred yards away that is never used. Can we talk there?"

"Sure. Lead the way."

I followed him, and sure enough, there was a tiny, one-hoop basketball court that no one was using. There was a park bench on the side of it, but he seemed to want to remain standing.

I'm unsure why he hadn't just given this as his original destination instead of giving me the restaurant we'd walked from. Maybe he wanted an escape plan if he didn't like the looks of me. That made sense, I guess.

THE VIDEO TAPE

"Thanks for meeting with me," I said. We still hadn't even shaken hands.

Mr. Z's face was weathered. He looked like he'd seen a lot in his life. He was a white guy, probably in his mid- to late fifties, but his expression was worn, like someone in his seventies.

"Mr. Weaver told me you may have a real snuff film in your possession."

"Everyone seems to think so."

"Everyone?"

"I've shown a few experts the tape and they've both agreed it's the real thing."

"Is Mr. Weaver one of those experts?"

"Yes."

He laughed. "I taught that old man everything he knows about snuff films. His book was a total mess until he met me."

"I see."

I was intrigued by Mr. Z. He would either be a complete blowhard or have some important information for me. I didn't think there was much middle ground with him.

"The floor is yours. I'd love to hear anything you want to tell me."

"Do you have your laptop in that backpack of yours?"

"Yes."

"And I'd assume you have the prospective snuff film on that laptop."

"Yes. Would you like to see it?"

I was worse than Oprah.

Here's a snuff film for you. And a snuff film for you! And here's one for you!

"Yes, I think we should make sure it's the one I've seen first."

I was flabbergasted. "Wait, you think you've seen the videotape I have?"

"If Mr. Weaver described it correctly, then yes."

My heart was racing.

"Is there a woman stabbed to death while enclosed in some sort of atrium?" Mr. Z asked.

"Yes."

"Is she then decapitated?"

"The videotape cuts off right before then, but that's clearly what will happen. So you must have seen that part?"

If Mr. Z was telling the truth, the original film had this poor woman being beheaded on camera. Thank God I didn't have to see that.

"I did. Be happy you didn't."

BRIAN O'SULLIVAN

I quickly removed my laptop from my bag. I hadn't expected this.

But I now knew why Alfred Weaver had reacted so oddly. He knew he was watching the snuff film Mr. Z had told him about.

I walked over to the bench on the side of the basketball court. Mr. Z followed.

I usually preferred showing people the actual videotape, but that wasn't possible. I pressed play on the laptop.

"Play it one more time," he said, and I did.

"Yes, that's the same snuff film I first saw thirty years ago."

I couldn't believe it. This was the break I needed.

"Who showed it to you?" I said, asking the million-dollar question.

"How about I tell you a little about myself first?"

I'd waited a month and a half to get a lead like this. I could wait a little longer.

"Sure. Tell me anything and everything you want."

Mr. Z looked around nervously and saw that the basketball court was still empty, and no one was heading toward us.

"Okay, so I'm an LA baby. I was born and raised in El Segundo. My parents were great and tried their best. Whatever hardships I've encountered in my life are all on me. They are still together and have been married for over sixty years. You believe that shit? But I was a lousy kid. I guess you can tally one up for nature over nurture, because my parents nurtured the fuck out of me, and I still ended up a bad seed. I was kicked out of God knows how many high schools. I tried to join the military at eighteen, but even they wouldn't take me. Shows you how difficult I was. I started getting odd jobs anywhere in Los Angeles. And by odd, I truly do mean odd. I worked at dirty movie theaters. I bounced at the toughest bars. I even worked as a sanitation worker for a stretch. I should have kept that job. They get paid pretty well. Anyway, at this point, I'd been kicked out of my parents' house. I'd bring girls home, or be high on drugs, and my parents just weren't having it. I was also an argumentative prick to them. I can't blame them for anything they did. So I moved to Hollywood. Not the Hollywood you're thinking of with all the glimmer and glam. I was on the other side of the proverbial train tracks. Porn stores, rub-and-tugs, drug dealers on every corner. You hear what I'm saying?"

"I'm following." I didn't want to say much for fear of having him second-guess his decision to tell me everything.

"Okay, good. At some point, I'm pretty sure it was 1995, when I would have been twenty-five, I got hired at Hard Hank's, one of the more famous peep show places back then. Great name, right? I'm

116

THE VIDEO TAPE

kidding. It's gross. But it was a job for me, and I at least had enough to pay rent at a grimy studio apartment. It's not like now, where everything costs at least two grand to rent. I had a studio back then for about four hundred a month. Sure, the place was gross, but I preferred it to returning to my parents' house. Plus, they'd kicked me out. I began to get close to the owner of Hard Hank's. His name was Hank Jewel. Makes the name of his spot even worse, doesn't it? Hank thought I worked hard. He could tell I was a hellion. I'm sure he saw himself in me. From all I've heard, he was a troublemaker of all troublemakers when he was young. But now Hank was old. He was already in his mid-fifties when I started working there. He'd seen it all, including snuff films. He brought them up one day, probably about six months into my working at Hard Hank's. It was later in 1995, by this point, maybe the summer, if memory serves. I thought he was kidding, but he asked me if I wanted to watch one. Remember, I was a troubled kid, and my morals were lacking, if I had any at all. Plus, he was my boss, and we were becoming friends. It would have been rude not to. So I said, yeah, I'd watch one. After we closed one day, Hank put in an old VHS tape. And you'll never guess what I saw?"

"The videotape I just showed you?"

"Exactly."

Holy shit. It was all coming full circle. Hard Hank's. The videotape. Even the year he viewed it—1995—lined up.

"How did you feel when you saw it?"

"I knew what I'd watched was terribly wrong, but it fascinated me."

"I understand." I couldn't understand, but I had to keep this conversation cordial at all costs. "What happened next?"

"We didn't talk about it. I may have been a high school dropout, but I wasn't a dummy. I kept my damn mouth shut. I didn't even bring it up to Larry or Manny, the two other people Hank was close to. As the months passed, I expected Hank to ask me if I wanted to see another. I don't know why, but I assumed he had more than one. I know that's sickening, but I didn't think this had been a one-time thing. But he never asked me again. When we were alone, I asked him if we would ever watch another videotape. He knew what I was referring to. He got pissed and yelled at me. 'Don't ever fucking bring that up again,' he screamed. So I didn't bring it up again."

"So the videotape I just showed you was the only snuff film you ever saw while employed at Hard Hank's."

"Yes. That isn't enough?"

I could have reminded Mr. Z that he brought up watching another one to Hank Jewel, but I kept my mouth shut.

"Yes, that's more than enough," I said. "How much longer did you work at Hard Hank's?"

"Only a few more months. Hank was killed later that year."

"In 1995, right?"

"Yes."

"How was Hank killed?"

"He was stabbed to death."

"Where?"

"At his home."

"Did they catch the guy who did it?"

"No."

"Did they have any suspects?"

Mr. Z laughed. "Yeah, they narrowed it down to five hundred people. Hank was an asshole, and treated most of his employees like shit. I was the exception. He also worked in the porn industry and dealt with a lot of lowlifes. My point is that there would not have been a shortage of suspects."

I tried to take everything in. I certainly hadn't expected this bombshell when Mr. Z agreed to meet with me.

"A man named Ernest Riley turned this video in to the police." I pointed to my laptop. "Does that ring a bell?"

"No, it doesn't," Mr. Z said.

"You mentioned two people earlier that were close to Hank."

"Manny and Larry."

"Who are they?"

"Manny was his business partner, and Larry was an employee like me."

"Do you know what happened to them?"

"Larry had quit a few months before Hank died. And Manny inherited the place when Hank died."

"Inherited it?"

"Yeah, Hank left it to him in the will."

"Why?"

"Manny Torres was Hank's right-hand man. They were business partners, too. He took over the day-to-day operations of Hard Hank's after Hank died, but he wasn't the businessman that Hank was, and I think it went downhill. At least financially."

"So, Hank left him his half of the business in his will?"

"Yes."

THE VIDEO TAPE

"Was Hank married?"

"He had been married once, a long time ago."

"Did he have any kids?"

"Not that I know of."

"Any girlfriends around the time of his death?"

"He never really had girlfriends within twenty years of him. He always had young girls around. They'd often just turned eighteen. So no, no specific girlfriend that I can remember."

"Classy."

"Hey, it wasn't some after-school program for underprivileged kids he was running. He dealt in sex."

"Did he ever prostitute these girls out?"

"Not that I ever heard. He'd use them in the booths that men would pay for, but not prostitute them out."

"I could probably argue that's just a lesser version of the same thing."

Mr. Z nodded. "You probably could. And as for the ex-wife I mentioned, they couldn't stand each other. I'm sure that's why he willed Hard Hank's to Manny and not her."

"Is Manny still alive?"

"No, he died about five years after Hank."

"How did he die?"

"Don't worry, it wasn't anything suspicious. Manny died of a heart attack."

"And then what happened to the business?"

"Manny's family sold it. As I said, the place was going downhill."

"Did you still work there when Manny took over?"

"Yes, but I left after only a few months. We didn't always see eye to eye, and it wasn't as interesting as when Hank ran it."

Yeah, you weren't shown snuff films in your downtime.

"And did Manny ever mention the snuff film to you?"

"Never."

"Did you ever ask him what had happened to it?"

"No. Under no circumstances would I bring up something like that. For all I knew, I was the only one Hank ever showed it to. Maybe he burned it after he showed it to me. It wasn't my place to broach that subject with Manny. Shit, I worried I could have been held criminally responsible for just watching the damn thing. I wanted to forget about the whole thing. Not bring it up anew."

"Did you ever consider that Manny could have killed Hank? Money

BRIAN O'SULLIVAN

can be a tempting motive, and if Manny knew he would inherit half the business ..."

"I didn't like Manny all that much, but he wasn't a killer. You're just going to have to trust me. He loved working with Hank and being his second in charge. He was fine with that. And he was as distraught as anyone when Hank died."

"Is there anything else you can tell me?" I asked.

"This isn't enough? Fuck, I feel like I've told you my whole life story. Hank's, too. And fuck, most of Manny's. You know what, I think I should go."

I could have tried to shotgun a few more quick questions, but I feared losing him forever. I decided to let him go in hopes that he might answer more questions on a later day.

"Thank you, Mr. Z. You've been very helpful. Can I call you again if I come into any new information?"

"I'll think about it. No guarantees."

"That's fair," I said. "Thank you very much for your time."

"Yeah."

And with that, Mr. Z hurriedly left.

⚜

BEFORE RETURNING TO MY CAR, I TOOK OUT MY PHONE AND GOOGLED Hank Jewel.

I should have done it when I'd first heard Hard Hank's mentioned, but I didn't have anything specific to search for. I did now.

The *Los Angeles Times* wrote an obituary for him. It was a brutal obit, basically a hit piece on the guy. *Don't talk ill of the dead* was not taken to heart.

More than the article itself, what caught my eye was the date of Jewel's death. It's what I was looking for.

Hank Jewel died two days before Ernest Riley turned the videotape into the LAPD.

𝕾 26 𝕾

I had a lot more homework to do, but I needed information from the LAPD before I embarked on it.

And by that, I meant Noble Dunn, not Detective Heald.

I met with Noble and asked him about Hard Hank's.

"Yeah, I know about Hard Hank's. It had a bad reputation. Some of these adult stores cater to people who are horny and might have a few sexual kinks, but they aren't deviants. BLISSFUL was like that. Hard Hank's was different. Its clientele wasn't people you'd want to encounter in a dark alley. The videos they had were rougher. So were the sex toys. Shit, even the owner was rough. Hank Jewel."

"Did you ever meet him?"

"I had the *pleasure* of meeting him one time. West Hollywood wasn't my jurisdiction, or I'm sure we'd have crossed paths several times. But I was working on the West Side: Santa Monica, Venice, etc. Anyway, I'll never forget the one time I met him. They were doing a stakeout of Hard Hank's because there were rumors that he was using underage girls to dance for men. I'm not talking strippers. I'm talking private rooms where you'd put quarters into the machine or risk a screen falling and you no longer being able to watch the girl. That's the way it was back in the day. Not anymore. Anyway, Hank was able to ditch the officers and leave the premises without getting caught. They put out an APB. An All-Points Bulletin. That's what we called it back then. Now, it's called a BOLO—Be

BRIAN O'SULLIVAN

On the Lookout. But I digress. We were told to be on the lookout for a white, convertible Cadillac. Real subtle, right? I was working up in Brentwood, just west of the 405, and sure enough, I saw a big white caddy pass under the 405 and officially enter the Westside. I got a look at the license plate, and it was Hank Jewel's car, so I put on my lights and pulled him over. He had a young-looking girl in the passenger seat. I asked for his driver's license, and he had this shit-eating grin. 'Would you like to check her ID as well?' 'Yes, I would,' I said. She gave me her license. She'd just turned eighteen a week before. 'How long have you worked for Mr. Jewel?' I asked. 'Six days,' she said, and Hank Jewel erupted in laughter. 'It looks like Hank Jewel is one step ahead of the LAPD—as always.' Several other officers arrived shortly after but agreed we had nothing to arrest him on. I returned to his car and said, 'You can go, Mr. Jewel. Hopefully, I'll run into you again.' 'I'm sure you will,' he responded. 'Why don't you stop by Hard Hank's sometime? You can see young Kami here strutting her stuff.' And with that, he drove off. He was a piece of work. A real scumbag."

"That's quite the story," I said. "Did you ever run into him again?"

"I didn't. And I have no idea what happened to Kami. I'm sure it didn't end well for her. From what I'd heard from cops in Hollywood, most of his girls ended up getting addicted to drugs, and often became full-on prostitutes once they stopped dancing at Hard Hank's."

"Scumbag wasn't a strong enough word to describe him," I said.

"Yeah, you're right. Why did you bring him up anyway?"

Noble Dunn had been honest with me from the get-go. He deserved to hear the truth.

"I met a guy who claims that Hank Jewel showed him a snuff film. Our snuff film."

Noble couldn't hide his shock. "You're kidding."

"I'm not."

"And you believe him?"

Mr. Weaver could have told Mr. Z the bullet points of the video, and that's why Mr. Z knew the details about it. But I didn't believe that. I think he'd actually seen it back in 1995.

"I think he's telling the truth."

"I'll trust your judgment."

"Did you know that Hank Jewel was murdered?"

"Yes. I think I knew about that way back when."

"Do you know what year he was killed?"

"I'm going to guess 1995."

THE VIDEO TAPE

"Yes, sir. A few days before Ernest turned the videotape into the LAPD."

"You don't think ..."

"I don't know what to think. Nothing about this case makes any sense. But if you told me that someone killed Jewel to get his snuff film back, I'd say that makes as much sense as anything else."

"It's as good a theory as any."

"Can I ask a favor?"

"What is it?"

"I'd like to see the police report on Hank Jewel's murder. I'd especially like to know what the officers collected from the scene."

"You want to know if any other snuff films were found?"

"Yes. Do you happen to know?"

"Westside LAPD and Hollywood LAPD didn't intermingle much, but I'd be shocked if they found a snuff film. That would have been huge news, and I would have heard about it."

"Can you still get me the police report?"

"I would think so. It may take a few days."

"Thanks."

"Are you sure you don't want to contact the LAPD?"

"I'm sure. This is very much still circumstantial. Let's see what happens over the next few days."

"Okay, Bobby."

❧❧

IT HAD BEEN A LONG DAY, AND I WAS GRATEFUL FOR IT.

With Nori leaving, I needed to dive into my work, and I'd done just that. After I met with Mr. Z and Noble, I felt like I was back in the game.

I was about to call Nori when I saw a call coming through. All it said on the screen was LAPD. Shit.

"Hello."

"Is this Bobby McGowan?"

"Yes, it is."

"This is Detective Heald. Do you remember me?"

How could I forget?

"Yes, I remember you."

"We need to talk. Can you come back to the Hollywood precinct tomorrow morning?"

"What time?"

"Let's say nine."

"I'll be there."

Had Noble already ratted me out?

I highly doubted it, but the timing was suspicious.

❧ 27 ❧

I arrived at the Hollywood precinct of the LAPD.

I walked in and told the officer at the front desk that I was there to see Detective Heald. He made a quick phone call, and Heald was there within a minute.

"Thanks for coming, Mr. McGowan. Please follow me."

I followed him back to his office. The walls were adorned with cases he'd solved. He looked to be an accomplished detective.

He asked me to take a seat. "I figured this was more appropriate than an interrogation room," he said. "You're not a suspect or anything like that. I invited you here as a friend."

A friend? I highly doubted that. "Any progress on Darian's murder? Since we're friends and all."

Heald smirked. "We're not that close of friends."

I couldn't help but laugh. "How about just a little nugget? Something to tide me over."

"Don't forget, Mr. McGowan. I'm the detective here. I'm the one who will be asking the questions."

"Damn. I thought we were just two old friends shooting the shit."

"Don't be disagreeable. I can easily go back to the more confrontational detective that you've already had the pleasure of meeting."

Our bromance hadn't lasted long.

"How about the video I sent of the guy leaving the note? Any progress on that?"

BRIAN O'SULLIVAN

The second note—my camera hadn't been installed the first time—was left by a white man in his early twenties. He wore a Lakers hat and hung it over his face. He also used his arms to cover his face, so there was no clear look at him.

"No, he did a good job covering his face. We saw what you saw. Nothing more. If we find out anything, I'll let you know."

I doubted that.

"And that's not why I invited you here today," he said.

"Then what am I here for?"

"I'm sorry about your girlfriend leaving town."

"She'll be returning when you catch Darian's killer. Excuse me, *if* you catch her killer."

"Oh, we're going to catch the guy, all right."

"No offense, but your track record on this case says otherwise."

I deserved whatever came next, but all Heald did was smile. "You're a piece of work. I'll let that comment pass since I want your help with something."

"I'm listening."

"The reason I brought up Ms. Bridgewater is because the killer of Darian Hague has taken quite a liking to you and her. Leaving notes at your place not once, but twice."

"Well, yes and no."

"What do you mean?"

"I'm not ready to concede that the young man in the Laker hat is the killer."

"That's fair, but would you admit it's likely he was commissioned to leave the note by whoever the real killer was?"

"I think that's fair."

"He also may well have followed you to Ms. Hague's business. Would you say that's possible?"

I could have said I didn't want to be blamed for her murder, but what was the point? And Heald wasn't wrong; the killer may have followed me there.

"Yes, it's possible."

"Which brings me to the reason I invited you here."

He waited a few seconds to add to the drama.

"My guess is that this guy is keeping tabs on you. Possibly even following you without you realizing it. I want to install a camera on your car and monitor you for a few days. But I need your approval."

126

THE VIDEO TAPE

I'd had the same plan before abandoning it after encountering that jerk at Home Depot.

"Believe it or not," I said. "I had that same idea."

"Is this the spot where I'm supposed to say, *great minds think alike?*"

"I'm not sure either of us wants to be linked to the other."

Heald smiled. "You don't give an inch, do you?"

"I'm here, and I just said I think it's a good idea. I'm not trying to be an ass."

"Okay, Bobby."

"Did you plan on doing this today?" I asked.

"Did you drive here?"

"I did."

"We could install the cameras in less than an hour."

Although I preferred being a lone wolf, my gut told me this was the right thing to do. The main goal should be to catch Darian's killer, after all.

"Okay. I'm up for it," I said.

"Thank you. We'll keep them running for a week."

"And you will tell me if I'm being followed, right? I'm doing this because I want to catch Darian's killer. Not because I want to be your guinea pig."

"I understand. We will call you if we think you are in imminent danger."

"But only if it's imminent danger. That's reassuring."

Heald laughed. "You're insufferable."

"Since I'm being a team player, can you answer a question or two?"

"No promises, but you can ask."

"Were you able to determine Darian's killer's predominant hand?"

Heald raised his eyes to mine.

"That's an excellent question. I guess it can't hurt to give you the answer. He's right-handed."

"I'm going to assume she was killed the night before we found her."

"No comment."

"She was in her clothes from the night before, correct?"

"That's right."

"So it logically follows that she was killed the night before."

"Is that a question, or are you trying to show how smart you are?"

"A little of both."

Detective Heald shrugged. "It's never-ending with you."

"Thanks."

127

"It wasn't a compliment."

"To me, it is."

"As to your question, yes, she was killed the night before. Now, I'm allowing you one more question, and then we are getting your car equipped with some cameras."

"I guess I'd better ask a winning question."

"I guess so."

I paused, trying to rack my brain. "I know you never had a suspect in the videotape murder, but did you ever find out who Jane Doe was? And if not, was there ever a suspicion about who she was?"

"No, we never found out who she was. And as far as I know, we never suspected anyone specifically. What we did presume was that it was probably someone from out of town. Possibly a drug addict. And possibly someone living on the street."

None of this came as a surprise. Noble and I had been over this.

If it were someone with many friends and a nine-to-five job, they likely would have ID'd her from her eyes alone. Heald was right. This likely was someone living on the outskirts of society.

Hard Hank's came to mind, but I wouldn't mention that to Detective Heald. They were using me to try to get to the killer. I wasn't ready to give them my most valuable information to date.

"Thanks for that info," I said. "Now, where should I bring my car?"

An hour later, I was driving back to my place, two hidden cameras recording everything in front and behind me.

Hopefully, the killer would follow me.

And the LAPD would notify me before I was in imminent danger.

Not exactly the plan of the century.

28

The following two weeks were a disappointment for several reasons.

I couldn't find any valuable information on Hank Jewel.

He'd never had any children, and his ex-wife was dead. I could only get two of his old employees to agree to talk to me, and neither could provide anything helpful.

Neither one had ever heard the rumor that Hank possessed at least one snuff film. Both seemed happy to get off the phone with me.

I guess I couldn't blame them. It's not a place you'd brag about working at thirty years later.

Hank Jewel was killed in 1995. A lot happens in thirty years, and Hank Jewel had become a forgotten man. Or, at the minimum, someone whom people wanted to forget.

Noble was able to get me the police report on his murder.

Hank Jewel had been killed at his house, but no DNA was left at the scene.

He had fifty enemies, but none of them ever reached the level of being considered a suspect.

Manny Torres was mentioned several times, but he had an alibi for the night in question. Larry Gilden wasn't mentioned, nor was someone named Mr. Z. Not that I was expecting that.

My overall impression was that the LAPD hadn't been all that fired up

BRIAN O'SULLIVAN

about catching Hank Jewel's killer. They probably thought the *scumbag* deserved it.

I contacted Alfred Weaver again and told him I'd like to meet with Mr. Z, but Weaver got back to me and said Mr. Z had said all he was going to say.

⁂

I DID A DEEP DIVE INTO MANNY TORRES, BUT COULDN'T FIND ANY evidence of wrongdoing. Everyone I talked to said he was a good person who just happened to be in a bad business.

He didn't treat his subordinates like trash. He didn't cater to young women. He didn't even try to sleep with any of those women.

Everyone said he was a good family man.

This begged the question of why he was friends with someone like Hank Jewel. I got my answer when I met with Torres's delightful daughter, Teresa.

She said that both Hank and Manny had served in the Vietnam War. They were in the same platoon. One day, Hank was hit in both legs by enemy fire, and Manny carried him to safety.

They both got out of Vietnam alive.

Teresa claimed that Hank often mentioned what Manny had done to save his life. Hank gave Manny the opportunity to buy into his new business, an adult store named Hard Hank's, and Manny accepted.

I told Teresa that Manny's heroism in Vietnam would explain why Hank felt indebted to Manny, and why he'd let him buy into his business and then leave him Hard Hank's in his will. But it didn't explain why Manny would stay friends with Hank, who was universally viewed as an asshole.

Teresa disagreed.

"When you save someone's life, you hope that person will contribute to society. So my father looked at Hank as a kind of project. He knew he wasn't perfect—far from it—but they'd shared too much to give up on him."

"If you say so," I said, unconvinced.

"I do say so. And so did my father. It was always his excuse when we mentioned him being friends with Hank Jewel."

I talked to a few other family members. There were no snuff films, nor any suspicious videotapes given away upon his death.

Manny Torres appeared to be a dead end as well.

THE VIDEO TAPE

I wasn't the only one striking out.

The LAPD hadn't accomplished much, either. They couldn't find anyone tailing me. Or, if they did, they didn't tell me about it.

Making things even worse, Nori and I were talking less. What had been twice a day soon became once a day, and now we were down to talking once every few days.

Maybe it was my fault. Maybe it was her fault.

And maybe we were just drifting apart, and it was nobody's fault.

I met with Ernest Riley and told him it had been a rough few weeks, but I was still very dedicated to working the case.

He decided to extend our agreement for another six weeks.

Ernest didn't look great and had a coughing fit that lasted almost a minute. I told him to get some rest, but I was fearful that something more might be going on.

Was his cancer getting worse?

On our way out, almost as an afterthought, he said, "Maybe you should meet up with Tez Lamar."

"Who's that?"

"He's a private investigator who worked for me about five years ago. He was the last PI I hired before you."

"Was he any good?"

"He was excellent."

"But he still didn't catch the killer."

"Hey, I think you're excellent, Bobby, but you still haven't caught the guy yet."

"That's fair."

Ernest smiled. "Here, let me get you Tez's number."

❧ 29 ❧

I met with Tez Lamar the following morning.

We'd agreed to meet at a Taco Truck near me.

Tez wore jeans, a white T-shirt, and a Baltimore Ravens hat. He was a black man in his thirties, but probably closer to forty than I was.

"Thanks for meeting with me, Tez," I said. "You hungry?"

"No, but since you dragged me out here, I might as well get some food out of it."

I laughed, and we both ordered three tacos. Tez got Carnitas tacos, and I went with Carne Asada.

After receiving our order, we moved away from the gathered crowd.

"So, you're Ernest's latest guinea pig?"

"Why do you say that?"

"I'm joking. He's a nice guy. It's just that I spent five months on this case and have nothing to show for it. I'm not sure it's solvable."

"I beg to differ. I think I've made some serious progress."

He looked at me with genuine interest. "Yeah? What type of progress?"

We found a table that was out of earshot of anyone else and sat down. I ran through most everything I'd learned, only leaving out a few things.

"Impressive stuff, Bobby. And I heard about that Darian woman's murder. They didn't mention that it might be related to the videotape."

"The LAPD didn't want that to get out."

THE VIDEO TAPE

"I guess I shouldn't be surprised. They weren't much help with me, either."

"Did you deal with Detective Heald?"

"Not at first, but at some point when I kept hitting dead ends, I decided to go directly to the LAPD. Eventually, I found my way to him. He wasn't the biggest fan of mine."

"Join the crew."

Tez laughed. "He told me I'd never work in this town again. He made it sound like I was an actor and he was some old Hollywood exec from the 1930s."

I smiled. It's something I could imagine Heald saying. "He's now got me working with them."

"That's painful to hear. What are you doing exactly?"

I explained the cameras on my car.

"I'd have taken a pass on that."

"I considered that, but then thought of Darian and the woman in the video."

Tez shrugged. "Yeah, I understand. I guess I'm just more of a lone wolf."

"So am I."

"No offense, but it doesn't seem like it. You're updating Ernest every other day, dealing with Noble, and working with the LAPD. That's not the work of a lone wolf."

I wanted to disagree, but I had no leg to stand on. Tez Lamar was right.

And he could tell it hit home.

"I'm sorry," he said. "I'm just calling it as I see it."

"Don't be sorry. You're right."

An uncomfortable silence followed, which he finally broke.

"So, gun to your head, who do you think had the videotape on the morning of the garage sale? I'd always assumed it had ended up in Ernest's house somehow. Not that he knew anything about it, of course."

"I tend to disagree."

"I'm going to need more than that. C'mon, Bobby."

"What if someone visiting the garage sale accidentally left the video-tape in Ernest's section?"

"I'm not sure exactly what you mean."

"This was a garage sale for the whole block. There were about ten stations or so. What if someone picked up the videotape from one of the neighboring piles, thinking he might eventually buy it? He then decides against it and accidentally sets it in Ernest's pile. That could easily happen. I know if there were ten stations, I could easily forget which one I'd originally grabbed it from."

"The only problem is that Ernest claimed he was watching his section the entire time. He said he'd have noticed if someone set something in his pile."

"He told me the same thing. But what about when you're making a sale? You could have your back turned, and someone could easily place something down without you noticing. Plus, Ernest had about thirty videotapes in his pile. The guy in question could have thought that's where he'd originally grabbed it."

"Here's the problem I have. The videotape in question wasn't labeled. Who would want to buy a random VHS tape? That's why I always thought it came from Ernest's own house. And again, let me repeat. He would have had no knowledge of this. He's as innocent as they come."

"We agree on that part. As for who would want to buy a random VHS tape, I don't know. But I could see the allure of wanting to purchase it, not knowing what might be on it. Shit, maybe they were hoping there was something lurid on it. Or, maybe, they grabbed the wrong videotape, and when they saw it was unlabeled, they mistakenly set it back in Ernest's pile. That's more believable than the videotape somehow coming into Ernest's possession. He lived alone, and his daughter was in Italy. Who exactly would have left it at his house?"

"You make a fair point—not that I want to admit it."

"I'll bite. Why wouldn't you want to admit it?"

"Don't you know that all PIs are rivals? We are all competitive with each other and hate to see our successor catch something we didn't."

I could tell by his eyes that he was at least half joking. But there was some truth in there as well.

"It's no different than you not wanting to deal with the LAPD," Tez added. "Do you want them to solve the case?"

"Yes, of course I do. There's a killer out there, and I want justice for the Jane Doe in the video and for Darian Hague."

"But a part of you would be jealous it was them—and not you—who solved it."

He was right, of course. "Yes. But a very small part."

"I'd gladly place a wager it's a bigger part than you are willing to admit."

I smiled. "Okay. You got me."

"On the bright side, there's also loyalty amongst PIs."

THE VIDEO TAPE

"Meaning what?"

"Meaning I'd much rather have you break this case than the LAPD. PIs can be both loyal and cutthroat. I know those sound mutually exclusive."

"You're all right, Tez."

"You too, Bobby."

We were both finishing our third taco at this point.

"If you're convinced a neighbor's videotape found its way into Ernest's pile, there's someone you should talk to."

"Who is that?"

"Her name is Elena Estrada. If there was a ringleader of the entire block, it was her. She knew everyone."

"And she's still alive?"

"I can't be sure, but she was five years ago when I was working this case. She seemed to be in good health and was relatively young. Maybe only seventy or so. Definitely younger than Ernest."

"Do you have her number?"

"I'll have to go through some old files. I'll get it to you by the end of the day. Is that cool?"

"Of course. And thanks."

"As I said, the loyalty of PIs."

"I'll take anything I can get."

"Keep me abreast of your investigation. Maybe I'll think of something else."

"Will do," I said.

We stood, shook hands, and he turned to go.

"Hey, Tez. If you thought the videotape came from Ernest's house, why were you interviewing the neighbors?"

"Just covering all my bases," he said and gave me a slight smirk.

I had a sneaking suspicion that Tez Lamar suspected a neighbor as well.

Or had at least considered it.

﷼ 30 ﷽

I met with Elena Estrada on a Monday morning.
 It was supposed to be a hundred degrees by eleven a.m., so I was
 happy when Elena agreed to meet me at nine a.m.

You might think this was me being an ageist, assuming Elena would tire out as the day went on.

No, this was specifically on me. I didn't do well in the sweltering heat.

One thing about growing up in Santa Barbara is that the climate is more temperate than in LA. One hundred-degree days in SB were extremely rare.

Elena answered the door on my third knock. She lived in downtown Los Angeles in a two-bedroom house on a busy street. Kids were playing in the streets despite it being nine a.m.

It reminded me of summers as a child. No school. No homework. All fun.

Elena was a diminutive Hispanic woman with large, intelligent eyes. And yes, there is such a thing as intelligent eyes.

"Are you Bobby?"

"I am. Thanks for meeting with me, Elena."

She led me into her home, and a woman probably around my age approached. She wore an apron and was cooking something up.

The house smelled good, and thankfully, the air-conditioning was on. It felt very homely.

"I'm Leti," she said. "I'm one of Elena's daughters."

THE VIDEO TAPE

"Leti is my youngest," Elena said. "She thinks I need supervision, but she's wrong. I can look after myself."

It's safe to say that I liked Elena Estrada from the get-go.

"What month and year is it, Mom?"

"June of 2025. Does that stave me off from an old folks home for a few more months?"

"She's insufferable," Leti said. "Anyway, I'll let you two talk, but Mom, if you need help answering questions, just let me know."

"Don't have kids," Elena said. "They always think they know what's best for you."

They both laughed, and Elena led me to a couch in their living room. I could hear Leti continuing to cook in the kitchen. We both took a seat and faced each other.

"So you're here about the videotape?"

When I called her to set up the meeting, there was no way to sugar-coat why I wanted to see her.

"Yes. Your old neighbor, Ernest Riley, hired me. And Tez Lamar suggested I reach out to you."

"Tez is a good PI. If anyone was going to solve this, I thought it would have been him. Sadly not, though. As for Ernest, he was one of my favorite neighbors."

"Did you know his wife?"

"I sure did. She was delightful and died way too young. After my husband died, Ernest and I were two of the three longest living residents of Collier Court."

"Who was the third?"

"An angry old woman named Ms. Keaney. All the neighborhood kids started calling her Ms. Meaney, and it kind of stuck. She was the type of person who left vegetables out in a bowl on Halloween. And turned all the lights out in her house. She sucked."

Something about hearing a woman in her seventies say, "She sucked," warmed my soul. Elena Estrada continued to be a hit with me.

"Did Ms. Keaney live alone?"

"She did. Never married. No kids. But trust me, she had nothing to do with this videotape. She was already in her mid-eighties when this went down and died a few years later."

"Did everyone on the block know about the videotape?"

"After the fact, yes. I know it was the mid-nineties, and we didn't have the internet, but we lived on a cul-de-sac. That was like the internet back

137

then. If one person found out, everyone was going to find out. So once the cops came around, it was inevitable."

"Did the cops interview everyone on the block?"

"They interviewed me. And I'm assuming everyone else. I heard they put old Ernest through the wringer. They seemed to think he was involved. Like someone was going to turn in their own snuff film, it's ludicrous."

"What do you remember about the day in question. Were you at the garage sale?"

"You're darn right. I helped set the damn thing up."

A darn and a damn, back to back. Impressive.

"What can you tell me about that day?"

The LAPD provided scant details about the garage sale itself. Ernest described it, but never went into detail.

"This was more than just a garage sale. I know that's what everyone calls it, but this was different. A garage sale is usually held at one house. We had everyone on the block bring all their stuff to the end of the cul-de-sac, and we sold everything from there. Ten families total. Well, ten families lived on the block. Ms. Meaney didn't take part in the quote-unquote garage sale. So we were all lined up next to each other, selling our stuff. And guess what, I was one of the two people on either side of Ernest."

Elena had a fantastic memory.

"Was he selling a lot of things? I know he had around thirty VHS tapes, but do you remember what else he had?"

"A lot of pots and pans. I remember that for sure. He kept saying that his wife did most of the cooking, and with her gone, he only needed a few pans to make do."

Elena had twice referred to Sally Riley as Ernest's ex-wife, without mentioning her name. Her memory was impeccable, but I wonder if she'd forgotten her name. Sally had died forty years ago. Who could blame her?

"What other things was he trying to sell?"

"He had some dolls and an old EZ-Bake oven. Ernest's daughter was in her twenties by then, so I'm sure he didn't want those things lying around anymore."

"Anything else you can think of?"

"Your usual knick-knacks you'd have at a garage sale. An ugly old rug. Towels. I think he might have had some flower pots he was selling. It was all pretty standard stuff."

"You have a tremendous memory about that day."

THE VIDEO TAPE

"I have a good memory in general. Plus, when you're interviewed by the cops a few days later, the day fortifies in your mind."

I thought back to being interviewed by the police on the day my mother was killed. I remember it like it was yesterday. I knew precisely what Elena meant.

"I understand," I said, and left it at that.

"How is Ernest, by the way?"

I didn't want to divulge his prognosis, but I also thought it might be nice if he got a call from an old friend.

"He's doing all right. You should give him a call, though."

She looked at me and seemed to understand where I was coming from.

"Leave his number before you go. We always got along famously. If Raul hadn't been such a great husband, maybe we'd have had a little fling."

"Mom!"

Elena erupted in laughter. I guess Leti could hear our conversation from the kitchen.

"Did Ernest have any women come around?"

I was not trying to pry into his personal life. I was attempting to determine if the videotape could have ended up in his possession without his knowledge. Maybe the son of a girlfriend. I was reaching, and hated asking about Ernest's personal life, but I had to do it.

"Very few, if any. He was dedicated to his wife, even though she was gone. I can't seem to place her name."

"Sally."

"Yes, Sally. Thank you."

"What was their daughter like?"

"Lily was a real go-getter. She went to an Ivy League school and then studied in Europe. Ernest was really proud. I know that."

"Did Lily have any boyfriends who used to come around?"

"I'm sure she had a boyfriend or two in high school, but I don't remember. She was a good girl. I can't imagine her dating someone who would be tied up in something disgusting like a snuff film."

"I'm sure you're right. I had to ask."

"So, Ernest isn't doing well?"

"I didn't say that."

Elena looked at me sympathetically. "Not in so many words."

"He's sick. I'll leave it at that. So give him a call soon if you can."

"I will. Is there anything else I can help you with?"

"I guess I'll just come out and ask it. Do you have any opinion on how the videotape ended up in Ernest's section that day?"

139

BRIAN O'SULLIVAN

"I really don't."

"Any wild theories? I don't care how crazy they sound."

"This isn't a wild theory, but I don't think it came from Ernest's house. He was afraid of having too many pans in his house. He was very meticulous. He would have known if there was a videotape that wasn't his. I was in his house a few times, and it was like a museum."

"Mom!"

Elena laughed again.

"I was borrowing some sugar," she yelled, and then leaned into me. "I was completely faithful my whole marriage, and Leti knows that. It's just fun to press her buttons sometimes."

"You guys are too much."

As was often the case, I wondered if I was asking enough questions. I never knew exactly when to end an interview.

"Is there anyone else whom you'd suggest I talk to? Does anyone else remember your neighbors as well as you?"

"Maybe not as well as me, but Jane certainly knew everyone on that block."

"What's Jane's last name?"

"Giles. Jane Giles."

I smiled. Elena had said it like you'd say "Bond. James Bond."

"How old is Jane?"

"I'm pretty sure she's between my age and Ernest's age. Probably in her late seventies. Something like that."

"And you still talk to her?"

"Not as much as I should, but we still talk occasionally."

"Do you have her phone number?"

"I sure do."

Elena took out her phone and gave me Jane Giles's number.

"Thanks for everything, Elena."

"Is this it?"

"For now. But you might see me again. Once I get my foot in the door …"

Elena laughed.

"You're a delightful young man and are welcome any time. Leti, come say goodbye to Bobby."

Leti walked over just as I was standing. We shook hands, and I thanked both women for their time.

"You guys are great together," I said as I walked out the door.

Both of their faces lit up.

❧ 31 ❧

I returned to my apartment and made a sandwich consisting of mortadella, pesto, burrata, and chopped pistachio nuts on a focaccia roll.

This case took a lot out of me, and I hadn't been eating enough. I'd looked at myself in the mirror that morning, and while I wasn't exactly skinny, I didn't look as strong as I usually did.

I reminded myself to start eating more.

❧

AFTER THE SANDWICH, I GAVE JANE GILES A CALL.

"Hello?"

Her voice sounded frail.

"Hi, Jane. My name is Bobby McGowan, and I just met with your friend Elena Estrada."

"Oh. How is Elena?"

This time her voice stuttered, and it sounded like she may have had a stroke.

"She's good. She said to say hi."

"Okay. Tell her hello back."

"I will. She said you were friends with most of your old neighbors on Collier Court."

"That was a long time ago, but yes, I knew everyone on Collier."

BRIAN O'SULLIVAN

She continued to have a slight stutter when she spoke. Despite this, I could tell she was totally with it. She spoke deliberately, almost as if to ensure she got every word right.

"I've been hired by your old neighbor, Ernest Riley."

"I haven't heard that name in a while. Ernest was a good man."

That seemed to be the universal consensus.

"Do you remember when he found a videotape?"

"How could I forget? It started to divide people on Collier Court. We were never the same. People had suspicions about neighbors. You get the idea. I think the first people moved out three months later, and half the street was gone within a few years."

Ernest had told me a few families had moved, but he didn't make it sound as drastic as Jane Giles did. It did make me realize that Ernest, Elena, and Jane had all moved on from Collier Court, but that probably had more to do with age than anything else.

"I'm sorry to hear that. Ernest is getting up there in age and hired me in hopes that I could find out where that videotape came from. I'm going to try my best."

"I wish I could help you. What was your name again?"

"Bobby."

"I wish I could help you, Bobby. But I didn't know anything back in 1995, and I don't know anything now. I'm sorry."

That she remembered it was exactly 1995 showed it had a significant impact.

"You never had any suspicions?"

"Not of anyone on our street. I always thought it came from somewhere else. We were the perfect little American street. We did block parties. We did garage sales. All the kids played with each other growing up. You get the idea."

"Did you have children?"

"I sure did. A son and a daughter."

"And were they living at your house in 1995?"

"My son was in his mid-twenties and living on his own. And my daughter was living with her father. Why does that matter?"

"It doesn't really. I'm just trying to find out more about each family. And Ms. Meaney, of course."

I heard Jane laugh on the other end.

"Thanks for that. That's still one of my favorite nicknames all these years later."

"Don't be a meanie if your last name is Keaney," I said.

142

She laughed again.

"That's exactly right, Bobby."

"Were there any weird boyfriends or girlfriends who hung out on the block?"

"I don't know. There were nine families on that street. Over twenty kids. I can't remember every boyfriend or girlfriend that used to come around."

"I understand. So no one jumped out?"

"No, like I said, we were the perfect little American street."

Her voice struggled to finish the sentence, and I felt guilty for keeping her on the phone.

"I only have a few more questions," I said.

"Good, I'm getting a little tired."

"Have you ever heard of someone named Darian Hague?"

"No, I don't think so."

"How about a man named Hank Jewel?"

"No, I'm sorry."

"How about Hard Hank's?"

There was a long, awkward pause. "Who did you say you are?" Her tone had changed. She suddenly sounded accusatory.

"My name is Bobby McGowan."

"Well, like I said, I'm getting a little tired, so I think we should end this call."

I hated badgering an old lady, but I didn't know if I'd ever get her on the phone again.

"Why did you react that way when I brought up Hard Hank's?" I asked.

"I don't know what you're talking about."

She obviously did.

"Would you prefer if we did this in person?"

"No," she yelled loudly.

"How do you know Hard Hank's?" I asked.

"I have to go. Goodbye." She hung up the phone.

Something was up. Her reaction to hearing Hard Hank's had nothing to do with her stroke. She was shocked to hear me mention it.

But why?

Interviewing Jane Giles in person was suddenly at the top of my list of things to do.

BRIAN O'SULLIVAN

An hour later, I had an incoming call from Nori.

We hadn't talked in two or three days.

"Nori! Good to hear from you."

"I miss you," she said. "I miss Darian. I miss LA."

We usually started with pleasantries and small talk, but Nori jumped right into it.

"Well, I miss you, too. LA misses you. And I'm sure Darian is somewhere remembering the good times you two had."

"Do you believe that?"

"You probably don't want to know my opinion on this."

"Of course I do."

"You might be disappointed."

"I can take it."

"All right. I was raised Catholic and grew up believing in God."

"But things changed?"

"I'm all for believing in God. I'm just not sure that Darian is up in Heaven looking down at us."

"Then life on earth would all be pointless," Nori said.

"Actually, I believe the opposite."

"What do you mean?"

"This isn't always the easiest for me to articulate, but here goes. If all we have is this time here on Earth, then every year, every month, and even every day are more vital. If you know that when you die, you're going to be reunited with all of your deceased friends and loved ones, then death isn't nearly as big a deal. But since I don't subscribe to that, life here on earth means everything. Will I get to see my mother again in the afterlife? I sure hope so. I hope I'm wrong about all of this. But I can't be sure, and that's why losing her was so brutal."

"I sure am glad I made this call."

"A little too heavy?"

"No, I asked for it. But now I feel short-changed."

"In what way?"

"We had a fantastic month together, but didn't have enough of these conversations. I didn't even know that you were a God-denying atheist who thinks we are worm food when we die."

I laughed out loud. "That's the Nori I miss."

"See, you know I'm joking when I say that. Most people wouldn't."

I agreed with Nori. This was the banter I missed.

"How's home life?" I asked.

"It sucks. My mother and I butt heads all the time."

THE VIDEO TAPE

"Why don't you move out?"

"Because then I have to sign a lease, which means I'm less likely to return to LA. To get back to you."

"I don't know what to say."

"Say you're close to catching the guy. Say this will all be over soon, and I can move back and we can have heart-to-hearts about all the big questions out there."

"I'm not sure I've ever heard you this introspective."

"That's my point," Nori said. "We didn't have enough time together."

Her mother said, "Nori, keep it down a bit" on the other end.

"See what I'm dealing with?"

"Maybe I'm the lucky one, getting to chase a killer around."

"I miss those, too."

"What?"

"Your cheesy jokes."

"Hey, that was a good one."

"Don't quit your day job."

I didn't respond for a second, so Nori spoke again. I could tell she didn't want to get off the phone.

"Have you made any recent progress?"

"If you'd called me early this morning, I'd have told you it was the same old, same old."

"This sounds promising. What happened?"

I told her about my meeting with Elena Estrada and my call with Jane Giles.

"Her reaction to Hard Hank's is pretty fishy."

"I'd agree. Something stinks."

"There you go. Another cheesy joke."

"I can't help myself."

"What do the cops think?"

"I don't know. They attached two cameras to my car, and then basically told me to fuck off. If I'm being honest, I still think I have a better chance of solving this. Unless there's DNA or something, and if there was, they'd already have made an arrest."

"Sounds like you need an assistant."

"I miss you greatly. You know that. But as I said before you left, I could never forgive myself if something happened to you. So I do think you should stay in Missouri."

"What's the date today?" she asked.

"That's a random question. It's June 28th."

145

"All right, so there are two days left in June. I'll give you until the end of July to solve this, or I'm moving back to LA."

"I don't know. I've heard Missouri is beautiful in August."

Nori laughed. "You trying to keep me here longer?"

"I'm trying to keep you safe."

"Look in the mirror, mister. You're the one in harm's way."

"Nori, I need your help," her mother yelled in the background.

"Sorry, Bobby, I have to go."

"Talk soon."

It may have been brief, but it was the best conversation we'd had in a while.

Maybe the best since she'd moved.

I realized in that moment how much I'd missed her. I'd been so busy with the case—intentionally—that I hadn't had time to dwell on the fact that she was gone.

Which was probably for the best.

32

I woke up the following morning and looked in the mirror.

Not because of Nori's advice, but because it was the morning, and it's just something you do. I still looked too skinny.

Start eating more.

I hadn't shaved in three days and had a little more than a five o'clock shadow.

Was there such a thing as a six o'clock shadow?

I decided I liked the look of it. It fit the mood of this investigation.

Clean-shaven Bobby wouldn't have felt right.

After showering, I did a little research on the World Wide Web and was able to locate Jane Giles's address. She lived in Pasadena.

I set off to meet her at 7:15 a.m., not wanting to risk her being gone when I arrived.

She wasn't going to be too thrilled to see me.

I GOT TO PASADENA AN HOUR LATER, HAVING DEALT WITH THE BRUTAL LA traffic that I'd mostly managed to avoid lately.

The majority of people and businesses I'd dealt with had been in Santa Monica and Hollywood, and I could just take Wilshire back and forth. I'd been lucky enough to avoid freeways for the most part.

BRIAN O'SULLIVAN

But not on this day, and I arrived twenty minutes later than I'd planned.

I hoped Jane Giles wasn't already doing errands or something else.

I parked outside her house.

It was a little cottage with two bedrooms, possibly three small ones. It was painted white and yellow and would probably be described as either quaint or cute. Both words fit.

It was reminiscent of Elena Estrada's house, but Jane's was on a much quieter block. No kids were playing in the streets.

A white Chevrolet Malibu was in the driveway, which only had room for one car, so I assumed it was Jane's.

I approached the house and pressed the doorbell. No one answered, so I rang it again.

Thinking the doorbell might be tough to hear, I knocked three times. Still no answer.

I took out my cell phone and called her number.

It went unanswered, but I heard it ringing inside the house.

I called again, and the phone kept ringing menacingly.

Why wasn't she answering it?

A car was out front. I had to assume she was home.

I wasn't ready to panic, but an ominous feeling came over me.

You talked to her last night. She's fine.

Why would she leave her cell phone if she went somewhere?

Maybe she was just old and couldn't hear it ring.

She'd answered when I'd called yesterday, though.

My mind was running through all the possibilities.

I looked at my surroundings.

There was one curtain on each side of the front door. I was standing on the left of the porch, and the curtain on that side was drawn, and I couldn't see in. I walked the ten feet to the other side of the front door and peered in the window.

There was no body on the floor nor signs of an altercation. It didn't look disheveled.

I must be overreacting. Right?

I extended my left hand and knocked on the front door, while keeping an eye on the barren living room. I knocked five more times, but still nothing.

I considered calling 911, but what exactly would I tell them?

A woman who is getting up there in age isn't answering her phone?

148

THE VIDEO TAPE

If people called 911 every time that happened, they'd be log-jammed for decades.

I decided to walk around the house's perimeter, heading to my right to start.

After about twenty steps, I arrived outside a tiny room with what looked like a twin bed. There was also a dresser, and that was it. It was likely a guest room, and nothing looked out of the ordinary.

I continued along the perimeter, arriving at another room.

A woman was lying on the bed, but looked very still—too still.

I couldn't tell if she was sleeping or dead.

There was no obvious sign of trauma, but there was a stillness that was impossible to avoid. I looked intently at her chest, but didn't see it moving up and down. Her skin looked wan and pale, but that didn't necessarily mean she was dead.

I considered trying to break in, but decided against it.

I returned to the front door when I saw a neighbor walking by.

"Excuse me," I said.

He eyed me suspiciously. "Yes."

"Are you a neighbor of Ms. Giles?"

"Yes, I live right here." He pointed to the house next door. "Are you friends with Jane?"

"I talked to her last night on the phone," I said, not divulging who I was or what we had talked about.

"Congratulations," he said, not impressed. "Were you supposed to be meeting with her today?"

"I'm a little worried about her," I said, ignoring the question. I didn't want to admit that I'd shown up unannounced.

"Why?"

"Well, she didn't answer her phone or door, so I walked around the house and looked in her room. She didn't look like she was moving."

He stared at me with extreme skepticism.

"How do you know where Jane's room is? And why are you walking around the side of her house?"

"Because I could hear her phone ringing and she wasn't answering. Forget about me for a second. I think Ms. Giles might be in trouble."

He looked me over, debating whether to trust this weird guy in front of him.

"She didn't look like she was breathing," I said. "Do you have a key to the house? If not, I think we should call the cops."

That hit home.

149

BRIAN O'SULLIVAN

"You stay here," he said. "I'm going to walk around the edge of the house."

I stayed put, and he ran back to the front less than a minute later. His face showed genuine concern.

"You're right. She doesn't look good. Call 911. I'm going to break a window. Maybe I can perform CPR before the medics get here. And you can pay Jane back if this is all some big mistake. Deal?"

"Deal."

He grabbed a small shovel sitting in the flower beds on the porch and approached the window, slamming the shovel into the top left corner. He quickly moved to the relative safety of the front door. The window shattered, and the man was inside the house seconds later.

I didn't know if this guy was a cop, a military man, or a cat burglar, but he knew what he was doing.

Several seconds later, I heard him scream.

"No! Jane!"

I climbed over the broken glass and followed the scream to the bedroom on the left.

I wish I hadn't.

Jane Giles was lying on her bed, very much dead.

The good Samaritan next to me broke out in tears, and I just stared at the body. There were no signs of trauma, and from the looks of it, she might have just been an older woman whose heart gave out.

My eyes made their way to her neck.

To me—and maybe I was just hoping to find something—the sides of her neck were slightly redder than the rest of her throat and face.

Could she have been strangled?

Had I stumbled upon another murder?

Was another person dead because of my investigation?

33

I should have known.

After 911 arrived, the good Samaritan neighbor and I were interviewed by the arriving police. I gave my name, mentioned talking to Jane Giles the night before, and twenty minutes later, Detective Heald showed up.

This wasn't his district, but someone must have alerted him to the fact that I was in the vicinity of another dead body.

I saw him walking in my direction and knew the shit was about to hit the fan.

"Bobby fucking McGowan. Why the fuck are you always at my crime fucking scenes?"

Three f-bombs in two sentences may have been a record, but I wasn't going to be the one who told him.

"How do you know this is a crime scene?" I asked.

That only pissed him off more.

"I'll decide whether this is a crime scene. Not you."

"Okay," I said, trying to quell his anger.

"What the fuck are you doing here? When someone told me Bobby McGowan was at the location of another dead body, I almost shit myself. Bad luck must just follow you around."

He'd used the term "dead body" this time, probably not wanting to repeat saying *crime scene*. There was the chance that Jane Giles had died of natural causes, despite what I'd seen on her neck. The red coloring was

151

very subtle, and it wasn't like there were huge bruises or handprints on her neck.

If she were having a heart attack, maybe she grabbed her throat. Unlikely, but not impossible.

"What do you want me to say, Detective? I was just going where my investigation took me. You think I want to keep stumbling upon dead people?"

"I'm not putting anything past you."

He spoke loudly, and several police officers kept looking in our direction. By the time he arrived, there were three or four cop cars, a fire truck, and the medical examiner.

"Give me a quick rundown of how you ended up here."

I rehashed what I'd already told the arriving officer.

"Who the hell is Tez Lamar? And who the hell is Elena Estrada?"

There was a dead woman fifty feet from me, and I wasn't trying to make this about me, but Detective Heald was continuing to press my buttons. I'd just spent five minutes explaining who Tez and Elena were.

"Would you like me to repeat what I just said? He's a PI who used to work on this case, and she lived on Collier Court when Ernest Riley found the videotape."

"Watch yourself, McGowan. I might take you downtown again, and I don't just mean for an interrogation. Maybe I'll keep you there a few days."

"Sometimes I feel like you have it in for me more than you do the killer."

"Screw you. I'm trying just as hard as you are."

"Then why am I always a step ahead? Why am I always finding the bodies?"

"Maybe you're unaware of this, but Los Angeles is a big city. Every day, I've got new murders to investigate."

This was becoming a pissing contest, and we were both starting to look like big dicks. Not the kind to be proud of. The kind people didn't want anything to do with.

"You're right," I said. "I'm sorry. I know you want to catch this guy just as much as I do. I now think the videotape likely came into Ernest Riley's possession via someone on that street. Sadly, that's what led me to Elena Estrada, which led me here today."

"It's just a coincidence that you keep ending up around dead bodies. Right?"

"You know that's ridiculous, and I resent you for saying it."

THE VIDEO TAPE

"Why is it ridiculous? You were at Darian's murder, and you're here for the death of Jane Giles."

He had to look down at his phone to remember Jane Giles's name.

"The last time I saw Darian Hague alive, I left with Nori. And I returned with her the next morning to find her body. And today, I came over to ask Jane Giles a few questions. I never entered the house until the man over there did. Sorry, just because you can't solve this case doesn't mean you can pin it on me."

"I'd love to put the handcuffs on you."

"I bet you would."

"Don't be fucking weird, McGowan."

One of Heald's fellow officers walked over. His expression told me he wasn't pleased with Heald.

"Is everything okay over here?"

"Yes, I'm sorry," Detective Heald said. "I got a little carried away."

"It's fine, Officer. We're old friends," I added.

The officer didn't believe that, but started to walk away, before saying, "Keep it down over here, guys. This woman may have died of natural causes. Having a detective yell at a civilian might give these neighbors other thoughts."

"We'll keep it down," Heald said.

The officer walked away.

"Okay, where were we?"

"You were accusing me of being involved somehow."

"You said your fingerprints will be found on a few of the outdoor windows, and once you came inside with Tom Wells?"

He had looked down at his phone again. I guess Tom Wells was the good Samaritan's name.

"Yes."

"I've arrested people for less."

"Why are you doing this? I'm trying to find a killer just like you are."

"Because you're a young, cocky hotshot who comes in here and thinks he can solve this case before we do."

Despite the warning, we continued to argue.

"Ernest Riley hired me. This has never been about me vs. the LAPD."

Detective Heald turned his back on me and walked away, putting his hands on the back of his head. He talked to a few assembled police officers before returning to me.

He didn't look to have mellowed any.

"I want you to drop this case," he said.

153

BRIAN O'SULLIVAN

"I can't do that."

"I can make you."

"How?"

"I could make your life a living hell."

"It kind of is right now, anyway."

He shrugged, as if to say, *I can't win with this guy.*

I took it as a win. Screw Heald.

"I need you to come to the station," he said. "I need to ask you some more questions, and we're getting nowhere standing out here. I'm also going to remove the cameras from your car. They haven't amounted to jack squat. The LAPD will be happy to be getting out of the Bobby McGowan business."

I was of two minds. One, I was certain Heald did want me off the case, and removing the cameras was one way of cutting ties with me. Two, if he truly intended to make my life a living hell, it would be easier if there weren't cameras on my car to record it all.

"Can I drive my car to the station?" I asked. "You're going to need it to remove the cameras, after all."

"Yes, but drive directly there."

He stormed away, and I saw Tom Wells finishing his interview.

I approached him.

"Thank you for your help," I said.

He still looked like he was pretty shaken up.

"I can't believe she's gone. Jane was such a lovely lady."

"Do you know if anyone came by her place last night?"

"I have no idea. One of the cops told me that you're a private investigator. Is that true?"

"More or less."

"What did you guys discuss on the phone?"

I thought back to our conversation, mainly when she acted peculiar when I mentioned Hard Hank's.

"Can I throw a few names at you and see if they mean anything?" I asked.

"Sure."

"Darian Hague."

"Doesn't ring a bell."

"Hard Hank's."

"Is that a person's name?"

"It was a business. How about Hank Jewel?"

"No, I've never heard that name. What type of business was it?"

154

THE VIDEO TAPE

"An adult-themed store."

Tom Wells laughed and quickly caught himself.

"What is it?" I asked.

"The idea of Jane knowing some guy who owned an adult-themed store is so utterly ridiculous as to be funny."

"Then why did she get flustered when I dropped his name on the phone last night?"

"You must be mistaken," he said.

Tom Wells was merely a helpful neighbor, and I didn't need another discussion to go off the rails. Heald was enough.

"You're probably right," I said. "I'm sure I'm mistaken."

"I'd be shocked if she'd ever even seen a nudie mag back in the day."

"You don't happen to have a house camera, do you?"

"No. Neither did Jane. And the neighbor across from here doesn't either. This is a tranquil, safe area. I guess no one felt the need. I'm sure that's going to change."

I took out a business card and subtly handed it to him so none of the gathered police officers could see.

"Can you give me a call if you think of anything?"

"Instead of the police?"

"I don't mind if you call them, but I'd suggest not mentioning me. They aren't too fond of me right now."

"I hope you or the police catch whoever did this."

"Me too."

The next people I wanted to meet were Jane's family. That would be brutal, and when they found out I was at the crime scene and had talked with her the night before, that conversation could turn ugly.

"One last thing," I said. "Did you know anyone in her family?"

"Her son and grandson would visit a couple of times a month. She also had a daughter whom I'd see maybe twice a year. She didn't live in LA."

"Okay, thanks. Do you happen to have either of their numbers?"

"I actually have both. Jane was an older woman and not always in the best of health. I had to call her son a few times and tell him she might need to call an ambulance."

Tom Wells was closer to Jane Giles than I'd first realized.

"I'm sorry you had to see her like that," I said.

"You didn't know. I'm just sad we couldn't save her."

"She was already gone."

"Yeah." He glanced skyward as he got emotional.

I gave him a few seconds.

155

BRIAN O'SULLIVAN

"Do you want those phone numbers?"

"Please."

He took out his cell phone and gave them to me.

I looked at the names for a second.

"Wait, it's Layne and Rain."

"Yup. Jane wanted all their first names to rhyme. Jane. Layne. Rain. She could be peculiar like that."

His eyes moistened again, and I patted him on the shoulder.

"Thanks," he said, and then Tom Wells walked away.

I looked back at the house.

I said a quick prayer for Jane Giles.

I could hear Nori's voice in the back of my mind.

Look who is the religious one now.

34

"Hello."

"Hey, Dad. It's Bobby."

It was the night after I'd found Jane Giles's body. I'd convinced her son, Layne, to meet with me the following day, but I hadn't accomplished much besides that.

Besides a quick visit with Ernest, I'd stayed home most of the day.

I'd gotten the sudden urge to call my father. Coming across another dead body surely had something to do with it.

"Hello, son. It's been a while. Everything good in Los Angeles?"

"The city itself is fine, but this case is brutal. Someone else died, and since I don't believe in coincidences, my guess is she was killed."

"Who?"

"A woman who used to live on the same street as Ernest Riley."

"And you're sure it's related?"

"I'm fairly confident it is. I talked to her the night before and drove to meet her the following morning."

"Are you the one who found her?"

"Me and some other guy."

"But you saw her body?"

"Yes."

"Bobby, that's the second dead body you've seen. This can leave scars."

"No offense, Dad, but Mom was murdered when I was young. Nothing is ever going to leave the scars that did."

BRIAN O'SULLIVAN

"I understand, but this isn't normal to keep finding dead bodies."

"I know."

"What if you're next? If you were ever murdered, I wouldn't want to go on living."

"Don't say that, Dad."

"It's the truth. You can't understand because you haven't had kids yet."

"I can understand how paralyzing it can be to lose a family member."

He understood my point immediately.

"You're right. I'm sorry."

"I think I might come visit in a week. Probably just for a day since my investigation is so fluid. But it would be nice to get out of town for a bit."

"Why don't you just move back to Santa Barbara?"

"I'm not moving out of Los Angeles, Dad. But I have given a few thoughts to dropping this case."

"Now you're talking some sense. How is Nori doing? Staying away from you, I hope. And I don't mean that as a joke."

"I know you don't. She's still in Missouri. But she's getting a case of cabin fever. We had a nice talk a few nights ago. It was our first in a while."

"Are you guys drifting apart?"

"She's far away, and I'm working a horrific case. It doesn't exactly lend itself to dating bliss."

"If it's meant to be, it will happen. God is funny that way."

Then why didn't God save Mom?

I could never say that out loud, but I'd thought it dozens of times throughout my adult life.

"I still really like her," I said.

"Like her? You haven't told her you love her yet?"

"We dated for like a month. We started saying I love ya instead."

"That's about the dumbest shit I've ever heard," my father said, and it got me to laugh. He wasn't one to use swear words very often.

"It was her idea."

"Then you can tell her I said it's stupid."

I laughed a second time. It felt great after the last few days.

"It feels good to laugh now and then, doesn't it?"

"You have no idea."

"I can tell how stressed you are. How about going out in Los Angeles and grabbing a few drinks?"

"I don't need a few drinks to laugh, Dad."

"That's not what I was saying. But since you bring it up, it doesn't hurt, either."

158

THE VIDEO TAPE

"Maybe when I come up to Santa Barbara. Down here, I'm busy working on the case and don't want to wake up groggy."

"I said a few drinks. I didn't say to go all Nick Busey on me."

I didn't know if he meant Nick Nolte or Gary Busey, but it didn't matter. I got his point.

"I'll wait for a drink when I get to SB."

"Okay. Just trying to get you to loosen up."

"Like you said, I've seen two dead bodies. It's not like a snap of the finger or a quick drink will change that."

"I'm just being a dad."

"I know. I'm not blaming you."

And that's when I heard a knock at the door.

I looked at my phone. It was 9:15 and dark outside. There was no reason for anyone to be knocking at my door.

Maybe it was a neighbor looking to borrow some flour.

That seemed highly unlikely at this hour.

"Hold on, Dad," I said, setting the phone down.

I approached the door when I heard another knock.

My heart was about ready to jump out of my chest.

I slowly walked back and picked up my phone. If I had to call 911, I wanted it by my side.

I returned to the door, looked through the peephole, and was shocked by what I saw.

Nori was standing there, a brown backpack over her shoulder and a dark green suitcase by her side.

Her red hair and nose ring were gone, but it was her in the flesh.

I flung the door open, and she jumped into my arms.

We started kissing.

"I have so many questions," I said.

"There's only one answer you need to hear. I missed you. And I couldn't stand being half a country away."

"It's so good to see you."

"It's great to see you, too."

We kissed again.

"Here, let's go inside before the neighbors wonder what the racket's all about," I said.

I grabbed her suitcase, and she walked in with her backpack.

As I shut the door, she saw the phone in my hand.

"Are you on a call?"

"Oh, shit."

159

I put the phone up to my ear.

"You still there, Dad?"

"Yeah, I'm still here."

"Did you hear all that?"

"All I heard was some screaming and wrestling around. Are you okay?"

"I'm fine. Do you remember when you said that Nori was stupid?"

"I didn't say Nori was stupid. I said the 'I love ya' thing was stupid."

"Well, tell her yourself."

"What?"

"You heard me."

"Nori?"

"Hello, Mr. McGowan."

"Is this some group call or something?"

"Nope. I couldn't handle being away from your son anymore."

"This is really you? You're in Los Angeles? And standing next to my son?"

"Yes to all of the above."

"Then don't say stupid things like *I love ya*. If you love my son, then tell him."

Nori turned to me. "I love you."

"I love you, too," I said, and we shared a long kiss.

"Okay, this is weird now," I could hear my father saying.

"Goodbye, Dad."

I hung up and swooped Nori off her feet in one swell move.

I carried her to my room and threw her on the bed.

We were going to have a fantastic night together.

And we did.

But it was all downhill from there.

35

"What happened to the red hair?"

It was 7:45 the next morning, and we were cooking breakfast together. I was making an egg scramble consisting of cheese, eggs, cheese, onions, cheese, red pepper, cheese, ham, and cheese—sensing a trend yet? And she was chopping some fresh fruit and making coffee.

We'd fallen back into our old routine immediately.

"My mother said the only way she'd let me return to California is if I got rid of it. She worried I'd be too easy for the killer to recognize."

"That's darn smart on her part. Same with the nose ring?"

"Yup. I've become presentable. You can take me home to your father now."

"Hey, I did that even with your amenities."

"Amenities. I like that. And by the way, when you catch this guy, I'm bringing all the amenities back. I'm thinking bright yellow hair this time."

"You'd make it look good."

"Thanks. And don't worry, I'm going to look for a new apartment right away. I didn't come here to have you put me up. I am an independent girl, after all."

"You can stay as long as you want."

"That was my mother's other suggestion."

"To move out?"

161

"To get my own apartment. The killer knows Bobby, she said. But maybe he's forgotten about who you are, Nori."

"Once again, she's not wrong."

"Maybe not. But I just got here and want to spend the day with you. I don't care if that means tagging along while you work."

"Someone is chipper this morning."

"I'm just happy to spend time with you again. So, what's on the docket for today?"

"You may have changed your look, but if the killer is out there watching, he'll catch on quickly."

"I'll stay in the background. I promise."

"You're a striking woman. Not exactly background material."

"Thanks, but I can blend in anywhere."

"If you say so."

"I do. So what's the plan for the third time?"

"I'm going to meet up with Jane Giles's son. His name is Layne."

"Lame?"

I laughed. "Layne. L-A-Y-N-E."

"I heard you. I was just being a meanie."

I told her about Elena Estrada and Ms. Meanie. Thanks to our long-distance talks, Nori had a pretty good sense of how my investigation had been going, and I caught her up on the rest that morning.

"I'm surprised he's willing to meet you this soon," Nori said.

"Me too. After all, and I hate saying this, but it's a possibility his mother was killed because I reached out to her."

Nori quickly rubbed my shoulders.

"It's not your fault. And there's also the chance that she died of natural causes."

"Yeah," I said, still finding that unlikely.

I hadn't heard anything back from Detective Heald—nor would I—about the cause of death. I'd probably have to wait until it reached Noble Dunn.

"And even if it is related, you're just doing your job. It's nothing intentional on your part."

"No, it's not deliberate on my part, but Darian and Jane Giles might still be alive if I hadn't taken this case."

"You can't think like that."

"I try not to, but it does rear its ugly head now and then."

"Don't let it."

"Thanks, Nori."

THE VIDEO TAPE

"Anything else planned?"

"I may swing by and see Elena at some point, too. That may have to wait for tomorrow, depending on when and how long I meet with Layne Giles."

"Do you know if they are going to have a funeral for his mother?"

"I have no idea. Maybe he will tell me, but I have no intention of going. Not that I'd be invited, anyway. Jane seemed like a nice lady on the phone, but this isn't like Darian. I'd met Darian several times, and we were on our way to becoming friends. I never met Jane Giles in person and talked to her for all of five minutes."

Nori handed me a coffee. "You're wrong about one thing."

"What's that?"

"You weren't on your way to becoming friends with Darian. You two *were* friends. She talked about you to me, and she was a big fan. She told me that you were a catch."

"See, Darian grows in stature every day."

"She would have probably kicked my butt if she knew I headed back to Missouri instead of staying and standing by my man."

"You made the right decision by going home. And if you were Darian's daughter, she'd have done the same thing as your mother."

"Yeah, you're probably right. Anyway, here's to Darian."

We clinked our coffee cups.

"And you can take a seat. This scramble is just about ready."

Nori sat down. I brought over two plates with the cheesy scramble and a piece of toast. I then joined her at the table.

"Did I tell you about BLISSFUL?"

"No, what is it?"

"They are reopening. A co-worker named Carisa Delaney has agreed to take over Darian's duties."

"Are you disappointed it's not you?"

"No. Remember, it was supposed to be a stop-gap job until I found something in publishing. And then I kind of fell for Darian. Whatever. Carisa will do a better job than I. She's more in tune with that industry."

"You would have been great, but I understand your point."

"You know what's great?"

"What?"

"This scramble."

"Don't be a kiss ass," I said.

"Then how about just a kiss?"

She leaned over and kissed me.

163

"You know what? I will let you tag along with me today, but you have to promise you'll stay in the car. I'm meeting the son of a murdered woman, and she was likely murdered because of me contacting her. This conversation could get a little tough."

"Are you sure you don't need me there to lend a feminine touch? Just in case the guy gets hostile."

"I know you're playing around, but sorry, I'm sure. He'd ask you your name, and then we are either lying or it's out in the stratosphere that Nori Bridgewater has returned. I don't like either option. So, if you're coming, you're staying in the car. I'm sorry."

"That's okay. I understand that you're just trying to protect me."

We took another bite of our food and sat in silence.

I was thrilled to have Nori back in my life. She was as sexy, fun, and free-spirited as I remembered.

But part of me knew this was upping the ante going forward.

When it's just you, it's different.

When there is someone you genuinely care for, the stakes are raised dramatically.

❧ 36 ❧

Layne Giles lived in Hollywood, but not in the seedy part I'd become accustomed to visiting.

We were in the suburbs, and other lovely homes surrounded Layne's house on a tree-lined street. This wasn't Beverly Hills, but it wasn't the apartments above BLISSFUL, either.

I parked across the street, and despite Nori's initial pleading to the contrary, she agreed to stay in the car.

Layne Giles answered the door on my first ring, and I couldn't help but be brought back a few days earlier, when his mother never answered. I reminded myself to be overly respectful when talking about her.

Layne looked to be in his mid-fifties and had thinning brown hair. He was in good shape and had big arms, but wore wire-rimmed glasses that almost made him look like a professor. He resembled a roided-up librarian.

We shook hands, and he invited me inside. That quickly led to a trip outside, where he had a nice backyard with a pool. There were two chairs, along with a coffee and a water in front of them.

"I didn't know if you'd want water or coffee," Layne said.

"You didn't have to do all this."

"It's no problem."

"Well, thank you."

"And let me get this out of the way before we continue. From what I've gathered from the police, their initial impression is that my mother died of natural causes. So you don't have to worry about me blaming you for her death. You were just doing your job."

He smiled, but I sensed the slightest bit of sarcasm. Like maybe he did blame me.

"Thanks for that," I said.

"This conversation will probably be awkward enough as it is. Let's not make it more than it has to be."

"Works for me."

"So why are you here, Bobby? Let's start there."

"Well, it's pretty much like I told you over the phone. My investigation led me to interview Elena Estrada, who recommended I talk to your mother. I called her and she got off the phone pretty quickly. I ended up at her house the next morning because I had a few more questions for her. You know what happened after that."

"Indeed. I feel bad for Tom Wells. He is a good guy. I'm sorry he had to see that."

"He was great, and obviously liked your mother."

"He was an awesome neighbor to her," he said quietly. Layne paused, and when he spoke again, it was more forceful. "Okay, no more talk about my mother's death for now. It's still too raw for me."

"Of course."

"Elena Estrada was a very nice woman. I was around the same age as a few of her older children."

"I only met Leti, her youngest."

"I would have been too old to know her very well. I'm sure we crossed paths back then, but I only knew the two oldest."

"Elena liked your mother. She told me so. I hope that's okay to say."

"That's nice to hear. Thanks. And yes, you can compliment her. I just don't want to talk about her death."

"Understood."

"I'm sure you came here to ask me some questions regarding Ernest Riley and the videotape, so fire away. I wasn't even living on Collier Court then, but I'll help if I can. Nothing is off-limits, so fire away."

"Okay," I said, deciding on my first question. "When I was on the phone with your mother, I mentioned Hard Hank's and Hank Jewel, and she seemed to tense up. Do you have any idea why?"

"Hard Hank's as in the old sex store in Hollywood?"

"Yes. As well as its owner, Hank Jewel. I brought up both."

"Sure, I've heard of the store. Any red-blooded American male who grew up in Los Angeles in the seventies and eighties has heard of Hard

166

THE VIDEO TAPE

Hank's. But I don't know why my mother acted in that way. I'm kind of surprised she'd even heard of that place."

"I'm pretty sure she had."

"Pretty sure?"

"Well, she became flustered when I brought the store up."

"That could very easily be for another reason," Layne said.

"Do you mean the stroke?"

"Yes. She does get flustered occasionally. I'm sorry, she *did* get flustered occasionally. I'm still getting used to referring to her in the past tense."

"If it means anything, you're taking it better than I expected."

I regretted saying it immediately. How did I know how Layne Giles—someone I'd never met—would react to his mother's death?

"Well, she lived a fairly long life," he said, ignoring my faux pas. "She was just about to turn eighty. Do I wish I had a few more years with her? Of course, but I'm also grateful I had her this long. I'm fifty-four, and not all that many people can say they had a meaningful time with their mother while in their mid-fifties."

In situations like this, my mind instinctively thinks about my mother, and how I didn't get the time with her. He seemed to notice.

"Are you okay, Bobby?"

"Yeah. My mother was taken from me too early."

"I'm so sorry. I had no idea. Now you realize why I feel lucky to have had my mother as long as I did."

"Yes, I get it."

"Where did you grow up?"

"In Santa Barbara."

"And that's where you lost your mother?"

Something in the back of my mind told me that Layne Giles already knew this information. Maybe he'd done some research before meeting with me. That would make sense.

But this felt rehearsed. I couldn't pinpoint why, but my gut was telling me so.

"Yes."

"Well, I'm very sorry. Santa Barbara is usually such a safe city."

"Yes, it is."

I was growing tired of this conversation.

"They have a great university up there. UCSB."

"Yes, I went there."

Once again, I felt he already knew the answers I was getting.

"There are some famous alumni who went there."

"Yes, we have a few."

"Didn't Michael Douglas graduate from UCSB?"

This was getting odd. Why was he bringing up Michael Douglas?

"He did."

"What an underrated actor. He's in this great movie with Gwyneth Paltrow. You should check it out."

"I will, but Mr. Giles, we're getting off track."

"Okay, right. My bad. As for your question about Hard Hank's, I'm at a loss. I would guess that my mother was having one of her senior moments, brought on by her stroke."

"Maybe."

"Probably," he said.

That lone word felt surprisingly confrontational. Layne Giles had marked his line in the sand. If his mother acted oddly with the mention of Hard Hank's, it was because of the stroke.

"Did you happen to know Hank Jewel?"

"I'm sorry. I didn't."

I decided to change the subject.

"Can I mention a few more names and see if you recognize any of them?"

"Sure."

"Darian Hague."

"Sorry. It doesn't ring a bell."

"How about the clothing line Halo?"

"Nope. No idea what that is."

Layne Giles was trying to be helpful—or pretending to be—but this wasn't going anywhere.

"Have you ever had an opinion on how Ernest Riley came into possession of the videotape?"

"That's the great mystery of Collier Court, isn't it? I wish I had an opinion, but I never really formed one. I was already in my twenties and not living at home by then. I first found out about the videotape when my mother called me a few days later and told me the cops were interviewing everyone on the block."

"Did you ever get interviewed?"

"No. I'm sure when my mother told them I didn't live there, they felt no need to interview me."

"What did you think of Ernest Riley?"

"Ernest is good people. I can assure you that he had nothing to do with this."

THE VIDEO TAPE

"I'm running out of questions. I guess I'd better take a big sip of this coffee."

Layne Giles laughed. "Sorry, I couldn't be of more help."

Outwardly, he was polite and helpful, but I still sensed something was off about him.

"No problem."

"Anything else?"

"That's it for now. Can I call you if I think of any more questions?"

"Of course."

I took one more sip of coffee and rose from my chair. Layne escorted me toward the front door.

Hanging next to the front door was a family photo. Not an old school one where everyone is dressed up. This was an action photo with everyone doing a weird pose.

There was Layne, a woman I assumed was his wife, and a teenage son.

Layne had more hair; I guessed the photo was about three or four years old.

I found one thing interesting.

There was a 99.99% chance it was nothing, but it couldn't help but register.

"I love your son's hat. He must be a Laker fan."

"He is," Layne said, and then quickly added. "Isn't every kid in LA?"

⚜

"How did it go?" Nori asked when I arrived at my car.

"Fine. I'll tell you all about it on the ride home."

"He's still looking this way."

I looked over, and sure enough, Layne Giles was still peering in my direction. It was a bit creepy.

I waved at him, and he waved back. Then, he slowly shut his front door.

"What was that all about?" Nori asked.

"He just wanted to make sure I got to my car, I guess."

"You'd been in the car for thirty seconds, and he was still staring in our direction."

"He's a bit of an odd guy."

"Tell me more."

I rehashed my conversation with Layne Giles, culminating in seeing his son in a Lakers hat.

169

"I'm not sure that would stand up in a court of law," she said.

"I know. I just said I found it interesting."

"Do you think it's the kid who left the note?"

"The person hid their face well, so it's impossible to tell if it's him, but they are at least of similar build, and probably about the same age. Again, that's not convicting anybody in a court of law."

"But you're intrigued."

"Yes."

"Highly intrigued?"

"I don't want to get my hopes up, but something about Layne rubbed me the wrong way. He was an odd duck."

"Sorry to keep playing devil's advocate, but maybe he's just acting odd because his mother just died."

"That's possible. But then why agree to meet me so soon after her death?"

"Maybe he was trying to size up his competition," Nori said.

I looked over at her and nodded. "Maybe."

I was about to drive away when I remembered the hokey Michael Douglas reference.

"You're a movie buff, right?"

"I like to think so."

"Have you ever seen a movie with Michael Douglas and Gwyneth Paltrow?"

"I remember one for sure."

"What's it called?"

I saw Nori purse her lips.

"Are you okay?" I asked.

"You're not going to like the name of the movie."

"What is it?"

"*A Perfect Murder.*"

Holy shit.

37

LAYNE GILES

Bobby McGowan focused on our family photo for a second too long. I had been so close to getting him out of my house.

Why hadn't I removed every picture in the house? Or at least the ones with my son wearing a Lakers hat.

Why had I agreed to meet with Bobby to begin with?

I could have claimed that I was too broken up by my mother's death, and it would have been a perfectly valid excuse.

It would have been a whopper, but he'd have had no reason not to believe it. And yet, I'd agreed to meet him.

I knew why.

I welcomed the battle. I thought I'd committed the perfect murder— well, murders. That's why I'd made the Michael Douglas reference, after all.

And I wasn't going to avoid meeting with some punk wannabe PI.

WHEN BOBBY ASKED ME ABOUT THE PHOTO, I COULDN'T DENY THAT MY son was a Laker fan, but I added, "Isn't every kid in LA?" to try to make it sound like this is standard fare in Los Angeles, which it is.

Two-thirds of all teenagers in LA have a Lakers hat.

BRIAN O'SULLIVAN

A son with a Laker hat and a reference to a movie with an interesting title. That's all Bobby McGowan was ever going to get. I was going to be just fine.

Bobby left ten seconds after asking about the Lakers hat, and I watched as he walked across the street to his car.

I saw a woman in the passenger seat, but didn't recognize her at first.

A few seconds later, it hit me.

It was Nori Bridgewater without that filthy red hair and disgusting nose ring.

She looked pretty good, I had to admit.

Well, this changed everything.

Thanks for coming back, Nori.

I hope to make your acquaintance at some point.

38

BOBBY

I decided to take a detour to Noble's house.

I felt a bit bad for him. I always assumed he would be at home.

I get that he was a widower and had a nasty knife wound, but he was too much of a homebody. He needed to get out now and then. Not that he was asking for my advice.

As we neared his house, Nori turned to me. "I'll stay in the car."

"You can come in. It's only when I meet new people. Noble is on our team."

"Thanks."

Noble greeted us at the door.

"Hey, Bobby."

I hadn't warned Nori about the knife wound, but she didn't make some ghastly face or say anything inappropriate. Not that there was any chance of that. I never had anything to fear with Nori. She would always be classy, and I appreciated that about her. And yes, I know she used to work at an adult shop. That doesn't prevent someone from having class. Darian had it in spades.

"This is Nori."

They shook hands, and Noble led us into the house.

"I've heard a lot about you, Nori."

"You have?" Nori sounded surprised.

BRIAN O'SULLIVAN

"Yes. And I'm sorry about your boss."

"Thanks."

"I have something to tell you, Bobby. But first, why don't you tell me why you're here?"

"You sure you want me to start?" I asked.

"Yeah. Go ahead."

"I met with Jane Giles's son today. His name is Layne. Did you ever interview him?"

"No. I didn't."

"Do you remember if anyone from the LAPD did? I don't remember the police reports ever mentioning it. He said he never had, but I just want to follow up and make sure."

"I want to say no, but I'd have to go over it with a fine-toothed comb. Would there have been a reason to?"

"Not really. He said he wasn't living on Collier Court during that time."

"Then he's probably telling the truth, and they probably didn't. But by the tone of your voice, I'm guessing you've taken a little interest in Layne Giles. Why?"

"There are a few things. I saw a family photograph with his son wearing a Lakers hat."

"Oh, I get it. And the young man who left the note on your door wore a Lakers hat. No offense, Bobby, but isn't every kid in LA a Laker fan?"

"That's almost verbatim what he said."

"So? That just means it's an appropriate response."

"It didn't feel that way. It felt more like he was giving an excuse as to why his son would be wearing the hat."

"That's pretty flimsy."

"He also stared at us from his front door for about thirty seconds before we left."

"Also flimsy."

"One more. When he learned I was from Santa Barbara, he referenced Michael Douglas and said I should check out a movie with him and Gwyneth Paltrow. Any guess as to the name of that movie?"

"You got me."

"It's called *A Perfect Murder.*"

Noble straightened up. That had got his attention. "He told you to check out a movie called *A Perfect Murder?*"

"He sure did."

"That's still flimsy, but I'm a little more interested in that than a Lakers hat or a stare that lasted too long."

174

THE VIDEO TAPE

"That's fair, but I'm telling you, this is the first time I've felt like maybe there's something here."

"Okay. I've said you have great instincts. Now what?"

"This goes back to Hard Hank's somehow. When I mentioned the business, Jane Giles was put off or shocked. The reaction was not due to her stroke. I'm sure of it."

"Same question. Now what?"

"I need to meet with Mr. Z again. Ask some more questions. He's my only tie-in to Hank Jewel."

"Such a stupid name."

"Mr. Z or Hank Jewel?"

"Both. But I'm referring to calling yourself Mr. Z."

"We agree on that one. Now, what did you want to tell me?"

Noble's face tensed up. This was serious.

"Ernest has had a setback. He's getting sicker, and the doctors have amended how long they think he will live."

My heart sank. "Oh, no. How long does he have?"

"A few weeks. If that."

"That's terrible. Can I go see him?"

"Not today. His daughter is in town looking after him, and I've touched base with her. They are going to be spending most of the day today with specialists."

"Are they hoping to get a second opinion?"

"No. They are talking about putting him in hospice."

A tear came to my eye. "Fuck."

"Yeah. Fuck."

Nori looked in my direction and saw how affected I was.

"He sounds like a special man," she said.

"He is," Noble said. "For a long time, he hated everyone in the LAPD with the exception of me. That's got to count for something, right?"

That brought a smile to my face. "Well, even the good ones miss one now and then."

Noble let out a small laugh and looked at Nori. "Your boyfriend always finds the right thing to say, even if it's not always at the opportune moment."

"Ernest wouldn't want us to hang our heads," I said.

"That is true. If I can arrange it, would you guys like to see him tomorrow morning? He probably won't use his phone much, but I can arrange it with his daughter."

"We'd love to see him," I said.

175

Nori looked at me, and I knew what she was going to say. "Yes. *We* would."

We said our goodbyes, and Noble promised to keep me updated on Ernest Riley.

And I promised to keep him in the loop on Layne Giles.

❦ 39 ❦

BOBBY

I woke up the next morning and received a call from Noble Dunn at six-thirty.

Ernest Riley would see us at eight. His daughter and possibly a nurse would be there, but he'd be able to talk. Noble insisted that I try to make it quick.

"Let's not ask him a million questions while he's in this state," he said.

"I won't. And thanks for setting this up."

When the call ended, Nori turned to me. "Can we have a serious talk?"

"Of course."

"Before I came back to LA, I had this vision. You would be one of the Hardy Boys, and I would be Nancy Drew. Or I was going to be Scully to your Mulder. But it doesn't quite feel like it's headed in that direction. It's not your fault. Not at all. You've worked this case all along, and I'm out of my league. I'm not cut out to be a PI. And I just can't imagine myself continuing to sit in cars while you do the investigating. And please, Bobby, I want you to understand that this does not reflect on you. You've been great."

"I thought we've been getting along fine."

"We have. This isn't a judgment on our relationship. It's a reflection of me not being cut out for detective work. I'd rather watch from the sidelines."

177

"Okay, I get your point. What did you have in mind?"

"You're going to Ernest's this morning, right?"

"Yeah."

"And then what?"

"Hopefully, I'll meet up with the guy, Mr. Z, I've told you about. Or potentially Elena. And I might even meet up with the woman whose mother owned Halo."

"I think her name was Jaycee."

"You're right. Jaycee Mullen. See, you have been paying attention."

She gave me a courtesy smile. "My point is that you have a full day. I think I'm going to look at apartments. Maybe help Carisa get BLISSFUL ready for their eventual reopening."

"Are you sure? I told you I don't mind you staying here until you get settled."

"Like I keep saying, you've been awesome. I like you very much, Bobby. I like how easy you are to talk to. I like how dogged you are in going after this killer. I like making love to you. There are a lot of things I like about you."

"So, what's the problem?"

"There's not a problem. But don't you find it weird that the only time we've officially said we love each other was at your father's urging? That's not a great sign."

"We've said I love ya."

"I started saying I love ya, and you followed my lead. Hardly the stuff of romance novels."

"I can't tell if this is a breakup or what?"

"It's not. I'll be back here tonight. But I do want to find my own place to live. I think we should take this a little slower. We've been together a short time, but it's been a whirlwind. In every way. Including Darian's murder. And now someone else has been murdered. It's not exactly fertile ground for a new relationship."

I wanted to play devil's advocate, but everything Nori said was true. I liked her very much. She was fun, playful, intelligent, and sexy. I remember being smitten the first day I met her.

And when she saw the videotape, I wanted to protect her.

I cared about her.

The sex had been great as well. I didn't have much to complain about.

But did I love her?

She was right that we'd never officially said it except at my father's urging.

THE VIDEO TAPE

"Bobby, are you there?" Nori said. "You look like you're in a daze."

"Sorry, I was just running over things in my head."

"And ..."

"And, I hate to say this, but maybe you're right."

"Okay, good. Remember, we're not breaking up," Nori said. "We're just going to move a little slower."

"I understand. It would be easier to figure out where we stood if I didn't have this case hanging over my head."

"That's all I'm saying. You're an awesome dude, but maybe it's not the right time for us to move in together."

"Okay. I think you're right."

We gave each other a lengthy kiss.

"Love ya," she said, and we both thought it was the funniest thing ever.

❦

NORI LEFT WHEN I DID.

She went to look for a new apartment, and I went to see a dying man.

I noticed a few new cars parked out front when I arrived at Ernest's. Knowing what they were there for made me sad.

I knocked on the door and was greeted by someone I assumed was his daughter.

"You must be Bobby. I'm Ernest's only child, Lily McFarland. Formerly Lily Riley."

Lily was in her early to mid-fifties, and her light red hair fell to her shoulders. She had a pleasant vibe.

"Nice to meet you, Lily. Your father is a great man. I was sorry to hear the latest news from Noble."

"Thanks. Let's not try to focus on that."

"I won't."

We walked inside, and in the corner of the living room was Ernest, sitting up in a hospital bed. He had several tubes going through him, which were connected to an adjoining wall.

He looked like he'd aged ten years. I'd always thought he appeared young for his age, but he now firmly looked to be a man in his eighties.

A dying man in his eighties.

I told myself not to tear up. Try to be positive.

"Is that Bobby McGowan I see?"

I walked over and grabbed his hand.

"It sure is. How are you feeling, Ernest?"

179

"I'm feeling just fine. It's probably these drugs they are pumping into my system." He laughed.

"Your sense of humor hasn't gone anywhere," I said.

"Always. What is there to complain about? I've lived into my eighties. My only daughter is here. And tomorrow is the chef's kiss."

"What's tomorrow?"

"My grandkids are flying in."

"That's fantastic."

Noble told me not to have Ernest talk too much, so I turned to Lily. "How many grandkids does he have?"

"Three, and they are all flying in tomorrow."

"Where from?" I asked.

"One lives near me in Seattle. One is flying in from New York. And one from South Carolina."

"Sounds like you're pretty loved there, Ernest."

"As I said, I can't complain."

I turned back to Lily. "Has Noble been over?"

"I know what you're doing," Ernest said. "I can talk, you know. You don't have to turn to my daughter to ask basic questions. And speaking of Noble, I bet he put you up to this. When he visited, he'd barely let me talk."

I couldn't help but laugh. "You've still got it, Ernest. Yes, Noble asked very sweetly not to have you talk too much."

"Well, there's no reason to save your breath. After your last one, it's not like you get to take them with you."

Lily looked like she wanted to both laugh and cry.

Just then, two nurses appeared from the kitchen. They were both wearing large name tags with their first and last names. I wondered if the large name tags were so Ernest could more easily read them.

Piper Bloom, a young black woman, gave him a couple of pills to take. Alma Villanueva, a slightly older-but-still-young-Filipino woman, gave him some water to take it down with.

"Will you look at these name tags, Bobby? They are the size of the billboards you see driving in LA. Just because I'm dying doesn't mean I can't see. And no offense, Piper and Alma, you've both been great, but do I need to know your last names?"

Everyone in the room laughed. Ernest was the one loosening us up. It should have been the other way around.

"You'll have to take some more pills in about an hour," Piper said.

"Or what, I'll die?"

THE VIDEO TAPE

I busted out laughing. Maybe it was the wrong time, but Ernest was being pretty damn funny.

And come to think of it, maybe it was the right time. I thought back to Darian's funeral. I was delighted by how it became a celebration of life and not a sad reflection of death.

Ernest was doing the same in real time.

The nurses headed back to the kitchen, and Lily turned to me.

"They have been great, but Ernest doesn't like them to stay in this room too long."

"What am I going to talk about with them? The 1960 presidential election? I have nothing in common with those young ladies, as nice as they are. Shit, they even make Bobby here look old."

"I don't remember your father being this funny," I said.

"He's not usually."

"All right. I'll turn serious for a second. Any new news on the investigation, Bobby?"

I told him everything, with one exception. I didn't mention Layne Giles's son's hat, nor my lingering suspicion of him. I didn't want to get Ernest's blood pressure going.

"But I am making good progress," I said. "I feel like I'm getting close."

"That's good to hear. Hope you'll solve it before Piper and Alma move on to their next victims."

Ernest had tried to tell another joke, but this one fell flat.

"I think you're going to be around for longer than you think," I said.

"Thanks, Bobby. You've been great since I brought you on. I mean that."

I grabbed his hand and held it tight. "Thank you, Ernest. I appreciate your faith in me. I'm trying my best."

"I know you are. We're going to catch this asshole soon."

Ernest coughed violently, and the nurses quickly returned to the room.

"I'm fine. I'm fine."

Maybe he was, but I'd had him talking long enough. Noble was right.

"I've got to go, Ernest, but I'll come to see you in a few days."

He grabbed my hand and squeezed it. "Thanks for stopping by, Bobby."

"You're welcome. Take care."

I started toward the door, and Lily followed me.

"I appreciate you coming over," she said. "You two have a great back and forth."

"We certainly did this time. Maybe he's loosening up in his old age."

181

"He has been surprisingly frisky these last few days. Thinks he's a damn stand-up comedian now."

I smiled. "Can I ask you a few quick questions about my investigation?"

"Sure."

I mainly wanted to mention Layne Giles, but didn't want to make it obvious by starting with him.

"I met with Elena Estrada. Do you remember her?"

"Of course. She was like the first lady of Collier Court."

"She was awesome. And did you know her daughter Leti?"

"I know who she was, but she was one of the younger kids on the block."

"I also met with Layne Giles."

"My father told me about his mother. I'm sorry you had to see her."

"Thanks. What was Layne like growing up?"

Her eyes held my gaze just a touch longer than is socially acceptable. Something was up.

"Why do you ask that?" she said.

"I'm just trying to get a proper representation of everyone who lived on that block."

"I wish Layne had never lived there. He was an oddball."

"How so?"

"He was always creepy, even when we were kids. We were basically the same age, so I grew up seeing his antics."

"What antics were those?"

"When we were kids, it was just standard stuff. Teepeeing houses. Throwing eggs on Halloween. Nothing too bad. But then I remember him getting a little more brazen. Once, he threw a rock through Ms. Keaney's window and swore a bunch of us to secrecy. At the entrance to Collier Court, cars would go whizzing by on the main street. He and some kids would play chicken and run out in the street before quickly running back."

"That sounds extremely dangerous."

"It was."

"I had talked to Jane Giles on the phone. She seemed like a sweet woman."

"She was, but she couldn't handle Layne. She was a divorcee, and it's too bad, because Layne could have used a father figure."

Layne didn't sound like a very pleasant young man, but millions of kids did dumb shit like that. They didn't grow up to be killers.

"Why all the questions about Layne?"

THE VIDEO TAPE

"I told you. I'm just trying to get a read on everyone who lived on Collier Court."

"Bullshit," Lily said. "There's more to it than that. My father is sitting over there dying. Don't lie to his only child."

"Wow, you're playing hardball."

She smiled. "A little guilt trip never hurt anyone."

"Layne Giles said he wasn't even there on the day of the garage sale," I said.

"Maybe, maybe not. I don't know, I was in Italy. Plus, his denial doesn't mean anything. If it was his videotape—and I'm definitely not saying that it was—his mother may have accidentally grabbed it."

"By that logic, it would be more likely that whoever was in possession of the videotape would have been gone on the day in question. If they had been there, the videotape never would have made it to the garage sale and eventually your father's pile."

"Bingo."

"Do you think Layne Giles was enough of a sociopath to make a snuff film?"

"My answer would have to be no. I mean, how many people actually make snuff films? A handful of sickos across the whole world? So what are the odds that I grew up next to one who did? That being said, Layne was a bad seed. I'll leave it at that."

"Thank you, Lily. I'll give your father a break tomorrow, but can I come see him the following day?"

"Sure. Thanks, Bobby."

I returned to my car, thinking about Layne Giles the whole time.

Could it be him?

I didn't have much to go on. A bad joke about a movie, a son who liked the Lakers, and an old neighbor who said he was a bad seed.

It wasn't much.

But it wasn't nothing, either.

⚜

I CALLED NORI ON MY WAY HOME.

"How are things going?" I asked.

"I've already looked at two places."

"Where?"

"One in Hollywood and one just west of the 405."

"That one would be closer to me."

"Yeah, that's why I'm leaning toward the one in Hollywood."

I laughed.

"I know it's the middle of the day in late June and it's ninety degrees out, but still be vigilant. You never know."

"I no longer have a nose ring, and the red hair is long gone. The killer wouldn't recognize me if we passed each other on the street."

"Regardless, just be careful."

"I will be."

"And I'll see you tonight?"

"Yeah. I'll probably finish apartment hunting around four or so and head back. I'll wait to go to BLISSFUL until tomorrow."

"Okay. I'm a little tired, so I may just order a pizza. Are you cool with that?"

"Of course."

40

LAYNE

I was less than ten feet from Nori Bridgewater.

She was about to end a phone call with Bobby, and my mind was focused on ending her.

"Yeah. I'll probably finish apartment hunting around four or so and then head back," she said.

But I should probably explain how I got here.

***

IT HAD BEEN AN EMBARRASSMENT OF RICHES THAT MORNING.

Bobby and Nori left simultaneously, and I saw Bobby head toward the underground parking while Nori headed to her car on the street. I had my choice of who to follow.

I decided to follow Nori. While she'd seen me from fifty feet away, she hadn't seen me up close.

Not that I expected to be caught, but Bobby McGowan had a keen eye, and I'd have to be careful when I followed him.

On the other hand, Nori would be a piece of cake. A piece of pie, if you will.

Her car pulled out from the curb and headed toward the freeway, with me following from a distance.

185

Her first stop was at an apartment complex in Hollywood.

Was their love on the rocks?

To my knowledge, she'd just moved back, and now she was out apartment hunting already?

What did you do, Bobby? Not satisfying Nori in the bedroom? Or, is this case driving a stake between the two of you?

Now, that's an idea. Driving a stake through someone.

I might have to consider that option with the beautiful Nori.

Nori was inside the complex for about half an hour. Next, she drove back under the 405 freeway and looked at an apartment complex in Santa Monica.

I continued to watch from the relative obscurity of my car. I also own a truck, but the car was more nondescript, so it became an easy choice.

One stop at a random apartment complex could be explainable. Maybe you'd left something at a friend's place and were getting it back.

A second stop at an apartment complex said something different. Nori was definitely looking for a place to move.

Poor, poor Bobby.

HER NEXT STOP WAS AN UNDERGROUND PARKING GARAGE ON THE Wilshire and Centinela Avenue cross street.

I knew the area; a few stores were above the garage, including a coffee shop. I guessed she was headed there.

I waited a minute until I saw her reappear on the street level. I then drove into the underground parking garage and parked four spots from her.

It was a quiet parking garage. There was only one other car besides Nori's and mine.

One of the rare times in Los Angeles when things weren't overcrowded. That was good for me, and bad for Nori.

I exited my car and moved behind a pillar, shielding myself from view. When Nori returned and went to open her car door, her back would be to me.

I scanned the parking lot, making sure no one else pulled up in the meantime.

So far, so good.

THE VIDEO TAPE

A FEW MINUTES LATER, NORI CAME AROUND THE CORNER AND HEADED toward her car.

She had a coffee in one hand and a little bag in the other.

I was still hidden behind the pillar, but could see her silhouette.

More importantly, I could hear her voice.

She was talking on the phone, and I was delighted to hear the name *Bobby.*

Could there be a better time than this?

To kidnap her as she's talking to Bobby McGowan, my nemesis. This was going to be perfect.

As she approached her car, I quietly stepped out from the obscurity of the pillar. She still had her back to me, but I pulled my hat closer to my head, just in case.

It was not a Lakers hat. I was certain that Bobby had discussed the case with Nori in detail. Seeing someone with a Lakers hat would draw Bobby's or Nori's attention.

My hat was black and my shorts and T-shirt were gray. I wasn't trying to stand out—I was trying to blend in.

I took a few steps toward Nori, trying not to make any noise.

If she heard me and turned around, I'd cover my face and head to my car, but she hadn't noticed me yet.

It sounded like she was wrapping up her phone call.

That would be another fun way to record someone's death: Wrapping them up, mummy style. *Dexter*-style.

Don't get sidetracked, I told myself. Concentrate on the task at hand.

And that's when Nori said, "Yeah. I'll probably finish apartment hunting around four or so and head back."

I took one step closer to her. She had no idea how close I was. Within ten feet for sure.

What a dumb bitch. She never should have come back to Los Angeles.

The day she met Bobby McGowan was the unluckiest day of her life.

Her soon-to-be shorter-than-expected life.

I took one step closer.

❧ 41 ❧

BOBBY

I was surprised when I arrived back at my apartment.

Nori wasn't there.

I gave her my spare key, and she said she'd return by four.

It was only 4:10, but with my imagination running wild lately, even ten minutes late felt like a lot. If she weren't back by 4:20, I'd start worrying.

She wasn't back by 4:20, so I gave her a call.

No answer.

I called again.

Still no answer.

I told myself not to panic, but that was getting harder by the second.

Just then, I looked out my apartment window and saw that Nori was headed toward me.

"You scared me," I said when we returned inside.

"I'm only a few minutes late."

"Twenty minutes late. And that feels like two hours these days."

She looked at me with sympathetic eyes. "You're right. I'm sorry. But I do have a good excuse."

"I'd love to hear it."

"After looking at those two complexes and grabbing a quick lunch, I decided to head over to BLISSFUL."

THE VIDEO TAPE

"How was it?"

"They haven't reopened yet, but Carisa showed me around. She's the one who is taking over all of Darian's duties."

"I remember. Does that mean she's taking over the ownership as well?"

"I talked to her about that. No, Darian's daughter, whom I'm sure you remember well, was given the business in the will. But she has kids and doesn't even live in LA, so she can't do it. So she hired Carisa."

"She did come to you first," I said.

"True, but I didn't want it then. And I don't want it now. But I'm happy that it's staying open. Darian would have wanted it, too. And Carisa has been there a lot longer than I was, and she genuinely cares about the business. I think she's going to do a bang-up job."

"That's great to hear. When is she planning on officially reopening it?"

"Mid-July. She could open it tomorrow if she wants, but I think Carisa wants to make it her own before officially opening it. I don't blame her. And she's doing a great job so far. The main floor is going to have a lot more open space. It feels more modern. Darian was the best, but she was kind of old-school. This will feel more youthful."

"Just what we need. More of today's youth going to sex stores."

Nori laughed. "Okay, Mr. Funny Guy!"

We kissed.

"I'm glad you got to see the new place, but try to be on time from here on in. For my sanity, if anything."

"I'm sorry. I will. How was your day?"

"Busy. My meeting with Ernest was brutal. He is dying."

"Didn't you know that going in?"

"Yeah, but it's different when you see it in person. It's very sad."

"I'm sorry, Bobby."

"Thanks."

"What else did you do?"

"I cussed out Alfred Weaver, but he still wouldn't give me Mr. Z's phone number. He's a stubborn old bird."

"He can't just rat out his sources. Even if the book was written a long time ago."

"Yeah, you're right, but I hate being on this side of it. I need to learn more about Hank Jewel, and Mr. Z is the only one who can provide that. His family is all gone, and his other employees I talked to were worthless. I want to hear about who Jewel was friends with back then. I want to hear more about this Larry Gilden guy." I repeated the name. "Larry Gilden."

189

BRIAN O'SULLIVAN

And that's when it hit me.

"What is it?" Nori asked. She could tell something was up.

"Larry Gilden sounds similar to Layne Giles, doesn't it?"

"Yeah. I guess."

"The first names start with L-A and the last start with G-I-L."

"I know where you're going with this."

"Is it that crazy? Imagine you're in your mid-twenties and come from a nice upbringing on Collier Court. If you went to a business like Hard Hank's, would you want to use your own name?"

"Look who you're talking to. When you first met me, I used the name *Paige Turner.*"

I laughed. "Oh shit, that's right."

"So, yes, I buy the idea of using a fake name."

"There have been numerous examples of people using fake names that sound pretty darn close to their real name. A lot of them even use the same first name. That always seemed a bit aggressive to me, but I understand the idea behind it. At least you know when to turn around if your name is called. But I'd change it up a little bit."

"Like from Layne to Larry. And from Giles to Gilden?"

"Exactly," I said.

Nori could tell I was excited, which also caused her to get excited.

"I've got a feeling the next few days will be crucial."

"I think you're right."

"You really think Layne Giles might be the guy?"

"Yes, I do. It's hard to explain since you only saw him from the street. To feel his unpleasant aura, you have to be near him."

"A lot of people have unpleasant auras. They aren't all killers."

"Very true. But they don't all reference movies called *A Perfect Murder,* either. I think I may visit Mr. Giles again tomorrow. Then, I'll go see Ernest's daughter Lily."

"For what?"

"I want to see if she has any old pictures of Layne Giles."

"She's visiting. I doubt she'd have any."

"That's true. Maybe I'll go down and see Elena Estrada. She might have some old yearbooks or something lying around."

"And what do you want to do with those pictures?"

"I want to confront Mr. Z and ask if he recognizes Layne Giles. Ask him if Layne Giles is the man he knew as Larry Gilden."

"Why not just find a picture of Giles on the internet?"

"I'll look, but I'm almost certain he's not a social media guy."

190

THE VIDEO TAPE

"How about LinkedIn or something like that?"

"No, that won't work."

"Why?"

"Because we are talking about 1995. That's a long time ago. I'm sure Layne looks very different. I'm trying to give Mr. Z the best chance to identify him. And if Elena has a high school yearbook photo or something, that would be a lot better than a LinkedIn photo of the guy at fifty-something years old."

"Are you sure you want to go see Layne Giles in person? If he's as dangerous as you think he might be ..."

"He won't do anything to me inside his house."

"Any chance of notifying the police?"

"Not yet. This is still all circumstantial. I promise to use them when it's time, but we're not there yet."

"Sounds like you've got it all figured out."

That could have sounded condescending, but Nori meant it as a compliment.

"I don't have the whole case figured out—far from it—but I do have my plan of action nailed down."

"How does Darian come into it?"

"I have no idea. That shows you how far I am away from truly solving this. Layne—or whoever the killer is—wouldn't just kill Darian because we talked to her. If that were the case, why didn't they go after Ernest, Noble, Jaycee Mullen, or so many others?"

"So you think Darian might be tied up in this more than we realize?"

"That makes it sound like she did something disreputable. I'm not saying that. But she did own an adult store at the same time as Hank Jewel, and maybe they had mutual friends. Something like that."

"And the killer feared that Darian might know something that could identify him?"

"Exactly. But my guess would be that Darian didn't know what that was yet. Or else, she would have told us."

Nori took the time to take a deep breath. I followed suit.

"There is a lot to digest," she said.

"You can say that again."

The doorbell rang, and we both jumped slightly.

"Are you expecting someone?" Nori asked.

It took me a second to remember that I ordered a pizza at four. I'd gotten so enmeshed in our conversation that I'd forgotten about it.

"It's just dinner," I said.

191

BRIAN O'SULLIVAN

"That sounds like a bad dating app."

I laughed as I approached the door.

Just to be safe, I looked through the peephole. To my relief, it was the pizza guy.

My nerves were on high alert.

And it was unlikely to get any better in the days to come.

❧ 42 ☙

LAYNE

Nori Bridgewater should thank her lucky stars.

I was only ten feet from her, with a chloroform-dipped washcloth ready to work its magic, when a car pulled into the underground parking garage.

I quickly turned around and made my way to my car, my forearm covering my face just in case Nori turned around.

I left the parking garage, feeling exhilarated, if slightly let down.

Nori would have to wait.

❧

I WOKE UP THE NEXT MORNING AND DECIDED I WOULDN'T BE following Nori or Bobby around.

I was a big believer in the subconscious, and even though Nori never saw me, part of her, possibly unknowingly, would know that she was followed.

So I was going to wait a few days to follow her again.

I'd follow Bobby tomorrow.

At eight-fifteen a.m., I got a good laugh.

If I'd followed Bobby today, I just would have ended up where I started.

BRIAN O'SULLIVAN

That's right. Bobby McGowan was walking toward my front door.
The little pissant was tenacious.
I'd give him that.

43

BOBBY

I didn't like the idea of ambushing my #1 suspect at his home.

I'd told Nori I wasn't worried about it, but who knew how he'd react?

The problem is that I assumed Layne would soon eradicate me from his life. I would likely get a *no* if I called and asked to meet with him again.

And with Mr. Z a no-go for the time being, I felt like I had to confront Layne Giles.

So against my better judgment, I swung by his house in the Hollywood suburbs early that morning.

I hadn't even reached the door when it swung open.

Layne Giles had a huge, knowing smile on his face.

Had he expected me?

"Bobby McGowan. Back a second time. To what do I owe this surprise?"

"I wanted to ask you a few more questions. I promise I won't stay too long."

"You've got five minutes, because I have somewhere to be."

"No problem. Where are you headed?"

"I've got some investigating to do myself."

"Oh, yeah. What are you investigating?"

BRIAN O'SULLIVAN

"I'd rather keep that to myself for now, but if anything turns up, I'll be sure to let you know." The devious smile was still there. "Come on in."

I entered his house, and he closed the door behind me. My phone was in my pocket, and my hand was engulfing it. If I had a split second, I'd snap a picture of the photo of Layne's son in the Lakers hat.

But I had to be sly. I couldn't risk having Layne catch me doing it.

I was also looking around to see if his handwriting was on something lying around. I'd also take a picture of that; see if it matched up with the notes Nori and I had received.

He was by my side, and I didn't have a chance to turn around without being obvious. It would have to wait.

We sat down in two loveseats. The front door was a good thirty feet from us. Taking a picture would be worthless from here. Plus, most of my back was to the door, so it would be obvious if I quickly swiveled around.

"You said you had a few questions for me?"

"I do. Thanks for being willing to answer them."

"Well, I did let you into my house. So it would be rude if I didn't answer at least a few of your questions. Fire away."

"I was wondering if your mother contacted you the night before she got killed."

"Wow, you're getting a little personal right off the bat, aren't you?"

"I don't think that's personal."

"I beg to differ. What if I asked you if you talked to your mother on the day she died?"

I jumped up and punched Layne in the face.

At least, that's what I wanted to do. It took all of my strength to stop myself from doing so.

"See, it's not as fun when the shoe is on the other foot," Layne said.

He briefly looked away from me, and I took a quick glance back toward the front door. To my shock, the picture had been removed.

"What were you looking for?"

"What?" I tried playing dumb.

"You just glanced back in the direction of my front door. What were you looking for?"

"Nothing."

"Nice try. Well, don't worry. There's nothing to see there anymore. I used to have a family photo, but decided to move it."

"Why would you do that?"

"My son is a Clippers fan now. He was wearing a Lakers hat, and since he's switched allegiances, he asked me to remove that picture."

196

THE VIDEO TAPE

"Do you have any other pictures of him lying around?"

"No, I'm afraid that was the only one. We're not a big photo family. How about you? Does your father hang many pictures from his house on Calle Rosales street in Santa Barbara?"

I was incensed. He knew the street my father lived on. And he'd now gone after my mother and my father.

It took extra restraint not to leap at him this time.

"You look perturbed, Bobby."

"Don't fucking mention my mother or my father again."

"You don't like it when people fuck with your family? Well, neither do I. So stop asking for pictures of my son."

"I'm going to have a great time taking you down."

"Oh? I don't think so, young man. You see, I've done nothing wrong. There would be no need to take me down."

"Why was your mother so shocked when I mentioned Hard Hank's?"

"I already told you. My mother had a stroke a few years back. Her sounding shocked was just you misinterpreting an older woman who'd had a stroke. And it was also less than a day from her passing away, I might add. She was probably a very sick woman that day you called her."

"You're the one who is sick."

"You have no respect for the dead, that much is obvious."

"And you do, mentioning my mother?"

"She died in Santa Barbara, right? Did you ever check out that Michael Douglas movie I mentioned?"

"Interesting title."

Layne smiled.

"I thought so."

"But they are never as perfect as you think," I said.

"Generally, I'd agree with you. But there's always that murder that truly is perfect and forever goes unsolved."

It was surreal having Layne basically admitting in real time that he'd committed the perfect murder.

"Where's your son? I'd like to ask him a few questions."

"Well, wouldn't you know it? He flew to Spain yesterday to spend a few months with my wife. I'm sorry you never got to meet him."

"We may not have met, but he did visit my apartment once."

"That sounds very unlikely. I think you must be mistaken."

"Maybe I'll let the LAPD decide on that. They might take an interest in the fact that a note was left by the son of someone who lived on the same street as Ernest Riley."

197

BRIAN O'SULLIVAN

"Let me see a picture of the person who visited your house. I'll let you know if it's my son."

Layne Giles had an answer for everything. Had he trained his son to avoid the camera at my apartment? Did his son know what the note said? Had this animal in front of me involved his son in worse ways than just leaving a note?

"I don't have a picture of him on me," I said.

"That's a damn shame."

Layne's arrogance was truly world-class. He was a smug asshole at the very least. And I was becoming confident he was way worse than that.

"I can't wait to get enough evidence to prove you killed that girl," I said.

"What girl?"

"The girl in the videotape. Don't play dumb."

"From what I've heard, they could never ID that girl. It seems like it will be a pretty hard case to solve. And an even harder case to prosecute. No body. No name. No chance."

"You're a piece of work," I said. "But I'm on to you."

"Oh no. Am I supposed to be shaking in my boots?"

I stood. If I stayed any longer, I really was going to attack him.

As much as I wanted to, I couldn't let that happen.

"I'll be seeing you again soon, Mr. Giles."

"Oh, you can call me Layne. Just think of me as laying in wait. You get it? Layne in wait."

"I get it. You're quite the wordsmith."

"I'll see you around, Bobby."

I walked out the door, and he slammed it behind me.

There was no need to stare at me crossing the street this time.

We both now knew where we stood.

44

BOBBY

I tried not to get too excited.

While I was becoming more certain by the moment that Layne was the killer, I had nothing concrete. Nothing that I could take to the cops. And certainly nothing that could convict Layne Giles in a court of law.

But I did have a plan.

I drove down to Elena Estrada's.

"Hello, Elena."

"It was Bobby, right?"

"Yes. Good memory."

"I didn't think I'd be seeing you again. To what do I owe this surprise?"

"Can I ask you a few questions?"

"Sure, come on inside."

Elena led me into the same room as my first visit.

"No Leti, today?" I asked.

"No, this old woman has the house to herself for once. And don't you feel sorry for me. I wish I had more days by myself. My whole life has been hectic. Raising four kids will do that to you. So I enjoy the downtime."

BRIAN O'SULLIVAN

I couldn't wait for some downtime myself.

Italy. Wine. Gnocchi.

But it wasn't going to happen anytime soon. My investigation had hit the "pedal to the metal" stage.

"Well, I'm sorry to break up your downtime," I said.

Elena smiled.

"You're fine. You won't be here long. It's an all-day thing when it's one of my kids."

"I get it."

"So, what did you want to ask?"

"Did you hear about Jane Giles?"

Everything had been so frenetic that I hadn't reached out to Elena to tell her that Jane had died. I should have.

"One of my other daughters told me. I was very sad. Do they know how she died yet?"

"They are still investigating."

"Was it a natural death?"

"I don't think they know yet."

"Could this have something to do with your investigation?"

There was no reason to sugarcoat it. "It could."

"Mary Almighty," Elena said. "I remember the day the cops came to my door, the day after Ernest had dropped the videotape off at the police station. I can't believe it's not over even after thirty years."

"I don't blame you for getting mad."

"The Curse of Collier Court," Elena said. "Sounds like a bad movie."

I smiled. "It does. Did you know Jane's children well?"

"A little bit. The daughter's name was Rain. That was easy to remember because it was so different. I can't place the son's name, however."

"It was Layne."

"I should have remembered that. Damn. I knew they all rhymed."

"What was he like?"

"I wasn't the biggest fan. He was the closest that Collier Court had to a bully. I tried to shield my kids from him."

"Were your children close in age?"

"Well, not Leti. She was what we used to call a 'Change of Life' baby, meaning she was unexpected. She's over ten years younger than all of her siblings."

"How about your other children?"

"They were all fairly close to his age. Within five years or so."

200

THE VIDEO TAPE

"You said you have four children in total?"

"Yes. Three girls and a boy who died prematurely."

"I'm very sorry."

"Thank you. Luis died in a motorcycle accident when he was in his early twenties. That was 1992. Luckily, my three daughters are all still alive and have given me seven grandkids. I can't complain."

"So that would have made Luis about Layne's age."

"Yes. He was probably closest in age."

"Do you happen to have any pictures of Layne as a kid?"

"I've got about twenty old photo albums. There's probably a picture of all the kids who lived on the block in some huge group photo."

Hearing Elena mention photo albums brought me back to my mother. A photo album is what compelled me to start investigating her murder. Which indirectly led to me taking the Annie Ryan case. Which had indirectly led me to Ernest Riley, and now here, to the home of Elena Estrada.

A thought came to mind. "You said your son, Luis, was around Layne's age. Did you happen to keep his old yearbooks?"

"I sure did. I inherited all of his stuff after the accident."

"Do you mind if I look at those?"

"Of course not. Here, let me show you where they are."

I followed Elena to another room in the house. She opened a few drawers full of photo albums.

"I know it's here somewhere," she said.

She found two yearbooks a minute later and handed them over to me.

"Here you go. It looks like this is Luis's junior and senior year. I'm sure Layne will be in at least one of them. Maybe both. I can't remember if they were the same age or not."

"Thank you so much."

"I'll go back to the living room. You can come back when you're done."

"Do you want me to return these when I'm done?"

"No, leave them here. When you go, I'll come back here and take a trip down memory lane."

Elena was a good woman.

She strode back to the living room, and I opened the first yearbook. I flipped to the section of yearbook photos.

Luis Estrada and Layne Giles were on the same page and in the same class. In this yearbook, they were juniors.

I pulled out my cellphone and took a picture of Layne Giles. He was wearing a red polo and looked cocky. I could easily see him as the neighborhood bully.

201

I scrolled over and looked at Luis Estrada. He was a handsome young man with a big smile and his whole life ahead of him. It just shows you how unfair life can be.

I moved on to the senior yearbook, took another picture of Layne Giles's photo, and then returned to the living room.

"Thank you, Elena."

"You're welcome."

"Luis was a handsome young man."

"Yes, he was. A lady killer, as they call them."

I laughed, and then caught myself.

Layne Giles might also be a lady killer—in the literal sense.

"I'm going to get out of here in a minute, but I have one more question."

"Let's hear it."

"Back to the day of the garage sale. I know that you said your station was next to Ernest Riley."

"It was."

"Do you remember who was on the other side of him?"

"Give me a second. I'll remember."

It was less than ten seconds before it came to her.

"Well, I'll be damned."

"What?"

"It was Jane Giles."

Boom.

My working theory was that Jane Giles accidentally brought her son's videotape to the garage sale. Someone picked it up, possibly with plans to buy it, and then mistakenly set it down in Ernest's section when they decided against buying it.

This was much more plausible if Jane Giles's section was next to Ernest's.

"Thank you, Elena."

"You had several questions about Layne Giles, and then you discovered that Jane was next to Ernest at the garage sale. Something is up here, Bobby."

"Please don't say anything. I'm just doing my job."

"Do you suspect Layne Giles?"

Elena was a wise woman, but in that moment, she was causing me a little grief.

"I'm just following every lead."

"If that's what allows you to sleep at night." She smiled. "Your secret is

THE VIDEO TAPE

safe with me."

I stood and shook Elena's hand. "Thank you very much. And please don't mention our conversation to anyone."

"My lips are sealed."

"You're the best."

I called Alfred Weaver on my drive back to Santa Monica.

"Hello?"

"Mr. Weaver, this is Bobby McGowan. I need to talk to Mr. Z."

"I told you, Mr. McGowan. Mr. Z no longer wishes to talk to you."

"I will give him a hundred bucks."

"He said not to contact him under any circumstances."

"Two hundred dollars."

"Did you not hear me? Maybe you should get those ears of yours checked. I will not be contacting him under any circumstances. I'm sorry, but journalistic standards apply."

I wanted to say, "journalistic standards don't apply when your book has sold twenty copies. You're not David Brinkley."

But I didn't. There was a chance I might need Mr. Weaver's help, and we already didn't like each other.

"Do you have a picture of Mr. Z in your book?"

"No. That would be insane. He's talking about a snuff film. Do you think he wants his picture there for everyone to see? Maybe I should have included his address as well."

Despite myself, I laughed.

Mr. Weaver was right, of course.

So much for canvassing the neighborhood where I'd met Mr. Z, holding his picture, and trying to find out if anyone knew where he lived.

"I'll make one last offer, Mr. Weaver. If you can convince Mr. Z to meet with me, I will give him five hundred dollars."

"Mr. McGowan, I already said ..."

"And I will give you five hundred for setting it up."

A long pause followed.

"I'll see what I can do," he said.

"Great. Thanks. Looking forward to hearing from you."

Mr. Weaver hung up the phone.

I should have been sad. It proved that everyone has their selling point. Journalistic standards be damned.

Instead, I was excited. I fully expected a call from Mr. Weaver later that day.

Everything was coming together.

≉ 45 ≋

LAYNE

Everything was coming together.

After the back-and-forth with Bobby McGowan in which I trounced him and exposed him as the out-of-my-league amateur he is, I drove back to the house where this all started.

The place where we'd killed Emma Lynn Sutton.

Oh, who was I kidding? I'd killed her.

I now believed it had been a blessing that I wasn't able to abduct Nori in the parking garage.

I didn't realize it at the time, but I wasn't ready.

I had to recreate everything just as it was.

And now I had a few more days to do it.

It was going to be perfect.

❧ 46 ❧

BOBBY

Ideas were flowing out of me.
This must be what it feels like when NBA players say the hoop looks like the size of the ocean. I feel like I couldn't miss.

I called Noble.

"Hey, Bobby."

"Hello, Noble. I have a favor to ask."

I'd arrived back at my apartment from Elena's. After checking in on Nori, who was in Brentwood looking at an apartment, I'd come up with my latest idea.

"I'd expect nothing else."

"When the LAPD was first investigating Jane Doe from the videotape, they were looking for people who went missing in 1995 and before, correct?"

"Obviously, Bobby. No offense, but in 1995, you can't look for a girl who will go missing in 1997."

"I'll give you a few points for sarcasm. Well done."

"It may have been sarcastic, but it's also true."

"You're right. You'll understand where I'm coming from in a bit."

"I'm intrigued. What do you have?"

"How long would you say the LAPD made Ernest Riley's case a focus?"

"A focus?"

205

BRIAN O'SULLIVAN

"Yeah. How long was that case at the forefront of their murder cases?"

"I'm not sure if it was ever in the forefront. Remember, some people in the LAPD didn't even think it was a real snuff film."

"I'll ask it a different way. How long do you think the LAPD spent significant resources investigating Jane Doe in the video?"

"Once again, I'm not sure they ever spent significant resources."

"Humor me."

"Okay. I'd say by 1996, a year after they received the videotape, it was barely even on their radar."

"Thank you. That's what I'm looking for."

"I'm still not sure where this is headed."

"So, the LAPD and I don't agree on much, but we do agree that Jane Doe was likely from somewhere other than LA and may well have been either a drug addict or lived on the street."

"Okay."

"And can we agree that drug addicts and the homeless are less likely to be reported as missing?"

"We can agree on that."

"So if we accept that as fact, and agree that after 1996, the LAPD wasn't exactly focused on this case, we come to why I called."

"I'm waiting with bated breath."

"I'd like a list of women reported missing from 1996 to say 1999. I'm going with the assumption that Jane Doe was a runaway or something similar and her family didn't report her missing until a few years later, because they just assumed she would come home at some point."

"I think I follow. You think the LAPD could never match a picture to Jane Doe because she hadn't been reported missing yet."

"Exactly."

"You would have made a damn good detective, Bobby. There's only one problem."

"What's that?"

"We're assuming this girl wasn't from LA, right?"

"Right."

"So, in that case, we have to look at missing girls all over the United States."

"There's going to be thousands, isn't there?"

"Thousands? You wish. We are talking tens of thousands."

"But you can get them?"

"I can pull a few strings. One nice thing about being a former cop is that current cops genuinely give you the benefit of the doubt."

206

THE VIDEO TAPE

"I imagine the pictures of missing women are digitized these days?"

"Yes. We won't have to scroll through old binders like they did back in the day."

"How soon could you get those photos?"

"Considering they are all digital, I might be able to get it today."

"I'll owe you big time," I said.

"Let me make a few calls, and then I'll get back to you."

"I have one last favor to ask."

"What is it?"

"Do you want to join me and Nori in looking through the photos?"

"Sure, why not?"

"Thanks, Noble."

"I'll be in touch."

⚜

WHICH HE WAS.

At four p.m. that afternoon, Noble called back.

"Give me some good news," I said.

"You said you'd owe me big time, right?"

"I did."

"Then you owe me."

"You were able to get them?"

"I was."

"Fantastic. And you said you're up for reviewing them with me and Nori?"

"I am."

"Okay, great. And I have one more favor to ask."

"You are a pain in the you know what. What's the favor?"

"My apartment is pretty small. Could we come to your house to do this?"

"Sure. How about six p.m.?"

"Perfect."

"And pick up a pizza on your way, too."

Looks like we were having pizza again.

207

47

BOBBY

Nori and I arrived at Noble's at six p.m. with two medium pizzas.
"Hello, Nori. Hello, Bobby."
"We got pepperoni and the works."
"Thanks. Here, bring those back."
Noble led us into the dining room, and we set the pizzas down.
"Follow me," he said.
He led us into his office, and I was shocked at what I saw.
"Wow, you've outdone yourself," I said.
He had two large computer monitors, both of which had Jane Doe's face blown up. They were from two angles and offered the best look the videotape gave of her.
Below the monitors were three chairs lined up on a big table.
"I will email each of us one-third of the missing persons. And we will have the two pictures of our Jane Doe to look at."
"This is great," Nori said.
I nodded. "It is."
"Thanks. We'll be back in a few minutes, but I'm starving now, so let's go eat."

THE VIDEO TAPE

WE RETURNED TO HIS OFFICE TWENTY MINUTES LATER, READY TO GET down to business.

"How many girls are there?" I asked.

"You don't want to know."

"Five thousand?" Nori guessed.

"More."

"Ten thousand?"

"More."

"Twenty-five thousand?"

"More."

"You better just tell me."

"They sent me 28,000 photos."

"We got this," I chimed in. "Jane Doe is distinctive. She's very skinny, and her face is downright gaunt. She's got those bright blue eyes. She's got a small nose. And she's a natural blonde."

"I've got some bad news, Bobby."

"What?"

"In my history, the majority of runaways are skinny. Maybe they don't eat enough, or maybe they are addicted to drugs. We'll certainly have some heavy-set women here, but the skinniness you mentioned will not make her stand out."

It made sense.

"Okay, let's start then," Noble said, wanting to get this going. "What are both of your emails?"

We gave them to him.

"Okay, Bobby, I am sending you 1997. Nori, I will send you 1998. As for me, I did include 1996, so I'll start with that. And I also have 1999 for whoever finishes first. Is there anything else?"

"Let's fucking do this," I said.

WE WERE ONLY EIGHT MINUTES IN WHEN NORI ASKED US TO LOOK at one.

The woman resembled Jane Doe, and we compared her to the two photos. Ultimately, we decided Jane Doe's nose was much smaller, and it wasn't her.

We had our hopes up for a minute.

About twenty minutes later, Noble brought one to our attention. It

BRIAN O'SULLIVAN

was again close, but we decided they weren't the same person. The eyes just weren't blue enough.

Forty-five minutes in, I found one that I thought was close, but after looking at Jane Doe a few more times, I ruled it out.

⚜

AT 7:45, WHEN WE'D BEEN AT THIS FOR NINETY MINUTES, I GOT A phone call.

"Excuse me, guys. I need to take this."

I walked out of Noble's office and answered the phone.

"Hello, Mr. Weaver."

"Greetings, Mr. McGowan. Our friend Mr. Z has agreed to meet with you."

"Excellent. When and where?"

"He said you would know the place and meet him there tomorrow at ten a.m."

"Thank you, Mr. Weaver. I'll be there."

"And before you go, there is that matter of my five hundred dollars."

I vehemently disliked Alfred Weaver, but a deal was a deal.

"Do you have Venmo or PayPal?"

"Yes."

He gave me his PayPal.

⚜

I WALKED BACK INTO NOBLE'S OFFICE.

"Any luck?"

"No," they said simultaneously.

"Who was that?" Nori asked.

"Alfred Weaver. I'm meeting with Mr. Z tomorrow morning."

They both looked up.

"This could be very important," I said. "If he confirms that Layne Giles was Larry Gilden, then I might have enough to take this to the police."

"You're finally talking some sense," Noble said.

"And if we had the girl to match, that would be even better."

"Then sit your ass back down and start looking."

I gave him a courtesy laugh and sat back down. Investigative work is

210

often solitary, so I enjoyed my time with these two. It wasn't a stakeout, but it felt like one.

Three hours later, it was almost eleven o'clock, and we were all exhausted.

My eyes and neck hurt. I was looking down at my laptop too much and then back up at Jane Doe.

"Noble, I think we're going to call it. We'll be back tomorrow, though."

"Okay. What time?"

"I'll swing by after meeting Mr. Z. Nori, what are your plans?"

"I have a few other places to look at and have to swing by BLISSFUL. I told Carisa I'd help her out for a few hours. So, I think I could return here around two or three p.m. Would that work?"

"That's fine," Noble said. "All right, I'll see you guys tomorrow."

Nori and I were exhausted on the way home, but we both agreed it was a rewarding experience.

"It's the first time I felt I was contributing," she said.

"There were a few women I momentarily thought might be her."

"I know. Did Noble say how far we got?"

"No, but judging by how far down I'd scrolled, I think I got about a third of the way through 1997."

"It's sad to think that many girls go missing every year."

"I tried not to think about it, but it's impossible. I kept wondering how many of these girls were dead. How many were reunited with their families? How many were somewhere in between?"

"What does that mean exactly?"

"Well, not dead, but never made their way back to their families."

I pulled into my apartment's parking garage a minute later, and then we made our way to my apartment.

We both fell asleep within minutes.

48

LAYNE

Something in the recesses of my mind told me things were happening.

Things I wasn't privy to.

Maybe it was Bobby's confidence in approaching my house or his confidence in going head to head with me.

But he had an air of confidence, like he knew more than he was letting on.

And that gave me pause.

It was time to follow Bobby around town.

I woke up the following morning and drove to the street outside Bobby's apartment.

Once again, they left together. Nori headed to her car on the street, and Bobby went to the underground parking area below.

I ducked my head when Nori drove by, and when I raised it back up, I saw Bobby leaving the garage.

I followed.

THE VIDEO TAPE

TWENTY MINUTES LATER, WE ARRIVED SOMEWHERE DOWNTOWN.

I'd been a lifelong Angeleno but didn't know this area too well.

Bobby drove past a few businesses and parked beside an abandoned basketball hoop. I stayed far enough back where he couldn't see my car.

I could make out a picnic bench on the side of the court. That was also not being used.

I decided to drive past.

Now that I knew where he was, I could double back whenever I wanted.

❦

I WAITED A FEW MINUTES, IN CASE MY CAR HAD SOMEHOW REGISTERED with Bobby.

I didn't want him to see the same car circle around the block twice in such a short span. The problem was that the longer I stayed put, the more I risked missing something.

I decided to head back.

I parked about sixty feet down the street. Bobby was talking to a man on the picnic bench, but I was too far away to get a good look at him.

I needed to get closer.

Luckily, Bobby's back was to the street, so I could drive by and look at who he was talking to without risking Bobby seeing me.

I put the car in drive and slowly drove toward the picnic bench, pulling my hat down tighter. The picnic bench was about thirty feet from the road, and I wore sunglasses and a hat.

There was no way this other guy could identify me.

Once I was parallel to the picnic bench, I glanced over. The guy was deep in conversation and didn't look in my direction. I spent a solid three or four seconds staring at the guy. Something about him was familiar.

At that point, he looked up, so I darted my eyes straight ahead and continued driving down the street.

A half mile down the road, I pulled over so I could concentrate.

I knew this guy.

I didn't know from where, but I absolutely recognized him.

I thought long and hard.

It was one of those times when you think you'll remember it, but it stays just out of your grasp.

I must have sat there for ten minutes.

213

BRIAN O'SULLIVAN

And finally, it hit me.
Bobby was talking to my ex-co-worker.
How the fuck had he found Sid Zabel?

49

BOBBY

When I arrived at the basketball court and no one was there, I feared Mr. Z had gotten cold feet.

I needn't have worried because he showed up a minute later.

"Thanks, Mr. Z."

I still felt odd saying it.

"Hello, Bobby. Not to be an asshole, but can we get this payment out of the way first?"

"Sure," I said. "How would you like to be paid. Do you have Venmo?"

He did, and I sent it over. It was ridiculous that I had to pay him and Mr. Weaver, but it would all be well worth it if he could identify Layne Giles.

"Thanks. Now, what did you drag me here for?"

"I want you to look at a picture and tell me if you recognize the guy."

"That sounds like a fair deal for five hundred bucks," he joked.

I pulled out my phone and scrolled down to the yearbook photo of Layne Giles.

"Do you know this guy?"

He took a look and a second look.

"I know who that is, but that's not the name I knew him by."

215

BRIAN O'SULLIVAN

I wanted to ask if that was Larry Gilden, but that would be a version of leading the witness. I wanted Mr. Z to come up with this all on his own.

"What name did you know him by?"

"Larry Gilden. My old co-worker at Hard Hank's."

Bingo.

"You're sure?"

"I'm fucking positive. Who the fuck is Layne Giles?"

He was looking at the name in the yearbook.

"That's his real name," I said. "It looks like Larry was a fake name he'd given to work at Hard Hank's. What can you tell me about Larry?"

"I pretty much already told you everything I know about him."

"I gave you five hundred bucks. Try a little harder."

Mr. Z sighed, knowing I was right.

"He was close to Hank. Even closer than me. He worked there before me for probably something like eight months. We overlapped by about four months, and then one day I came in and he'd quit. I was shocked since he got along so well with Hank. And then, a few months after Larry quit, Hank was murdered."

Everything I'd hoped for was lining up.

I now thought there was a very good chance that Layne Giles killed Hank Jewel.

If I had to guess, something happened between the two, and Layne felt he had to get the videotape back. Maybe Layne discovered that Hank was showing it to people like Mr. Z.

So he had to kill him.

But I had no idea how the videotape ended up at Ernest Riley's.

Nor did I know if it was Layne in the videotape.

The videotape was thirty years old, and the man was wearing armor. The height seemed about right, but there was no way to possibly ID Layne from the video.

"Do you know if Larry was ever interviewed by the police after Hank's murder?"

I referred to Layne as Larry to make it easier for Mr. Z.

"I have no idea. The last day I ever saw Larry Gilden was the day before he quit."

"Hank Jewel didn't have a funeral?"

"No. He'd been murdered, and everyone knew he wasn't a good man. It's almost like everyone just wanted to move on."

I paused, and Mr. Z jumped at the opportunity.

216

THE VIDEO TAPE

"Do you think Larry Gilden is the one in the videotape? Do you think he also killed Hank?" he asked.

"I have no idea. I'm just here to find out more information about Larry Gilden."

That was a lie, and he saw right through it.

"Yeah, sure. You give me five hundred bucks to look at a picture of somebody who is not involved."

"I didn't say he's not involved. I said I'm not sure."

"Hell, what do I care? I got my money."

"Can I ask you something personal?"

"It depends. What?"

"I promise not to tell anyone."

"Tell anyone what? You haven't even asked the question."

"What's your real name?"

"Oh, hell no. Then you're going to tell Larry Gilden my real name and that motherfucker may have killed multiple people. Thanks, but no thanks."

It was time to bluff. "Fine. I'll just find it the old-fashioned way."

"What is that?" he asked, seemingly nervous.

"I'll go through the old pay stubs from 1995."

I had no pay stubs, but Mr. Z didn't know that.

"You would do that?"

"I would, but I'd prefer if you saved me some time."

"What have you ever done for me?"

"I just gave you five hundred bucks."

He shook his head. "That's true."

"Listen," I said. "I could go to the cops, and they could get a warrant to talk to Alfred Weaver, who would inevitably give them your real name. I'm not trying to do all that. I just want to know for myself, and I promise you I won't bring it up to Larry Gilden."

He was considering his options. "You promise not to tell that motherfucker?"

"I promise."

Another pause. "Fuck it. Why not? My name is Sid Zabel."

If I needed to find him again, it would be easier if I knew his name. I'd achieved my goal.

"Thank you, Sid. And that's the last time I'll mention it. You're Mr. Z again."

"Good."

"I can't imagine you'd like to give me your phone number."

BRIAN O'SULLIVAN

"I'll pass on that one."

I'd set this meeting up to get confirmation that Layne Giles was Larry Gilden and had accomplished that. It was time to get back to looking at more potential Jane Does.

"Thanks for your time, Mr. Z," I said, and headed to my car.

❧ 50 ❧

LAYNE

I met Hank Jewel on October 31st, 1994.

An easy day to remember.

I was at Hard Hank's with a friend, and we were looking for something "interesting" to wear for Halloween that night. No, Hard Hank's wasn't a Halloween Costume Store, but I was told they had a few wild things, so we decided to look.

I'd been there a few times over the years. I was a pretty precocious kid, to say the least!—and I was interested in sex at a young age. Hard Hank's was world famous, or at least, it felt that way to us Los Angeles high-schoolers.

Going there was like buying alcohol for your first time with a fake ID. You held your head high and bragged to your friends about it.

As a sophomore, I got suspended from high school for bringing a blow-up doll from Hard Hank's. "She" had a fake garter belt and not much else. I hung it in the quad for all to see.

Which also meant that somebody saw me hang it, and I got ratted out. The principal seemed unsurprised when I was sent to see him.

"Are you ever going to grow up, Mr. Giles?"

"I don't plan on it, Al."

"My name is Mr. Pendergrast."

"I'll try to remember that, Al."

"You're suspended."

"Oh, no. I don't have to come to this wretched fucking school that I despise with all my heart and soul. What a penalty."

"You don't have a soul," he said.

This was the late eighties, and I didn't have a cell phone or social media, but a comment like that would have gotten Principal Pendergrast fired in this day and age. You can't tell a student that he has no soul.

Although it was true. Hahaha.

Even back then, I could tell I was different. I didn't have empathy. I didn't care what happened to others. Blah blah blah. You get the idea.

⚜

BY THE TIME I VISITED HARD HANK'S ON HALLOWEEN IN 1994, I WAS A grown man of twenty-three, but I hadn't changed much since those teenage years. Al Pendergrast had been right about that one.

You'll be shocked to learn that I wasn't doing much with my life. I worked as a bouncer and was living at home for the most part. Sometimes, I'd spend weeks at a friend's house and then surprise my mother by showing up at her place.

She was never too happy.

So meeting Hank Jewel was a big moment in my life.

I was fascinated by him. He wasn't quite Hugh Hefner, but he was probably the next step down for a testosterone-fueled, blue-blooded male who grew up in LA.

I asked Hank for a tour, and he showed my buddy and me around. My friend wasn't as enamored with Hank, and I could tell he wanted to leave mid-tour.

"You can get out of here, Tyson," I said.

"Yeah, I think I might have something to do."

It was a bullshit answer. Tyson didn't have anything to do. Neither one of us had anything to do back then.

Once he left, I turned to Hank.

"Are you hiring here?"

I think Hank knew I was a bad seed. And I think he was attracted to bad seeds. Now, I couldn't be sure whether he was attracted to me. He always had beautiful young women around, and slept with some of them, so I know he liked women.

But I also think he liked having young, virile men around. Of which, I was one.

"We have some jobs open. What did you say your name was?"

"Larry," I quickly said, but Hank caught me.

"Is that your real name?"

"No. It's just, my mother knows a lot of people, and I'd hate to think it might get back to her that I worked here."

It sounded weird pretending I cared what my mother said. To be honest, I'm not sure why I used a fake name. Maybe it wasn't my mother but my friends that I didn't want to find out.

"I don't mind calling you Larry."

"And you could still make the paychecks out to me?"

"Yes, we could still make the checks out to ..."

"Layne Giles is my real name."

"Nice to meet you, Larry."

He smiled, and I understood what he'd done. He wasn't going to call me Layne anymore.

"Nice to meet you, Hank. I'm Larry Gilden."

"Gilden. I like it. Makes me think of gold. Can you start tomorrow, Larry?"

"Sure. Why not?"

And just like that, I was working at Hard Hank's.

A MONTH LATER, I WAS ABLE TO MOVE OUT OF MY MOTHER'S PLACE completely.

She asked what I was doing, and I said bartending. My mother was a wise woman, and I think she saw right through me, but she didn't say anything.

I remember the last thing she said to me when I left.

"Stay out of trouble, Layne."

Shit, even she knew she'd given birth to a bad seed.

FROM THE BEGINNING, HANK AND I SPENT A LOT OF TIME TOGETHER.

He was divorced and had a huge house all to himself. I'd later find out about another home, but I didn't know about that one yet.

We'd have wild sex parties complete with young women and a lot of cocaine. Again, he never hit on me, but I think he liked knowing I was having sex with these women. He never asked to watch, but I felt he wanted to.

⚜

ONE DAY, AFTER HE'D ORDERED A CAB FOR THE TWO REMAINING GIRLS, he turned to me.

"If one of those girls ever went missing, no one would know."

"What do you mean?"

"Missy is from Minneapolis and ran away from home. And Wanda is a drug addict who moved out to LA as a fourteen-year-old."

"They are nice girls," I said. "Why would you want them to go missing?"

"Nice girls? They are drug addicted hookers who will do anything for money. Fuck them."

I remember thinking Hank was tough on them, but I also knew he wasn't wrong.

"It's not worth going to prison, is it?" I tried to be reasonable for one of the few times in my life.

"Oh, I'd never go to prison. I'd plan it perfectly, and it would be a one-time thing. The perfect murder."

I laughed, but it was more from being nervous than anything else.

"You're kidding, right?"

"Do I look like I'm kidding?"

Hank's face told me the answer.

"No, not really."

"Because I'm not."

"How would you pick the one girl?"

"They are a dime a dozen. Like I said, there are so many runaways in Hollywood. It would be easy. Now, planning the actual killing. Setting up the cameras. All that stuff. That would take time."

"You're serious, aren't you?"

I ended every sentence with an 'aren't you?', 'right?', or 'is it?' because I was trying to give Hank an out. Only he didn't want one. He was deathly serious about it.

"Yes, I'm serious. Are you?"

"Am I? I'm not the one who brought it up."

"No, I did. I'm asking you, though. Would you be interested in carrying this out with me?"

THE VIDEO TAPE

I don't know what I would have done if the conversation had just stopped there. I was a shitty human. I didn't give a fuck about many people and certainly wouldn't give a second thought about some druggie runaway.

But I'd never killed anyone.

What he said next changed everything.

"I'll make it worthwhile. How does a hundred grand sound?"

I remember laughing. It wasn't exactly the right time, but one hundred grand sounded like such an outrageous number.

"You're serious?"

"Stop fucking asking me if I'm serious," Hank said.

"Sorry."

No one said anything for almost a minute.

"Fuck it, I'm in," I said.

"Excellent. We've got some planning to do."

"Let's do some more cocaine to celebrate."

*   *   *

Two months passed, and the planning had almost been completed.

There hadn't been much to it, really.

We bought a Sony camcorder. The first digital versions would come out later in 1995, and we were unlucky time-wise.

And I'm not just using the word unlucky to be flippant. If it were digital, I never would have ended up with a VHS tape of what we'd done. And it never would have come to this. Maybe unlucky is not a strong enough word.

Meanwhile, Hank was looking for the perfect girl. He wanted her pretty. He said if he was going to watch this for the rest of his life, he didn't want it to be some ugly chick. His words.

Not that I'm some saint. I did laugh at his joke.

She also had to be unemployed, from outside California, and not in contact with her family. Hank didn't want her employer out looking for her, or worse yet, going to the cops.

Lastly, she had to live alone or be homeless on the street—the same reason applied. Hank didn't want a roommate looking for her or raising a fuss with the police.

This sounded like a tall order, but Hank said women in similar situations always came into Hard Hank's, and they'd end up spilling their guts

223

BRIAN O'SULLIVAN

to Hank when they found out he was the owner.

He said it wouldn't take long.

And he was right.

He came to me a few days later and said he'd found the girl.

❦ 51 ❧

LAYNE

Her name was Emma Lynn Sutton.

Hank gave me the rundown. She'd fled an abusive father and an alcoholic mother, leaving Knoxville, Tennessee, to come to the City of Angels. She dreamed of becoming an actress, but as was often the case, Hollywood gobbled her up.

Emma had a "slight heroin addiction" and lived on the street for the most part, occasionally getting a night or two in a soup kitchen or some other place that catered to the homeless.

She told Hank that if someone just gave her a chance, she'd be able to kick her addiction. She was ostensibly asking for a job.

Thinking this was our girl, Hank had something different in mind and gave her an address. He told Emma to meet there tomorrow night at eight p.m. The address was a block from Hard Hank's, so if Hank and I decided it was a no-go, she wouldn't be loitering around the shop in case a cop came by. Not that the cop would have any idea what had truly been in store for her.

"I'm going to make you a star," he said. "You can always have a job at my place, but let's see if you have what it takes to make it in Hollywood."

"I'm so excited, Mr. Jewel. Thank you. I have one question."

"Sure."

"Why is it so late at night?"

225

"We're open till seven here at Hard Hank's, so I always have my auditions later at night."

"Oh, okay, that makes sense. But then why not just meet here?"

"I don't want my other girls seeing you and getting jealous."

"Oh, okay. Thanks. I'll be there."

"I think you're going to be a star, Emma Lynn."

"I think I'm blushing."

"And one more thing."

"Anything."

"I get so many girls coming in here asking for auditions. I try to keep it quiet who I select. If not, I risk offending the other girls. So please don't tell anyone that you got selected."

"Oh, I won't say anything, Mr. Jewel."

"Call me Hank, Emma. Call me Hank."

WE PICKED HER UP THE FOLLOWING NIGHT IN A VAN THAT HANK JEWEL rarely used.

She was excited and nervous in equal measures.

Hank probably told her ten times on the drive that she would be a star.

Her excitement gave way to nervousness when we arrived at the house, and no other women were there.

Remember, this was the second house I'd referred to, which I only found out about once we agreed to do this. It wasn't the house Hank lived in; according to him, he rarely used it.

When Emma Lynn asked once again why no one else was there, Hank made an excuse that another van would be arriving within twenty minutes.

"But you're my favorite, so we'll let you audition first."

"Okay," she said nervously.

Hank laid out some clothes he'd bought for her. He'd told me it was important she wear a classy white dress.

"It will age better in the video."

He'd bought one from a boutique store named Halo for this special occasion.

"At least she'll be wearing an expensive outfit when she's killed," he quipped.

After Emma Lynn changed, Hank led her to the atrium and told her this scene would involve her and a knight.

THE VIDEO TAPE

"It's a variation of *Beauty and the Beast*," he said. I remember that line well.

I then went and changed into the knight's armor.

I'm sure people will want to know what I was thinking at that time.

Did I want to back out? Was I excited? Was I going to enjoy doing this?

Truthfully, I felt numb. I'd been a shitty human up to that point, and now I was about to do the most horrible thing someone could ever do.

But did I care about Emma Lynn Sutton? No, not really.

And that hundred thousand sure sounded good.

I approached the atrium ten minutes later, and ten minutes after that, Emma Lynn Sutton was dead.

⬡

HANK AND I VOWED NEVER TO TALK ABOUT THE VIDEOTAPE.

He gained possession of it. It was his after all.

He paid me the hundred thousand, and I'd never been happier. If I had any guilt over Emma Lynn Sutton, it had washed over me by that point.

I remember Hank saying, "No one is missing that girl. She would probably have died of an overdose within a year anyway. Shit, we kind of did her a favor."

And then he laughed. Well, to be honest, I laughed too.

⬡

IN A RARE MOMENT OF HUMANITY—IF YOU COULD CALL IT THAT—HANK told me that he deleted the last ten seconds of the video.

"I prefer seeing her face in fear than seeing what happens after the sword comes down."

I tended to disagree, but what was the point in arguing? He'd deleted the last few seconds, and they were gone forever.

⬡

HANK AND I GOT CLOSER OVER THE INTERVENING MONTHS.

He hired a new guy, Sid Zabel, with whom he became friendly, but it was nothing like our friendship.

Hank would talk about the ex-wife he couldn't stand. And he'd say while he loved Manny Torres—he'd saved his life in Vietnam, after all—he didn't want him to get everything.

"Everything?"

"Yeah, that's why I invited you here today, Layne. I was thinking about including you in my will."

"Wow, Hank. I wasn't expecting this. I'd be honored."

"You deserve it. We share a secret that will go to our graves."

I nodded. That acknowledgment was enough for Hank.

"Don't you want to know what I'm going to leave you?"

"Yes. Of course."

"I'm going to will you the house in question. That seems apropos. And I'm going to give you another hundred thousand as well. I'd say that's apropos, too."

Hank laughed. So, as had become customary, I did as well.

"But keep this quiet," he said. "I'll be willing Manny my half of Hard Hank's, but I don't want him thinking you're getting as much as him. And with that house and a hundred grand, that's probably more than Hard Hank's is worth. And if you care, I'm leaving my main house to my brothers and sisters."

"Thanks for all this, Hank, but you're not going anywhere."

"I'd like to hope not, but you may have discovered that I rub many people the wrong way. Who knows, maybe a nemesis of mine might try to give me an early death. I guess that would be apropos as well."

At that moment, neither of us could have guessed I would be that nemesis.

⚜

A few months after that conversation, Hank started going downhill. He was drinking every night and doing way too much cocaine.

He would be fucked up at work and make comments like, "Where oh where are you, Emma Lynn?"

And then he'd laugh in my direction.

He was becoming a liability, and I feared his loose lips would get us caught.

It got worse in the following weeks, and that's when he dropped the bombshell. I remember this like it was yesterday.

"And by the way, I showed Sid the video," he said.

"You what?"

"Are you deaf? I said I showed him the video."

THE VIDEO TAPE

"What are you doing, Hank? Are you trying to lead the cops to us? When I agreed to do this, you said this would forever stay between us."

"I know what I said. But I've been thinking. What's the point of making a snuff film if you can't show a few friends? Am I right?"

He laughed, but I didn't follow suit this time.

"You didn't show anyone besides Sid, did you?"

"No. Sid was the only one, Layne."

He still called me Layne in private. Thus far, he'd been good about always calling me Larry at work, but who knew how long that would last. The guy was derailing like a runaway train.

This couldn't continue.

But it did.

Not only that, it got worse.

Hank was a coked-up liability.

Finally, it had become too much.

I had to do something, so I formulated a plan.

I QUIT ONE DAY.

It must have felt like it was out of the blue to Hank.

"You what?"

I had to tread lightly here. I didn't want to risk what he was giving me in the will.

"I don't want to, Hank, but my mother was just diagnosed with terminal cancer, and I need to be with her. I'll be back within a few months."

Those were both lies. I had other plans.

"I'm so sorry, Layne. How long does she have to live?"

"A few months. And then I promise I'll be back. You know how much I love you and Hard Hank's. I can't stay gone for long."

"It won't be the same without you," he said, and I saw a tear in his eye.

"I'll be back before you know it."

We hugged.

MY MOTHER DIDN'T HAVE TERMINAL CANCER.

But Hank Jewel was terminal; he just didn't know it.

229

BRIAN O'SULLIVAN

I couldn't trust him anymore. He'd shown Sid Zabel the video and God knows who else.

He had to go.

And soon, before he changed his will.

I'd decided to kill Hank because of his loud mouth and the fear he was going to get us caught.

But what he'd left me in the will certainly played a part.

52

LAYNE

I needed an alibi for the night in question.

I thought long and hard about it, finally coming up with something I thought might work.

My mother was not a big drinker, and I could use that to my advantage.

I told her we were having a few beers and tacos that Friday—my treat. She said she was in.

It probably wasn't her idea of a good time, but she'd get to have dinner with her only son, which was enough for her. She often lamented that we didn't spend enough time together. Well, here was her chance.

Little did she know that her lone son would be committing murder later that night. And he'd already committed the worst murder imaginable.

I PICKED HER UP ON THE NIGHT IN QUESTION AND DROVE US TO LA Cabana, a famous Mexican restaurant in Venice Beach.

I ordered a tequila shot for each of us to start the dinner.

"What is this for?"

"I got a raise at work," I said.

My mother still didn't know I'd ever worked at Hard Hank's—at least, I didn't think so—and I had no plans of divulging that.

"Oh, congratulations," she said.

I remember thinking she was so naïve.

I ordered another shot and a beer as a chaser.

"Like I said, we're celebrating."

I couldn't risk being drunk with what I had planned that night, so I'd subtly drop my tequila shot in my water as my mother took hers. If I just had a few beers, I'd be all right.

The tacos came, but too late for my mother. She was already drunk, and no amount of food was going to save her at this point. I ordered one more shot during dinner and one final one before we left.

I had to make sure my mother would be drunk by the time we got home.

I'd succeeded on that front.

We arrived at her house, and she immediately went to bed.

"Thanks, Layne. I think I had too many shots," she slurred.

"Just get some sleep, Mom."

She was asleep a minute later, and I was out of the house twenty seconds later. Every minute counted, and I couldn't have my mother waking up and finding out I was gone.

I DROVE TO HANK'S.

I'd played this over in my mind a dozen times.

When I started formulating this plan, about a month ago, I bought a giant knife at an off-the-beaten-path store that would never remember me.

It was still only nine p.m.

This was part of the plan. If I arrived at ten or eleven, Hank might have thought something was up and been on guard. I didn't want that.

I also didn't want to call ahead because then the police would want to know why I'd talked to a man on the night he was stabbed to death.

I parked one street over in case some neighbor peeked out their bedroom window and remembered a license plate.

It was nine p.m. and dark out, but you never knew, so I was overly cautious.

I approached Hank's house and put on my gloves.

I knocked on the door, and he opened it a few seconds later.

THE VIDEO TAPE

"Hey, Layne. To what do I owe this surprise?"

"You're not going to believe what happened to me today."

"What is it? Come on in."

He let me in and shut the door behind us.

"What's with the gloves?"

I immediately pulled out the knife and started stabbing.

The first one was deep into the left side of his chest. I was aiming for the heart. I don't know if it pierced the heart or not. I guess it didn't matter. I was going to keep stabbing regardless.

I stabbed quickly and with great force. I didn't want to give him time to scream.

My plan worked to perfection. I stabbed him probably eight times in rapid succession, and he didn't say a word.

Finally, as he stumbled to the floor, he managed one single word.

"Why?"

He never got that answer because I stabbed him five more times, until I knew, without a shadow of a doubt, that he was dead.

I had one more thing to do, and it was almost as important as killing Hank.

Collecting the videotape.

I knew where Hank hid it, because he'd made me watch it sporadically over the intervening months.

Sure enough, it was there.

I grabbed it and put it in the pocket of my black sweatsuit. It barely fit, but I just had to get to my car.

I made my way back to the front of the house and stepped over Hank's body while making sure to avoid the blood on the ground. I then closed the door and headed back to my car.

<hr />

If I'd had more time that night, I would have gotten rid of the knife and the videotape.

But I could do that the following morning. More than anything else, I had to get back to my mother's house before she woke up. If she happened to get up and notice I was gone, my alibi was fucked.

I returned to Collier Court and brought the videotape and the knife inside.

I approached my mother's room, and when I heard her snoring, I went

BRIAN O'SULLIVAN

to my childhood bedroom and grabbed a change of clothes and a plastic GLAD bag I'd brought.

Next, I went to the sink and washed off the knife I'd just used. I cleaned that knife perfectly and didn't leave a drop of blood in the sink.

I took off my clothes and noticed several bloodstains. Even though I'd worn a dark sweatsuit, the bloodstains were still noticeable.

I threw the clothes in the GLAD bag.

After showering, I put on my new clothes and returned to my room.

I looked at the freshly cleaned knife and the videotape.

I'd have to dispose of them tomorrow.

My room was small, and there was no hidden space under the floor where I could hide them. So I grabbed the knife and went back into the bathroom, putting it in the bottom drawer with several small towels over it.

My mother had her own bathroom and wouldn't enter mine, but I was still cautious.

I had a collection of about twenty VHS tapes—all the best movies from the eighties and early nineties.

Tonight, they would have to share that space with a more gruesome type of videotape. I'd be sure to take it with me the following morning.

Next, I had to wake my mother.

This would complete the alibi.

"*Yes, my son was here the whole time. He drove us home and even checked on me an hour later.*"

I knocked on her door and walked into her room.

"Are you okay, Mom?"

She took a little while to come to. "Remind me never to drink with you again."

I laughed. "Do you need water or anything?"

"Yeah. And a couple of Tylenol, too."

"Sure. I'll be back in a minute."

I returned with her water and Tylenol and wished her a good night.

I had to stay the night to complete the alibi.

If not, the cops might assume I still had enough time to drive to Hank's and kill him.

Was any of this likely to happen? No.

But like I said, I was being extremely cautious.

I'd dotted every i and crossed every t, and felt like I'd come up with a foolproof plan.

Plus, from afar, Hank and I were great friends.

THE VIDEO TAPE

I slept well that night—it turned out too well.
I had zero guilt over killing Hank Jewel.
Fuck, I'd felt almost no guilt over killing Emma Lynn Sutton.
I certainly wasn't going to feel it about a scumbag like Hank Jewel.
To be fair, a fellow scumbag.

53

LAYNE

The next morning was a clusterfuck from the very start.

Maybe it was because of all that transpired, but I slept until nine.

Since my mother had gone to sleep so early, she woke up well before me and had already cooked breakfast.

She entered my room and said, "Breakfast is ready, sleepyhead."

"Give me ten minutes. I need to shower."

I'd showered the night before, but one more shower was advisable. Just in case I'd missed a tiny spot of blood, albeit unlikely.

"Okay. Ernest Riley is coming."

I had no idea what she was talking about.

⁂

AFTER ABOUT FIFTEEN MINUTES, MY MOTHER KNOCKED ON THE bathroom door.

"Your food is getting cold," she screamed.

"I'll be out in two minutes."

Five minutes later, I was changed and stepped out of the bathroom. My mother was waiting there for me.

"Jeez, Layne. This food has been sitting there for a long time now."

THE VIDEO TAPE

I couldn't wait to get out of there with the videotape and the knife, but I had no choice but to follow my mother.

"I've made scrambled eggs, bacon, toast, and a piece of banana bread."

"Sounds good."

Ten minutes later, I was close to finishing. "I thought I heard a noise when I was in the bathroom. What was that?"

"I told you what it was."

"No, you didn't."

"I said Ernest Riley was here."

"So, what does that mean?"

"Aye aye aye. Don't you ever listen to me?"

I still didn't know what she was talking about, but I started feeling nervous. After all, I had some very valuable things in the house.

"Remind me, Mother."

"The garage sale."

Something registered, but I wasn't sure exactly. "What garage sale?"

"Are you kidding me?"

"No," I said, feeling perturbed.

"I told you earlier this week that Collier Court is doing a huge garage sale today."

Fuck! She had.

With all the planning I'd been doing, I'd completely forgotten about it.

"Don't you remember me saying to save anything you wanted from your room?"

She had said that as well. It was coming back to me now.

I was getting more nervous.

"So what was that noise I heard then?"

"I told you. It was Ernest. I didn't know you would be staying here last night, so he agreed to come over and help me take some of the stuff up to the garage sale. You can help me with the rest now that you're here."

And that's when I panicked. "He grabbed stuff from my room?"

"Yes, Layne. I've been over this now. You were told to get anything you wanted to keep out of there."

"What did he grab?"

"A few old rolled-up posters. A couple of jigsaw puzzles. Some VHS tapes. Things like that."

I jumped up from the table and walked to my room.

"Layne. What is the matter?"

I got to my room and to my utter dismay, all of my VHS tapes were

237

BRIAN O'SULLIVAN

gone, including one that could have landed me in jail for the rest of my life.

My mother barged in. "You're being weird."

"Those are some of my favorite movies," I said, and she seemed to buy it.

"Okay, well, why don't you head to the end of the street and check. I'm sure almost all of them are still there."

Almost!

Almost might be the difference between being a free man and spending my life in jail.

༺༝༻

I HAD TO GET RID OF THE KNIFE FIRST, JUST IN CASE ERNEST RETURNED and went to the bathroom.

I threw it in the trunk of my car and then jogged to the end of the street.

There were already like fifty people at the garage sale. I felt sick.

It was only nine thirty in the morning.

Didn't these fucking people have anything better to do?

I approached Ernest Riley, reminding myself to be subtle and not mention the videotapes specifically.

"Ernest, where are the things you grabbed of mine? There are a few items I don't want to sell."

"Well, hello, Layne. Elena was looking after it. Let's hope they didn't buy the ones you want to keep."

Ernest pointed me to my mother's section right next to his. Elena Estrada was there, a big shit-eating grin on her face.

"Oh, hey, Layne."

I gave her the courtiest of courtesy smiles.

I didn't give a fuck about Elena Estrada in that moment.

I looked through my videotapes.

A few were missing, and one of them was the murder of Emma Lynn Sutton.

I wanted to scream, but I had to keep my cool.

"Hey, Elena. Did you sell anything of mine yet?"

"Yup. I sold a poster. And three VHS tapes. Here's $25 that I made for you."

Elena was handing me $25 like I'd won the lottery. I'd done the exact opposite.

238

THE VIDEO TAPE

I'd won the you-are-a-fucking-dumbass-and-should-have-gotten-rid-of-the-videotape-the-night-before award.

"Do you know who bought my stuff?"

"I'm pretty sure they left. This was twenty minutes ago, and I saw them walk away after buying it."

"They?"

"Yeah, it was a husband and a wife."

"If you see them return, please let me know."

"Sure, Layne. I didn't know that stuff meant that much to you."

"It's not that big of a deal," I said through gritted teeth.

⁂

I LOITERED AROUND THE GARAGE SALE FOR THE NEXT TWO HOURS.

When it became apparent that the couple wasn't coming back, I told my mother I was going home.

"Okay, son. You know I'm only now feeling better. Too much tequila for me last night. Thanks for staying and looking after me."

⁂

MAYBE EVERYTHING WAS GOING TO BE OKAY.

I had an alibi for Hank's murder. You couldn't see my face in the videotape of Emma Jean Sutton's murder. And maybe whoever bought the VHS tape would just think it's some cruel joke and throw it away.

I was now quite happy that Hank had deleted the end of the videotape. It would be hard to think it was a fake if you'd seen that part.

Little did I know that the videotape was sitting twenty feet from me. That couple had bought a few of my VHS tapes, but not the one that mattered.

That one had ended up in Ernest Riley's stack, somehow.

239

54

LAYNE

It turned out I was worried about nothing.

I was interviewed once about Hank Jewel's death. I explained how heartbroken I was and how we'd become great friends over the last year plus.

They never treated me as a suspect, although they did ask me where I was that night.

I'm sure it was protocol.

"I was looking after my mother," I said. "We went out to dinner, and she had too many tequila shots."

The officer smiled at me.

"Sounds like a good time."

⁂

A FEW DAYS LATER, MY MOTHER CALLED AND TOLD ME THE POLICE HAD been to her house.

I felt about three seconds of unrelenting dread.

"Someone left a nasty video on Ernest's station during the garage sale."

"You don't say."

"Yeah."

"And what did the police ask?"

"They asked if any suspicious people were around."

I hated to ask, but it would be weird if I didn't. "What type of videotape was it?"

"Ernest told me that he thinks a lady might have been killed on it."

"I doubt that. It's probably a fake."

"Maybe you're right. I guess the cops will have to figure that out."

She never asked me about my videos or my reaction that morning. I don't even think it entered her mind. What mother would ever think that about one of their children?

My videotapes were movies like *Top Gun* and *Ferris Bueller's Day Off*, and she knew that.

I didn't even ask her if she mentioned me to the cops. That would have sounded suspicious.

I just wanted this to go away.

And it did.

The cops never came and asked me questions about the videotape.

NOTHING HAPPENED OVER THE INTERVENING THIRTY YEARS.

Well, nothing regarding the videotape or the murder of Hank Jewel.

As for me, I fell in love and had a family.

I did inherit the house and the money from Hank. Thanks, buddy! Hahaha.

I took that money and the money from making the snuff film and invested it in a few stocks, then a few more stocks, and then a few more stocks.

Before I knew it, it was 2004, and I had over a million dollars in stocks and a young son.

Life was good.

It only got better since then.

And no, I never made another snuff film or killed anyone else.

Until ...

EVERYTHING CHANGED WHEN I GOT A CALL FROM MY MOTHER ONE DAY in June of this year.

"You'll never guess who called the other day?"

"Who?"

"Lily Riley. Ernest's daughter. She's married now, but still Lily Riley to me."

"How is Lily?"

"She's good. But sadly, Ernest has got the cancer."

"That sucks."

Maybe you shouldn't have taken my videotapes without my consent, Ernest.

"It sure does. Hey, do you remember that whole thing with the videotape?"

Uh oh.

"Vaguely."

"Well, she said that Ernest hired someone new to investigate it. Supposedly, this guy is good. Bobby something or other. I guess he starts tomorrow."

"Hmm, that's interesting. Let's hope something comes of it."

"Yeah, let's hope."

"But wasn't that nice of Lily to call?"

"Very."

I got off the phone soon thereafter. The less my mother thought about the videotape, the better.

I FOUND OUT WHERE ERNEST RILEY LIVED NOW AND WATCHED HIS house the following morning.

A tall, well-built man in his thirties approached his house that morning.

Half an hour later, I saw him walk out with a videotape.

It had to be *my* videotape. Well, a copy of it, at least.

I followed this "Bobby" guy, and at his next stop, I saw Noble Dunn greet him at the door.

This just kept getting better and better.

I knew Noble Dunn. Not personally, but he was a well-known cop. I'd known he'd worked the Emma Lynn Sutton murder—not that they ever knew her name.

And I knew he had a massive scar on his face.

I assumed Ernest had referred Bobby to Noble.

THE VIDEO TAPE

THE NEXT MORNING, I FOLLOWED BOBBY TO A VIDEO STORE IN SANTA Monica.

He was getting around for being on the job for less than a day.

I decided I wanted to get back in the game. Not in the killing game necessarily, but back in the joy of the hunt.

I'd been a mostly upstanding citizen for thirty years, but part of me missed the action.

So I left Bobby a note asking if he'd seen any good movies lately.

On the way out, I looked at the community mailbox and checked the name corresponding to Bobby's apartment.

His last name was McGowan.

I'd unofficially met Bobby McGowan.

My only plan was to shadow Bobby's investigation.

Leave a note here and there.

And yes, I made one big mistake by involving my son and having him leave a note.

He didn't know what the note said, and I vowed not to involve anyone from my family from then on.

And I swear I hadn't planned on killing again.

Until I got that text from Darian.

I DATED DARIAN HAGUE BACK IN THE LATE NINETIES.

Unfortunately, I was also dating my future wife at the time. And we were living together in a two-bedroom condo.

So, when I wanted to have fun with Darian, I had her meet me at the house Hank had left me in the will—the same house where I'd killed Emma Lynn Sutton.

I'd been afraid to sell the house or even rent it out. This was less than five years after Ernest Riley had turned in the videotape to the police, and I was still spooked and didn't want any other people to see the house.

But it was the one place I could meet with Darian and know my future wife wouldn't find out. I hadn't even told her about the place yet. I hadn't told anyone I'd inherited it.

I'd made a few changes to the atrium, but if you'd seen the videotape, you could probably guess it was the same place.

Not to worry. The only people who saw the tape were Hank, Sid, Ernest Riley, me, and some cops.

BRIAN O'SULLIVAN

And it's not like Darian Hague would ever see the videotape, so I was willing to bring her over.

Our relationship didn't last long, but we did have sex several times at the house in question.

❧

FAST FORWARD TO A MONTH AGO, WHEN I GOT THE SURPRISE TEXT FROM Darian Hague.

The text read: *"Hello, Layne. We need to talk."*

Well, I guess it wasn't entirely shocking. I had followed Bobby to BLISSFUL on one occasion. Still, I couldn't have ever thought that he'd shown her the videotape. Was Bobby showing the tape to every fucking person in LA?

I panicked. There was only one reason Darian would be contacting me. She'd seen the videotape and recognized the house.

I debated my options. I couldn't allow Darian to go to the cops. I had to act soon.

I also couldn't call her back from my phone.

What the fuck could I do?

I went online and discovered that BLISSFUL closed at six. That was less than thirty minutes away. Darian had always liked closing up her shop. Hopefully, that hadn't changed.

Maybe I had a way out of this.

I knew what I had to do.

I grabbed gloves and a knife from my house, which I covered with a towel, and walked to my car.

I then drove to Hollywood. I knew they still had a few pay phones around town, and I could use one to my advantage.

Hopefully, Darian was working today.

❧

AT 5:44, I CALLED BLISSFUL FROM A RANCID MOTEL A BLOCK AWAY.

This motel couldn't spell camera if you spotted them the first five letters, so I knew I'd never be identified. I did wear gloves just in case the cops ever made it to the pay phone and dusted for prints.

"You've reached BLISSFUL."

Excellent! It was Darian.

"Darian, this is Layne Giles. How are you?"

244

THE VIDEO TAPE

"I saw a weird video the other day, Layne."

She didn't want to exchange pleasantries, wanting to get right down to it.

"Oh, yeah? How so?"

"I think it might have been a snuff film."

"Oh, that's terrible. But what's it have to do with me?"

"When I first saw the film, I knew it reminded me of something, but I couldn't place it. And then, finally, about an hour ago, it came to me."

"What came to you?"

Darian paused, and I knew what was coming next. "I think it might have been filmed at your old house. The one with the atrium."

"Atrium? I'm not sure what you're talking about."

"Really? You don't remember the house with the atrium?"

"We dated a long time ago, Darian."

"I know. But I also know you haven't forgotten that house, Layne. Don't play dumb with me."

She'd always been tough. I'd liked that about her.

I looked at my watch. It was 5:48.

I hadn't heard any background noise yet. That was great news. I thought there was a good chance that Darian was alone at BLISSFUL.

And it was only two minutes from this motel.

"I guess I kind of remember the house," I said. "But it has been over twenty-five years. Do you remember everything from back then?"

As soon as I got off the phone, I'd head toward BLISSFUL.

"I do. And I remember that house, and I know why you took me there. To avoid your future wife."

"What year do you think this videotape was filmed?"

"1995."

"Oh, see, Hank Jewel owned that house back then. I mean, he was up to some sneaky stuff, but I wouldn't have expected snuff films."

I inherited the house in early 1996, but there was no need to include that.

"You and Hank were pretty close back then, weren't you? That's what people in the industry said."

"We were friends, but not close friends."

"Then how did you end up with his house?"

She didn't believe a word I said.

"He didn't give it to me. Is that what you thought?"

"Then how did you end up with it?"

I had no good answer to that, so Darian kept talking.

245

BRIAN O'SULLIVAN

"Why did you buy it? It wasn't that great if I remember. Did it bring back old memories for you?"

That was her line in the sand. It was basically an accusation against yours truly.

"The only memories I have of that house are me and you getting hot and heavy."

"Gross. Don't say that."

It was approaching six. I had to get to BLISSFUL, but couldn't risk her calling the police right when I got off the phone.

"I'm sorry, Darian. This is all just hitting me like a ton of bricks. My wife just got home. Can I call you back in five minutes?"

"Fine."

⚜

I GOT IN MY CAR AND SPED TOWARD BLISSFUL, PULLING IN THE BACK a few minutes later.

There was the apartment building overlooking the back entrance, so I couldn't just kill her in the back alley. I'd have to get inside.

I also didn't know if Darian had a co-worker with her.

I waited a few minutes until I saw someone walk out the back entrance, Darian by her side.

I rolled down a window so I could hear. My windows were tinted, so there's no chance they could see me.

"Thanks, Carisa," Darian said. "You can go now."

"You sure you got the rest?"

"I'm sure. I'll see you tomorrow."

I watched as Carisa got in her car and sped away. Darian threw some bags in the garbage and then went back inside. She'd left the door ajar.

I slid the knife between my jeans and skin, put on my gloves, stepped out of the car, and headed to the back door.

I quickly looked up at the apartments above. No one was looking down.

I approached the back door.

I pulled the knife out from my side and pushed the door open.

Darian was standing five feet away.

"What? How?"

"Nice to see you again, Darian. Thanks for calling."

I was on her in two seconds.

Two minutes later, she was dead.

246

THE VIDEO TAPE

I had blood all over me and knew I wasn't going to be leaving until it got dark out.

With my extra time, I decided to send Bobby a message.

I started carving.

❧

WITH MY EXTRA TIME, I DID SOME MUCH-NEEDED HOUSE-CLEANING.

Not of BLISSFUL, mind you.

I went on Darian's phone and deleted the text she'd sent me. I also deleted it from my end.

Our text wouldn't show up on either phone, but I wasn't sure if that deleted them forever or not.

On the bright side, she'd merely said: *"Hello, Layne. We need to talk."*

It didn't prove shit.

And they'd never know that I was the one who called from the shithole motel I'd just come from.

I was going to get away with this, just like everything else.

❧

I HADN'T PLANNED ON KILLING AGAIN AND HOPED DARIAN WAS JUST A one-off.

Well, a one-off since Emma Lynn Sutton.

And Hank Jewel.

But then my mother called a few weeks later.

My own mother.

"Hey, Mom."

"I just got off the phone with a private investigator."

"Oh, yeah."

"And he brought up Hank Jewel."

"Who?"

"Don't play dumb. I know you worked at Hard Hank's. I always knew."

"I never worked at a place called Hard Hank's."

"And when I heard that name," she said, ignoring me. "It brought back the morning of the garage sale. And how frantic you were about your videotapes."

"Mom, calm down. Your heart will give out. Take a deep breath. I'm going to come over."

"I don't want you to come over. I was so naïve back then. Why were

247

you so worried about what Ernest Riley grabbed from your room? And why did you get me drunk the night before? Isn't that around when Hank Jewel was killed? I know I saw it on the news. Why didn't I put two and two together back then?"

"Mom, stop talking. You're going to have another stroke."

"I have so many questions for you." She started crying.

"I understand, and I'll answer them all. And then we'll call the cops together if need be."

I'd lowered my voice and tried to sound soothing. It seemed to have worked.

"Okay, Layne. I'm scared."

"Don't be. I will be there soon and explain all the mistakes in your logic."

"I hope you're right."

"I'll be there soon, Mom. Don't do anything until then."

You can guess most of the rest.

She was threatening to call the police.

I kept telling her she was wrong and that the stroke was affecting her thinking.

I was trying to gaslight her, but she was too smart for that.

She grabbed her phone, and I saw her press a nine and then a one. I couldn't let her press another one.

I hit the phone out of her hand.

I don't want to go into the rest.

She'd lived a long life, and it was her or me.

And I chose myself.

I'd done a slow squeeze around her neck so as not to leave any marks.

The cops interviewed me the next day, but as had become my calling card, they didn't suspect me in the slightest. How could they?

Two days later, Bobby came to ask me a few questions, and that's when he saw my son in a Lakers hat.

And more importantly, I saw Nori.

She'd made her triumphant return to Los Angeles.

THE VIDEO TAPE

I had to admit, she was quite a creature.

I'd regained my love of killing after Darian and looked forward to getting some alone time with Nori.

She'd gotten out of my grasp the last time I'd seen her, but that wouldn't happen again.

And when I discovered that Bobby McGowan had found Sid Zabel, I decided I couldn't wait any longer.

It was time for Nori to meet my acquaintance.

55

BOBBY

I arrived back at Noble's after getting the confirmation I needed from Sid Zabel.

"Holy shit," Noble said. "This all seems to be coming together."

"If we find out who Jane Doe is, I'm going to the LAPD sometime tomorrow," I said.

"Finally."

"The fact that Layne Giles worked for Hank Jewel explains so much—including his mother's reaction. And Layne lied to me and said he'd never met the man. That and all the other circumstantial evidence I have is enough for me. If we can match Jane Doe with one of these women, even better."

"It sounds like you are going to the police regardless."

"Let's find the girl first," Nori said.

It was a little after four p.m., and we all sat down in our chairs, the two photos of Jane Doe staring back at us.

BY THE TIME SIX P.M. HAD ROLLED AROUND, OUR DINNER HAD ARRIVED.

We still hadn't found a match.

This time, it was delivered from a Chinese restaurant, and we spent

THE VIDEO TAPE

the next twenty minutes getting some much-needed energy.

"Everyone ready?" Noble asked.

Nori and I nodded and returned to our "War Room" a minute later.

❂❀❂

AT A QUARTER PAST SEVEN, WE HAD ONE THAT LOOKED PROMISING, BUT eventually decided it wasn't her. We had the same at a few minutes after eight.

We decided to choose nine as our ending point.

Our brains were fried.

At ten minutes to nine, Nori jumped up from her chair.

"Holy shit. This is her. I'm sure of it."

She set her laptop between the two pictures of Jane Doe, so both Noble and I could see her.

We both mentally contrasted the pictures for almost a minute. I didn't want to celebrate too early. We'd been confident before, only to find something different about the two women.

"That's fucking her," Noble said. "There's not a question in my mind."

I looked over at Nori, who was beyond excited.

"What do you think, Bobby?" she asked.

"I mean, how can it not be? The eyes, jawline, skin tone, etc., are all identical. What is her name and where is she from?"

"She's from Knoxville, Tennessee, and was reported missing on January 11th of 1998. And her name is Emma Lynn Sutton."

"It's her," Noble said. "I think we all agree. Fantastic job, Nori."

Nori nodded.

"And as for you, Bobby," Noble continued. "You better stick to your guns. It's time you went to the police."

"It's nine p.m. I'll go tomorrow. I promise."

❂❀❂

AS WE BEGAN TO LEAVE THE "WAR ROOM," I STAYED BACK.

I stared at the photo of Emma Lynn Sutton for several seconds.

"I'm sorry for what you went through. Layne Giles is going to pay for this."

I looked back at her photo and saw that she was born in December 1975. She would have been nineteen when she was killed. Just terrible.

"I'm so sorry, Emma." I left the room.

251

56

LAYNE

Kidnapping Nori was a piece of cake.

If I were grateful for one thing in this life, it's that BLISSFUL didn't have cameras outside their business.

For when I killed Darian, obviously, and also for when I abducted Nori.

I once again followed her from Bobby's, and when she turned onto Hollywood Boulevard, I was sure where she was headed. I accelerated my car and darted in and out of traffic.

I arrived there a solid two minutes before Nori, which gave me time to hatch my plan, not that it was very intricate.

I was going to use chloroform on the bitch.

I had three things working in my favor.

One, it was before BLISSFUL opened, and I didn't have to worry about some customer driving up at the moment I abducted her.

Two, the concrete wall that you parked against gave some cover from the apartments above. If I could chloroform Nori before she took many steps toward the back door, no one would be the wiser.

Third, the parking lot behind BLISSFUL wasn't visible from Hollywood Boulevard. The large building that was BLISSFUL worked as a beautiful buffer. If Nori parked on the main street, my plan would be futile.

But luckily, she parked in the back, just as I'd assumed.

THE VIDEO TAPE

When Nori approached, I ducked behind my car, chloroform rag in hand.

As she opened her door slowly, I ran behind her and put the rag to her mouth.

She didn't stand a chance.

However, unlike the movies, knocking someone out with chloroform doesn't take seconds.

So, I applied a sleeper hold to expedite things. I'm crafty like that.

I quickly grabbed her limp body and moved her along the concrete wall until I got to my car. I then threw her in the back seat, attached duct tape over her mouth, zip-tied her arms and legs, and threw her on the floor between the front and back seats.

She wasn't going anywhere.

I arrived at the house and yanked Nori out of the car.

The closest neighbor was a quarter mile away, which was a significant advantage.

I looked down at Nori. She had the same scared eyes I'd seen from Emma Lynn Sutton.

I liked seeing it. I must have been lying to myself for the last thirty years.

I did enjoy this shit.

An hour later, she was secured in the atrium and not going anywhere.

"I'll be seeing you soon," I said before I left.

And then kissed her on the cheek.

She tried to squirm, but her forehead, chest, thighs, and ankles were all zip-tied around the table. And her mouth was duct-taped shut.

Just as in my car, she wasn't going anywhere.

I headed home to grab a few things, including my passport.

I hadn't planned on involving Bobby more than I already had.

I swear.

I was going to kill Nori and then get out of the U.S. for a spell.

Sure, Bobby would huff and puff at the police, but he would have zero evidence that I was the killer.

Nori would be a missing person, but then again, so was Emma Lynn Sutton.

A lot of good that did her.

57

BOBBY

I could have gone to the LAPD that morning.

No, that's not right.

I should have gone to the LAPD that morning.

That's more like it.

But I had to see the expression on Layne Giles's face when I said the name Emma Lynn Sutton. I'd come this far. I wanted that added assurance that he was my guy, and I was a good judge of body language. That included facial expressions.

Once I saw Layne's face, I'd know.

And then I'd call the LAPD. Shit, maybe I'd call 911 on the spot.

But I had to know.

❦

NORI AND I LEFT MY APARTMENT AT THE SAME TIME THAT MORNING.

It had become par for the course.

I kissed her goodbye, and we enjoyed the moment. Looking at the photos of Jane Doe and finding Emma Lynn Sutton had brought us closer. Nori now felt like part of the team.

I'd tried to convince her to spend the day with me, but she wanted to spend more time helping Carisa at BLISSFUL.

BRIAN O'SULLIVAN

She'd taken to it.

I wondered if she was reconsidering her decision not to return to work there.

Nori seemed to like Carisa, who seemed to know what she was doing.

I had a feeling BLISSFUL would be up and running again very soon.

⊛⊰⊛

I ARRIVED OUTSIDE OF LAYNE GILES'S HOME AT A LITTLE AFTER NINE.

It felt appropriate that I was back in Hollywood.

This was where I'd spent most of the investigation, and hopefully it's where it would end.

Did I still have questions? Of course.

I still didn't know how Darian Hague was involved.

Was it just because I had talked to her? Or was it something more?

I didn't know where Emma Lynn Sutton was killed. I didn't know if Hank Jewel was involved, but I tended to think so.

And there were a few more questions I wanted answered.

What I did not doubt was that Layne Giles was involved.

⊛⊰⊛

BY ELEVEN, LAYNE STILL HADN'T ARRIVED.

I asked myself if confronting Layne was the smartest way of doing this.

It obviously wasn't. I knew that.

It would have been safer—and smarter—to just go to the LAPD with what I had.

But what was the fun in that?

I'd been on this case from the beginning. I'd spearheaded everything. I was going to see it through.

And once I saw Layne's face—and I knew that Emma Lynn Sutton was the victim—then I could hand it over to the LAPD in peace.

⊛⊰⊛

FINALLY, A FEW MINUTES AFTER ONE, LANE PULLED INTO HIS DRIVEWAY.

He parked the car exactly where it was parked the other two times. If he'd thrown a curveball and parked in the garage, I probably still would have knocked on the door, but I preferred doing it this way.

256

THE VIDEO TAPE

He stepped out of his Range Rover and walked toward the door. I couldn't let him see me.

I had to have the young woman's name do the talking.

"Emma Lynn Sutton," I said.

His face turned toward me, and I knew.

I just knew.

His face didn't even seem to be hiding it. He sat there and didn't respond for what felt like thirty seconds. For a moment, I feared he was going to brandish a gun, but I looked at his sides. He didn't have a weapon.

He looked to be debating what he should say.

I was ready for a "Who's that?" or an even more outright denial, so I was shocked by what he finally said.

"Very good, Bobby. I'm impressed."

I looked at my phone lying on the passenger seat.

Call 911, my inner voice said.

"So, I'm right?"

"Yes, you are."

Why was he admitting this?

Why was he not nervous?

Even worse, why is he smiling?

Something was wrong.

"You've avoided detection for a long time, Layne, but your time is up. Once I notify the LAPD of this, it's over."

Layne Giles laughed. "Actually, the fun part is just beginning."

What the fuck does he know? Why is he still smiling?

"What fun part?"

"May I show you a picture?"

My brain told me to call 911, but my heart told me to wait. I had to know why this man was smiling.

"Raise your hands," I said. "I have to ensure you don't have a weapon on you."

"If I had a weapon, I'd have already pulled it on you. But sure, here goes."

He raised his shirt and turned around.

"I think the picture would interest you," he said.

As he walked closer, my mind went to Nori.

Please, please, please don't be her.

Layne took his phone out when he was a few feet from me.

257

BRIAN O'SULLIVAN

"Before you get any ideas, if you attack me, Nori is dead. Do you understand that?"

My heart sank.

Nooo!!!!

"You're going to see a contraption in this picture. If I press a button, the contraption will be initiated. So, when you see this picture, you mustn't attack me or try to steal the phone. Do you understand?"

I was shellshocked.

"Do you understand?" he repeated.

"I understand."

He was standing right next to me, leaning the phone toward me.

Lying on some sort of makeshift gurney was Nori. Her forehead, arms, chest, and legs were fastened by what looked like massive zip ties. Her mouth was duct-taped. She looked petrified.

I couldn't believe what I was seeing. I should have demanded that Nori come with me that morning.

Making matters worse, there were several large knives, maybe seven or eight in total, hovering about ten feet above her head. There was a mechanism—similar to the giant claw that grabs stuffed animals in an arcade—holding onto the knives. They would all fall onto Nori's face if it let go of them. And from ten feet up, they'd cause massive damage, and likely kill her.

"I'm going to kill you," I said.

"Not right now, you're not. You're going to listen and watch. If not, Nori is dead. Look at the phone again."

I managed to look at the phone again, hate for Layne Giles burning through my heart.

Layne pressed something on the phone, the mechanical arm moved ever so slightly, and the knives hung precariously, feet from Nori's head.

"Don't," I yelled. "I'll do whatever you want. Don't kill Nori."

"I'm not planning on killing her. Unless you call the cops. If you do, I will activate this thing in a split second."

"I won't include the cops."

"Good," he said, taking a few steps toward his house.

"What's next?"

"You've proved to be a worthy adversary, Bobby. Now, let's see if you can take that next step. Nori is being held in the same room where Emma Lynn Sutton was killed. I will keep Nori alive for twenty-four hours. If you find the house, you have a fighting chance."

258

THE VIDEO TAPE

"And you swear on the life of your son that you'll keep Nori alive for twenty-four hours?"

I had zero reason to trust Layne Giles, but I might get an honest answer when I phrased it like that.

"Yes. But I also swear on the life of my child that if I see one cop near the house—and that includes Noble Dunn—then Nori is going to die the most gruesome death imaginable."

❧ 58 ❧

LAYNE

I hadn't planned on involving Bobby further.

But the guy was a cockroach. He truly was.

He genuinely surprised me when I arrived at my house.

He knew things I never would have guessed.

How the hell did he find out the identity of Emma Lynn Sutton?

I didn't have a gun on me. If I had, I'd probably have shot Bobby dead, then and there.

And come up with a story, after the fact.

"He went for his side, Officer. I thought it was a gun."

But alas, I had no gun.

So, I came up with something on the fly.

And it was brilliant, if I do say so myself.

The most crucial aspect was convincing Bobby that if he told the police, I would kill Nori. I'd made that point quite clear. I didn't think he'd be going to the cops.

And if Bobby were the excellent investigator he'd proven himself to be, he'd find the house where I was keeping Nori.

And he'd be walking into his own death.

Willingly.

59

BOBBY

A minute after leaving Layne's, I was calling Noble.

"Hello, Bobby. Anything new?"

"I need to talk to you in person."

"I can't right now."

"This is of the utmost importance."

"What I'm doing right now is all important to me."

"What is that?"

"If you'd planned on saying goodbye to Ernest Riley, you better come do it now."

My heart sank again.

"No."

"Sadly, yes. They think he may only have hours to live."

I heard Lily talking in the background. "You can see him now, Noble," she said.

Fuck this case! Fuck Layne Giles!

Ernest Riley was a good man, and I was gutted that he was dying. But Nori had to take precedence right now—a hundred times out of a hundred.

On the other hand, I needed to talk to Noble, and he was at Ernest's.

And while the timing was terrible, I owed Ernest a goodbye.

Dammit!

BRIAN O'SULLIVAN

"All right, I'm coming to Ernest's."

"I'll see you soon."

⚬⚬⚬

I DROVE LIKE A BAT OUT OF HELL AND MADE IT TO ERNEST RILEY'S IN less than thirty minutes.

Time being of the essence, I tried to do several things simultaneously.

First, I called BLISSFUL.

"You've reached BLISSFUL."

"I'd like to speak to Carisa."

"Speaking."

"This is Bobby McGowan. Has Nori made it in yet?"

I didn't want to alert Carisa for fear that she'd call the cops, but I had to know at what point Layne had abducted Nori.

"No, she hasn't. I'm getting a little worried. I've tried her phone twice."

"Don't be worried. She was looking at a few apartments and is probably on her way now."

"If you say so," Carisa said, unconvinced.

"Have you ever heard the name Layne Giles?" I asked. "Or Larry Gilden?"

Carisa had been with Darian for many years, and maybe she'd know a connection.

"They don't ring any bells. Does this have anything to do with Darian's murder?"

"Yes, it might."

"I've been with Darian for a while, but I've never heard her mention either of those names."

"Do you keep in touch with anyone who might have known Darian Hague in the earlier days?"

"Yeah, I know a few."

"Could you do me a huge favor and call a few of them?"

"Sure. What were the names again?"

"Layne Giles or Larry Gilden."

"I'll be in touch."

I hated doing what I did next, but it was necessary.

"Thanks, Carisa," I said. "Hold on just a second. A text from Nori just came in. She says she's not feeling well and went back to my apartment."

"Oh, no. I'm sorry to hear that. At least she's safe."

262

THE VIDEO TAPE

She's the opposite of that.

"Yeah. Call me back if you hear anything from Darian's friends. Thanks."

I was ten minutes from Ernest's when I hung up—time for one more phone call.

I thought Nori had given me Darian Hague's daughter's phone number; sure enough, she had.

"Hello."

"Mira, this is Bobby McGowan. Do you remember me?"

"Of course."

"I have a few quick questions."

"Shoot."

"Have you ever heard the names Layne Giles or Larry Gilden?"

"They don't ring a bell."

Darian had Mira later in life. If I had to guess, Darian knew Layne before Mira was born.

"Could you do me a huge favor?"

"Does this have to do with my mother's murder?"

"Yes."

"Then I'll do anything."

"Can you reach out to some of Darian's old friends?"

I was trying to do the math in my head. Darian was around seven or eight years older than Layne.

"How old?"

"People who knew Darian in her thirties and forties."

"Sure, there are still a few of those I keep in touch with. In fact, a few were at the memorial."

"Great. This is very important, so could you try calling them ASAP and then get back to me in an hour or so?"

"I'll make some calls right now. Goodbye, Bobby."

"Bye, Mira."

⚜

I ARRIVED AT ERNEST RILEY'S FIVE MINUTES LATER.

I immediately felt guilt and sadness.

Guilt for finding reasons not to see him, albeit good reasons. And sadness that he really was dying.

He'd been delightful since we met, and we'd become friendly. I'd go so far as to say that we were friends.

BRIAN O'SULLIVAN

I looked at myself in my rearview mirror.

Give Ernest your undivided attention for ten minutes. He deserves that.

❦

I KNOCKED ON THE DOOR, AND LILY ANSWERED.

There were tears in her eyes as she hugged me.

"I'm so sorry, Lily."

"Thanks for coming, Bobby."

"You're welcome. How is he?"

"His breathing is shallow, and the hospice nurses are not sure if he is going to make it through the day."

"That's terrible."

"It is and it isn't. He's led a great life, and he's kicked cancer's ass for several years. He's outlived his prognosis. He got to spend yesterday with his grandchildren. He's got friends like Noble, you, and many others who have stopped by. If you must go ..."

My eyes watered, and Lily hugged me again.

"Would you like to say goodbye to him?"

"Of course."

We walked inside, and I saw Noble in the corner, wiping tears from his eyes. He nodded in my direction.

The two nurses I'd met were standing over Ernest.

Lily walked over, talked to one of them, and then headed back toward me.

"You can have a few minutes," she said.

I'd been debating what I should say.

I wanted to say something, but it would break every rule.

"Can I be alone with him?" I asked.

"Sure," Lily said, escorting the nurses and Noble to another room.

I approached Ernest's bed. He had ten tubes going in and out of him. End of life is not for the faint of heart.

"Hello, Ernest."

He grabbed my hand and laid it in his.

"Bobby McGowan," he said, his voice struggling to find enough oxygen. "How is the case going?"

Well, here it was. Now or never. Do I lie to a dying man?

"I wanted to say a few things, Ernest. I know it's difficult to speak, so you don't have to respond."

He nodded.

264

THE VIDEO TAPE

"Thank you so much for putting your faith in me. You've been great throughout this process, and I've enjoyed our meetings. You have a great daughter as well."

I saw him starting to tear up. It was time to make my decision.

Maybe I was wrong for doing what I did next, but I couldn't have him dying thinking we'd never catch the person responsible for the videotape.

"I've solved the case that you gave me."

His eyes lit up, and he mustered a meek, "Really?"

"Yes. The videotape belonged to Layne Giles—Jane's son. I don't know how it ended up in your stack of videos, but it's his. The cops will be arresting him later today for murder. He was the man in the video as well."

Ernest Riley started crying, and he squeezed my hand even harder.

"Thank you," he said through muffled tears. "You don't know how much that means."

"You're welcome."

His crying was louder than I'd expected and alerted everyone else. They started walking in from the other room, fearing something was wrong.

Lily looked annoyed as she approached, but then she saw that Ernest was smiling and they were tears of joy.

"What did you say?" she asked.

"That stays between us."

Ernest Riley squeezed my hand one last time. I caught his eyes quickly, and he winked at me.

The nurses were standing behind us.

"Goodbye, Ernest," I said.

"Bye, Bobby. From the bottom of my heart, thank you."

His voice was all but gone.

I walked away from his hospital bed, tears streaming from my eyes. Lily followed me as the nurses gave Ernest their attention.

"Thank you for coming," Lily said.

"Thank you for having me."

When I got to the other side of the room, Noble eyed me suspiciously.

"What *did* you say?"

"Maybe I'll tell you later. We have to talk."

"Follow me to my house."

"I will," I said, taking one last look in Ernest's direction before heading out the door.

265

60

BOBBY

"This better be important," Noble said.

We'd arrived back at his house. As with Ernest, I'd been waffling on what exactly to tell Noble. I'd made another debatable decision.

"I'm going to paint you a scenario," I said.

"Okay."

"Let's say a madman took a woman hostage, and he notified a friend of hers. The madman said that he would kill her if that friend notified the police. And that friend believed with certainty that the madman would kill the woman if he did. So, he didn't want to notify the police. But he also knew that the police had fifty times his resources. He knew he should go to the police, but he also knew that the madman wasn't kidding. He'd told him he'd kill the woman if he saw even one police officer. What would be your thoughts on this obviously made-up scenario?"

"Holy shit, Bobby. Is it Nori? And is it Layne Giles?"

"Can we please stick with this invented scenario?"

"If we must. I'm biased, but I'd say that someone in this scenario should go to the police. Can I ask a few questions?"

"Yes."

"Does said someone know where the woman is being held?"

"No."

THE VIDEO TAPE

"Did the madman say how long he had?"

"Twenty-four hours."

I saw Noble wince.

"That's not a lot of time," he said.

"No."

"I don't think he has any choice but to go to the police."

"You're probably right. But I'm considering a third option for that person."

"What's that?"

"He could give himself until eight p.m. tonight, and if he hasn't found her location by then, he could call the police."

"I understand why the someone would want to have it both ways, but he's also giving the police less total time if he goes about it that way."

"I think it's a price that someone would be willing to take."

"Did the madman hint at where he took the woman?"

"Yes. He said she's at the location where this all started."

"Where he filmed a woman being killed?"

"Yes."

"Does he have any leads on where that location might be?"

"Not really, but he's put out some feelers."

Noble paused. I could tell he didn't like how I did this, but he was playing along.

I was starting to wonder why I'd gone about it this way. Initially, it was so that Noble couldn't go to the police, since the scenario was made up. We were past that point, obviously.

"Do you know if this someone knows how to use a firearm?" Noble asked.

"He does."

"Do you know if he has a firearm himself?"

"He does not."

Noble paused.

"Hasn't this little charade gone on long enough?"

I shook my head. "I'm the one who has to make this decision, Noble. I can't have you contacting the LAPD until I decide that's what I want to do."

"And you thought this little scenario would prevent me from going to them?"

"I guess. Maybe I didn't think it out well enough. I've got a lot going on if you didn't notice."

"I get it. We're all going through a lot."

267

BRIAN O'SULLIVAN

I nodded.

Noble continued. "I noticed that Ernest's tears were tears of joy. Did you tell him that Layne was responsible for the videotape?"

There was no reason to deny it. "Yes."

"Jesus, Bobby. You lied to a dying man?"

"It's not lying if we get Layne."

"Do you know for certain he has Nori?"

"Yes."

"Did he send you a picture?"

"Worse. A live feed."

"What could you see? Anything that could help me?"

"I'm almost positive it's the same atrium as in the Emma Lynn Sutton murder."

"But you can't see out of the atrium?"

"No."

"There's something you're not telling me."

Noble frequently reminded me that he'd been a detective himself. Not by saying it, but by making a keen observation. And he was right. I was hiding something.

"He's got a contraption that's holding several knives, about ten feet over Nori's head. He can control the contraption from his phone."

"You're serious?"

"I am. It's horrible."

"Every fiber of my being says you should go to the cops, but I'll respect your wish for now."

"All I'm asking is to give me until eight."

"Okay. I'll give you that."

"Listen, I have to go. Every minute counts."

"Give me one more of those minutes," Noble said.

"Okay."

He headed to the back of his house and returned shortly.

"Let me walk you to your car," he said.

When we arrived at my car, he looked me directly in the eyes.

"If you tell anyone about this, we will never talk again."

"Tell anyone about what?" I asked.

Noble took out a gun and handed it to me.

"This is a Sig P365. It may not be very big, but it can do some serious damage."

I accepted the gift.

"Thank you, Noble. Thank you very much."

268

THE VIDEO TAPE

"Keep in touch. You at least owe me that."

"I do and I will."

I opened the door to my car and got in.

"Good luck, Bobby," Noble said.

He threw something else in the car, shut the door for me, and then slapped the top of my car.

I sped away.

🏵 61 🏵

BOBBY

I tried to avoid thinking about Nori, but that proved impossible.
Every few minutes, I'd envision her frightened eyes and the knives dangling above her.
It was unbearable.

🏵

I RETURNED TO MY APARTMENT AND QUICKLY WONDERED WHY I'D EVEN come.

All the action took place in Hollywood, not Santa Monica.

BLISSFUL was there.

Hard Hank's had been there.

Halo had been there.

Layne Giles lived there.

When I thought of Layne Giles living there, an idea emerged.

I called Noble.

"What do you need?"

"Can you find out if Layne Giles owns real estate other than the house in Hollywood?"

"Of course. Anything else?"

"That's it for now."

THE VIDEO TAPE

I looked around my apartment, wondering if I needed anything besides my laptop.

I decided to grab a change of clothes for Nori.

Maybe it was wishful thinking, but that's all I had at this point.

I got in my car and headed toward the freeway.

I was going to make Hollywood my base camp.

⚜

WITHIN TWENTY MINUTES OF ARRIVING BACK IN HOLLYWOOD—I'D got a cheap, centrally-located hotel room for the day—I got a call from Darian's daughter.

"Hello."

"Hi, Bobby. I got ahold of one of my mother's closest friends. They knew each other for forty years. You may have met her at the wedding. Her name is Emerald Green."

Usually, I'd have commented on the name, but this was not the time. Not even close.

"Thank you, Mira. Am I supposed to call her, or will she call me?"

"I just wanted to make sure you could talk right now."

"I can. Have her call me."

"I will."

"Thank you."

⚜

A FEW MINUTES LATER, AS I LOOKED OUT THE WINDOW AT THE FADED paint of the Hollywood Stars Hotel, I received an incoming call.

"Hello, is this Ms. Green?"

"Yes, are you Bobby?"

"I am, and thanks for calling."

"I heard you have some questions about Darian."

"Yes, I do. How long have you known her? I heard forty years?"

"A little longer. Since 1983."

I decided to dive right into it. As I kept reminding myself, every minute mattered.

"Have you ever heard the name Layne Giles or Larry Gilden?"

I was ready to be disappointed.

"I've never heard of Larry Gilden, but I sure as hell remember Layne Giles."

271

My heart accelerated. "Can you tell me everything you know about him?"

"There's not all that much to tell."

"Whatever you can tell me would be great."

"Okay. Well, the main thing is that he dated Darian. That's how I met him."

I expected a long summary of how she knew Layne Giles, but I wouldn't get that.

"What year was that?"

"Hmmm. It was somewhere in the late nineties, like 1997, 1998, or 1999. Right around then. I remember being surprised because Darian was almost a decade older. I remember making some 'rocking the cradle' jokes back then."

"How long did they date?"

"Not too long. I'm guessing six months."

"Did Darian like him?"

"I mean, they dated."

"I know, but did she ever badmouth him? Was it a combative relationship?"

"I feel bad talking about Darian this way."

"Trust me, she would want this."

"Is Layne a suspect?"

"No," I lied. "I just want to learn more about him."

"That doesn't sound very believable. Anyway, they weren't in a combative relationship. But Darian did say that he could be rough in bed."

I knew the answer to my next question, but had to ask anyway.

"Rough fun or rough dangerous?"

"The latter."

"Where would they have their fun? Did they both have houses? Apartments?"

"Darian owned a house by then. So they would go there. They most certainly didn't go to his apartment."

"Why is that?"

"Because he had a live-in girlfriend at the time. He ended up marrying her, I believe."

"Did the other woman know about Darian and Layne?"

"I don't think so. They were pretty hush-hush about it."

"You knew."

"I did, but I was Darian's best friend, and she swore me to secrecy."

"You said they never went to his apartment. Did he have any other place they might have gone, or was it always to her house?"

"He did have another house, which they visited a few times. Darian said it was kind of creepy. It was up in Sylmar, a good half hour from where she lived in Hollywood."

"Why did she say it was creepy?"

"It was unkempt. That was the word she used."

"Did Layne Giles own it?"

"I assume so. Who else would take a woman to a place like that if you didn't own it?"

"Did Darian ever mention the place having an atrium?"

"Not that I can remember. She just said creepy and unkempt."

My heart rate hadn't decreased one iota. This house had my full attention.

"You said it was in Sylmar. Any idea what street or what section of the city?"

I didn't know much about Sylmar, but I had driven past it several times. I knew that if you were going north, the 405 freeway turned into Interstate 5 somewhere around Sylmar. I think it had both suburban and rural parts.

Maybe I was jumping to conclusions, but when I hear creepy and unkempt, I imagined it being in a more rural part.

"I have no idea. I probably didn't even know back then, and I certainly don't know now."

"Is there anything else you can tell me about the house?"

"That's about it."

What else might Emerald Green know?

"Did you know Hank Jewel?" I asked.

"I knew who he was. That's it. Darian knew him much better, working in the same industry and all."

"Okay. Thank you, Ms. Green. You've been very helpful. If you get a call from this number later today, I hope you'll answer."

"I will."

I CALLED NOBLE.

"Layne Giles doesn't own any other property."

There were no pleasantries to start the conversation. He just got down to it.

"You're sure?"

"Yes, I'm sure."

I wasn't ready to tell Noble about the house in Sylmar.

At least, not yet.

"I'll be in touch," I said.

I WASN'T DETERRED.

Layne Giles may have owned the property and had to sell it at one point. Perhaps he'd rented it out for the weekend for old times' sake.

Regardless, finding out that Layne Giles used to take Darian to a house in Sylmar was the most significant clue I had to go on.

Layne wouldn't just have killed Darian because she was an ex-girlfriend. She must have known something, or Layne feared she knew something.

When Darian first saw the videotape, she said that it felt familiar somehow.

Maybe Layne had changed the atrium between the time he killed Emma Lynn Sutton until Darian went there several years later. That would have made perfect sense. Perhaps that's why Darian didn't recognize it right away.

I was spitballing, but things were coming into focus.

NEXT, I CALLED ALFRED WEAVER.

"I'm getting sick of these calls, Mr. McGowan."

"The feeling is mutual, Mr. Weaver, but I need to talk to Mr. Z again."

Even though I now knew Sid Zabel's real name, I'd promised never to use it, and I would stick to that. Even though I'm sure Weaver knew his real name.

"Are you willing to pay again?"

No wonder your books didn't sell! You're an asshole!

I wanted to say that, but I couldn't risk losing him.

"I want to ask him one question. What's the going rate for that?"

"Two hundred dollars."

"If he calls me back in the next five minutes, I'll Venmo you two hundred."

"How do I know you'll pay me?"

THE VIDEO TAPE

"I will pay you, Mr. Weaver. Please, just call Mr. Z."

"Stay by your phone."

I wasn't going anywhere.

Less than five minutes later, I got a call from Mr. Z.

"Hello, Bobby. I was told two hundred dollars for one question."

"I guess that's the going rate."

"Tell you what, you've been fair with me. This one is a freebie. I'll even give you my number, so you don't have to pay that jerk Weaver."

"I'm going to pay you for that sentence alone."

"Thanks. Now what's your question?"

"Do you know who executed Hank Jewel's will?"

"I have no idea. That was above my pay grade, and Hank didn't leave me anything in the will."

"Did Hank ever talk about a second house he had? Up in Sylmar."

"Sylmar? No, he never mentioned a house up there."

"And when he showed you the videotape, he never mentioned where it was filmed?"

"Never. He told me he just happened upon it. He never claimed it was his or had any idea who'd made it. Nor where it was filmed."

I wasn't surprised. Showing Sid the snuff film was crazy enough. Telling him they'd filmed it at his house would have been downright suicidal.

"Have you ever heard the name Emma Lynn Sutton?"

"No. I'm sorry I can't help you with that either."

"It's all right. Do you want to leave me your phone number?"

He did, and I thanked him for his time.

◈

WERE WILLS PUBLIC RECORD?

I wasn't sure.

I googled it and found that it varied by state and county. Sometimes it was public record, and sometimes it wasn't.

Los Angeles County didn't appear to have them on a public website. I'd have to go to probate court and talk to a clerk to submit a request for a copy of the will.

I didn't have time for that.

I put my hands on my head, trying not to think about Nori.

What to do? What to do?

Something came to mind.

I scrolled through my phone numbers.

BRIAN O'SULLIVAN

⁂

I called Teresa Torres.

She was Manny Torres's daughter and told me about Manny saving Hank's life in Vietnam.

She answered on the second ring.

"Hello."

"Hi, Teresa. This is Bobby McGowan. We talked a few weeks back."

"I remember. What's going on?"

"I have an important question for you."

"Sure."

"Do you know who executed Hank Jewel's will? Who did Manny have to deal with to secure his half of Hard Hank's?"

"I don't know offhand, but I have a lot of my father's old paperwork."

"Would you mind seeing if you can locate the will? This is very, very important to me."

"Sure. Give me a half hour."

"Thank you so much."

I spent my downtime looking at maps of Sylmar.

I wanted to soak in my potential surroundings if my hunch proved correct.

⁂

When Teresa Torres called me back, it was already six p.m.

It seemed like a week had passed since Nori and I left my apartment that morning.

Confronting Layne Giles and finding out the unthinkable. Calling Noble and being told the devastating news about Ernest. Having to say my goodbyes to Ernest. Making seemingly thirty phone calls throughout the day. Coming to Hollywood and this nondescript hotel.

And this was all while thinking about Nori in the worst situation imaginable.

"Hello, Teresa."

"I found the will, Bobby."

"Great. Does it list everything Hank gave away or just what he gave to your father?"

"I have the complete will in front of me."

"Can you tell me what Layne Giles received?"

"Sure. Give me one second."

276

THE VIDEO TAPE

I heard Teresa rustling through some papers.

"Okay, it looks like Layne Giles was willed two things. One being a hundred thousand dollars. And the second being a house in Sylmar."

Bingo!

It didn't automatically mean that's where Nori was being held—and where Emma Lynn Sutton was killed—but it was becoming more and more likely.

"Does it list the address of the house in Sylmar?"

"It sure does. It's 1057 Hawkins Street."

I quickly wrote it down on the stationery of the Hollywood Stars Hotel.

"Does it say anything else about Layne?"

"There's an introduction where Hank talks about a few people in the will."

"Can you tell me what is said about Layne?"

I heard more rustling of papers.

"It's basically just one or two sentences about each person. About Layne, he says, "Thanks to a great friend in Layne Giles. We had a wild time, and ELS will bond us forever."

It didn't take me long. ELS was the initials of Emma Lynn Sutton.

Holy shit. This was basically an admission of guilt.

"Thank you so much, Teresa."

"You're welcome."

She must have known I was heading down a dangerous path, because before she got off the phone, she added, "Stay safe, Bobby."

62

BOBBY

I had two more things to do before committing to launching a sneak attack on 1057 Hawkins Street that night. It sounded crazy when I thought of it like that.

First, I had to go online and find pictures of the house on one of these ubiquitous real estate websites. I wanted to see some semblance of an atrium just to make sure.

Second, I had to find out who owned the house. Noble had told me Layne Giles didn't own it. I had to make sure I wasn't wrong about this.

I didn't want to be surprising a family of four at three a.m.

I WENT ON ZILLOW AND TYPED IN 1057 HAWKINS STREET IN SYLMAR.

The house came up, and I first noticed the lack of neighbors. I'd been right about it being in a more rural section of town.

Hawkins Street was in North Sylmar, adjacent to the San Gabriel Mountains. There were three houses on Hawkins Street, and no neighbor was within almost a quarter mile.

I don't know how current the pictures were, but the lawn hadn't been mowed, and the weeds were running wild, especially close to the front door. It was just as Darian Hague had described it. Unkempt.

THE VIDEO TAPE

And maybe this was just because of what I knew, but the house had a menacing feel. A happy family of four did not live there. It looked like no one lived there.

I continued to search Zillow, but I couldn't find who owned the property.

I went online to find that, and discovered it was public record.

In January of 2001, Layne Giles sold the property to Marilyn Quell.

I had an inclination and googled, "Giles-Quell wedding."

Sure enough, Layne Giles had married Marilyn Quell in late December of 2000.

Looks to me like one of Marilyn's first gifts was this house.

Why didn't Layne Giles want this home under his name? And why was it sold to Marilyn Quell and not Marilyn Giles?

I was pretty sure I knew the answer to both.

Layne Giles didn't want anyone to be able to trace this house back to him. This is also probably why he never sold it to a third party and, if I had to guess, why he never rented it out.

The atrium must still be there, so he didn't want anyone to ever see the house.

Maybe it's why he didn't hire people to fix the house.

Asking someone to remove/change an atrium might stick in a contractor's mind.

This was all subjective on my part, but it did make a lot of sense.

❧

NEXT, I WENT TO GOOGLE EARTH.

I knew these photos were not downloaded in real time, but I just wanted confirmation that Layne Giles's truck had been at this address in recent months.

Sure enough, one of the pictures of 1057 Hawkins Street showed Layne Giles's truck sitting in the driveway.

I zoomed in on the house and saw something. Two video cameras were clearly visible. One was above the front door. And one was sitting on the roof, directly above the first one. The second camera had a bigger radius and could catch more of the street.

Shit!

Part of me had been leaning toward calling the police like I'd told Noble I would.

I was now against it once again. Layne would see the cops coming. I had no doubt.

Making matters worse, Layne controlled Nori's fate from his phone. For all I knew, he was out of Los Angeles, and once he saw any cop outside his house, he could bring the knives down on Nori.

I shuddered at the thought.

I played with Google Earth for a few more minutes, but saw no other cameras around the house.

Maybe, just maybe, I could go undetected through the back.

I LAY BACK ON THE NOT-SO-COMFORTABLE BED AT THE HOLLYWOOD Stars Hotel.

I'd accomplished a shitload since arriving there.

But I'd merely left myself with the Herculean task of getting into Layne Giles's house and rescuing Nori while avoiding at least two cameras. And possibly an armed Giles upon entry.

Noble called, and I hated doing it, but I lied to him. Technically, I lied by omission because I told him nothing of the house on Hawkins Street.

He asked me if I would still call the police at eight, which was fast approaching.

I told him I needed a little extra time.

I SPENT THE NEXT HOUR THINKING.

It's not like I was going to raid the house during the day, so I didn't mind seeing the daylight hours dwindle.

I finally settled on a plan.

While rescuing Nori was my number one concern, I knew I couldn't let Layne Giles get away with this, either.

There was a considerable risk of my going into the house and getting killed. Surely, Nori would be next, and then Layne Giles would go on living his life.

I couldn't let that happen.

So, I would call 911 moments before I entered the house.

If Layne was going to take me down, he was going with me.

THE VIDEO TAPE

As soon as I settled on the plan, I hated it.

So many things could go wrong.

But at least I'd be the one going after Nori.

If I included the LAPD, and Layne executed Nori because of it, I could never live with myself.

❦

Before I knew it, eight p.m. had passed, and the sun was beginning to set.

Was it going to be the last sunset of my life?

It was a distinct possibility.

❦ 63 ❦

BOBBY

Noble called at both nine-thirty and ten.

I continued to tell him I needed more time.

I once again lied by omission, and I could tell he knew. But what exactly could he do? He didn't know where to send the cops. I was in Hollywood and headed to Sylmar in the early morning hours. As Frank Sinatra sang, *In the Wee Small Hours of the Morning.*

❦

I TOOK A NAP FROM TEN-THIRTY TO MIDNIGHT.

I had started to tire, and those ninety minutes did a lot for me.

I woke up focused and ready for what was to come.

I looked at the gun Noble had given me.

If it became necessary, I'd gladly shoot Layne Giles as many times as it took.

If I was right, he'd killed Emma Lynn Sutton, Darian Hague, his own mother, and who knew how many more?

Not to mention, he was holding Nori captive.

He deserved anything he got.

Then again, I could be walking into a trap and be the one pumped full of lead.

THE VIDEO TAPE

At two a.m., I went back on Zillow and Google Earth and did one last reconnaissance of 1057 Hawkins.

I knew where to park and how to get to the back door without being seen by the cameras.

I also knew that despite my last-minute preparation, I was wholly unprepared.

Three quick online fact-finding missions hardly prepared me to storm a house.

But at this point, I was pot-committed.

If there was one thing I believed, it was that Layne Giles would kill Nori if he saw anyone but me.

I continued to believe that was true.

And it was what I predicated all my decisions on.

At two-thirty, I walked to the parking lot, got in my car, and headed north toward Sylmar.

The drive could take over an hour in daytime Los Angeles traffic, but it was only eighteen miles, and it would be quick this early in the morning.

I arrived in Sylmar a few minutes before three. I drove slowly, going over every contingency for a third and fourth time.

I parked on the ridge above 1057 Hawkins.

The beginning of the San Gabriel Mountains prevented anyone in the house from seeing where I'd parked. As I got closer, that would change, but I hadn't been detected at this point.

I left my keys in the car. I didn't want to take a chance of them jangling and making noise. I also left my wallet.

The two things I took were Noble's gun and my cell phone. I made sure to silence all notifications on the phone.

I took a few deep breaths.

And then I set off for 1057 Hawkins.

I HAD THE ADVANTAGE OF BEING IN A RURAL AREA BECAUSE THERE WAS less lighting.

I was wearing all dark clothes, and there were very few lampposts. As I slowly descended the hill toward Hawkins Street, I would be tough to see.

I walked slowly.

When I was about two hundred yards from the home, I got off the sidewalk. There was only one more streetlamp between me and the house, and it was on the sidewalk, which made my decision easy.

I started walking through the shrubbery adjacent to the sidewalk.

When I got within a hundred yards, I got my first good look at the back of the house. I didn't notice any cameras, but it was dark and I couldn't be sure.

I walked closer.

I was now about half a football field away.

I had my gun at my side. I wasn't exactly an expert marksman, but I wasn't an amateur either.

If at any point, Layne Giles appeared in front of me, I'd start shooting immediately.

I don't always believe in "Shoot first, ask questions later," but I certainly did in that moment.

Every step I took was a delicate one. I couldn't risk being heard. Or seen.

There was still no light or movement from inside the house.

Maybe, just maybe, Layne was asleep.

I inched closer. I was now heading down through the shrubbery to the house's backyard.

My heart was beating like a hummingbird.

How had I ever ended up here?

A MINUTE LATER, I WAS WITHIN FIFTY FEET OF THE HOUSE.

I'd traversed the small hill and was now on even ground with the house.

There was still no sign of movement or light coming from inside.

If I were going to call 911, now was the time.

But if I did, they'd show up in the front of the house, lights blazing.

Layne would see them, and he would kill Nori.

I was sure he could see what was happening in front of his home, via the cameras.

THE VIDEO TAPE

I just hoped he couldn't see the back.

I decided to make one concession.

In case I were killed, I had to leave some path back to me.

So, I typed a brief text to Noble.

1057 Hawkins Street in Sylmar.

And pressed send.

But it didn't go through.

Fuck.

This was a rural street, but it was still Los Angeles. They would have had Wi-Fi.

Unless Layne Giles had installed something to disable it.

For the first time, I realized how overmatched I was.

285

64

LAYNE

My plan was working to perfection.

I was looking at my laptop from a room that was not visible from the back of the house. I'd seen Bobby from the first moment he started heading down the hill toward me.

The cameras in the front of the house were visible to all, while the ones in the back were hidden.

Bobby didn't know.

I got a good laugh as he slowly headed toward me, dressed in all dark clothes, thinking he was somehow gaining the upper hand.

What a loser.

BUT THAT'S NOT EXACTLY FAIR, IS IT?

Bobby finding this house is a miracle in itself. Yet somehow, I knew he would.

That told me all I needed to know about his investigative skills.

They were top-notch.

Twenty LAPD detectives had handled this case, and none of them had come half as close as Bobby now was.

That didn't mean I wasn't going to love killing him.

THE VIDEO TAPE

I'm just saying, he deserved a little credit.

"Bobby McGowan. He would have made a great detective."

They could add that to his tombstone.

Hahaha.

⚜

AFTER I DISPOSED OF BOBBY, I'D SPEND SOME TIME WITH NORI BEFORE finishing her off as well.

Maybe we'd have a little fun first. I hadn't had the opportunity yet.

I wasn't naïve enough to think that would be the end.

Although Bobby didn't seem to have notified the police, signs would still be pointing back to me.

I wasn't immune to that fact.

I had a flight booked to Europe later that night.

But I wouldn't be on it.

Instead, I would be on a flight to Argentina under the name of Larry Gilden. Using an alias I'd used in the past wasn't ideal, but it was my only choice.

While working for Hank Jewel, I realized a few crimes might be in my future, so I secured a driver's license and a passport for Larry Gilden. This was a lot easier in the nineties, and once you got in their system, it's kind of like you were a real person. It became easy to keep up the charade.

And whenever I had to renew either, the face was always a spot-on match.

As for securing a credit card, that shit couldn't have been easier.

So, while I don't know what the future holds, I have a decent chance of getting lost in South America.

Especially if Bobby McGowan never told the cops.

One thing was for certain.

I'd be outliving Bobby and his precious Nori.

⚜

I LOOKED BACK AT MY LAPTOP AND SAW BOBBY APPROACHING THE BACK door.

Which I'd conveniently left unlocked.

I grabbed my gun.

It was go time.

65

BOBBY

The back door was unlocked.

I didn't take it as a good sign. This was too easy.

I said a quick prayer and stepped into the house.

I didn't dare move for a few seconds, giving my eyes time to adjust.

The gun was in my right hand and pointed directly in front of me.

There was a small kitchen to the right, and what looked to be a long hallway to the left.

And right there in the middle of the house, there it was: the enclosed atrium.

A little light in the atrium was coming from the sky above. There must have been a small glass ceiling above the atrium.

I gave my eyes a few more seconds to adjust and then saw what I'd already seen on Layne's phone.

Nori was in the center of the atrium, fastened to a long, narrow bed. Her mouth was duct-taped, her body was zip-tied, and the knives dangled precariously above her head.

She looked alive, although her eyes weren't directly facing mine.

The kitchen gave me a good view of everything in front of me. Considering this was Layne's house and I barely knew the layout, I had about the best position I was going to get.

I crouched behind the kitchen table, my gun extended in front of me.

At some point, I had to get to the atrium, and that's when I'd be most vulnerable.

But I was okay with where I was for now.

I wanted to yell to Nori and ask her if Layne was in the house.

Maybe she could give me a slight nod, despite being harnessed in.

But in case Layne was here, I couldn't risk alerting him.

I didn't know what to do. It was like a standoff; only I didn't know where my opposition was.

66

LAYNE

Everything continued to go as planned.
 I assumed Bobby would stay in that corner for at least a while.
It was smart. He was partially hidden and could still see the atrium.
There would be no need to move.
But at some point, he would make his way toward Nori.
And that's when I'd take advantage of my position and start shooting.
So, I sat and bided my time, knowing the end was near for Bobby McGowan.

But then I was thrown a curveball.

67

BOBBY

I continued to take in my surroundings.

My eyes had adapted and were seeing okay, considering the limited light.

I spent time getting a read on the room, looking at what angles would have a good shot at me if I made my way to the atrium.

I still couldn't tell if Nori had seen me.

I doubted it.

Her head was zip-tied against the bench, and her eyes could not look in my direction. Maybe she noticed something in her peripheral vision, but I doubt it. The room was dark, as was my clothing.

I kept going over my options.

The safest position was my current one.

I felt like Layne Giles would want me to move.

So, I stayed put.

And that's when I heard him.

Layne had somehow arrived at the back of the house without me knowing. He was entering through the back door I'd come through. I swiveled my gun in his direction and was about to pull the trigger.

And then I abruptly stopped myself.

It was Noble.

What the fuck? How the hell had he ended up here?

He inched toward me and put a finger to his mouth.

Noble had no idea how close I'd been to shooting him.

He stood next to me, also wearing all dark clothes, and waited a few seconds for his eyes to adjust.

At least, that's what I thought he was doing.

He leaned in close to my ear and whispered the following. "Do exactly as I say. I called the cops. They will probably be here in about three to five minutes. I'm going to the atrium, and you provide cover. Hopefully, I can dismantle the knives above Nori. If Layne approaches the atrium, yell what side he is approaching from. Just yell left or right. Got it?"

At any other time, I'd have probably told Noble off. Told him he had some balls calling the cops and putting Nori's life at risk.

Instead, I just whispered, "Got it."

Less than twenty seconds later, Noble made his way toward the atrium.

68

LAYNE

I should have killed Nori when I saw Noble Dunn approaching my house.

Bobby hadn't lived up to his end of the bargain.

I would have been well within my rights.

But I liked the fact that the stakes had been raised.

Noble added a wrinkle, but that's it.

I was still going to win.

I knew the house. They didn't.

Nori was still going to die as well.

And I would make sure Bobby was front and center to see it.

My plans had changed.

Kill Noble. Then incapacitate Bobby. Then make him watch what I did to Nori.

I smiled.

That was a good plan.

❧ 69 ❧

BOBBY

Noble had his hand on the atrium door.

I still had not seen or heard anything.

Maybe Layne wasn't in the house, and maybe he wasn't currently watching the live feed of Nori.

It was past three a.m. It wasn't impossible.

I watched Noble turn the doorknob to enter the atrium.

He stepped into the atrium and didn't shut the door behind him.

❦

AND THAT'S WHEN THE HOUSE ERUPTED IN GUNFIRE.

It sounded like it was coming from behind the atrium.

I looked over, and I could no longer see Noble.

There was some wood paneling at the bottom of the atrium, so I wouldn't have seen him if he'd dropped to the floor. That's undoubtedly what had happened.

"Noble," I screamed. "Are you hit?"

Before a response could come, a voice came over some sort of loud-speaker.

It was Layne.

"Oh, Bobby. I thought I'd told you not to involve the cops. Even retired, washed-up cops. I was all ready to have a little mano-a-mano battle between you and me. And if you won, Nori would have been yours to take home. But you cheated and told Noble about our little contest. So, I had to cheat a little, too. Here's the deal. If you are not in the atrium within one minute, I will drop the knives on Nori. Maybe she'll get lucky and just end up being scarred like Noble. But that's doubtful. You see, these knives are sharp as fuck and being dropped from almost ten feet. They are probably going to take out an eye or two. Probably kill the damn bitch."

Although it was nearly impossible, I tried to remain as calm as possible. I wanted to run in the direction of the voice, firing my gun and hoping I hit Layne before he hit me. But that was emotion talking. It wasn't a strategy. So, I had to remain calm despite his incendiary words.

"One minute, Bobby. And then I unleash the knives. Starting now."

I didn't move for a few seconds, trying to come up with something. Anything.

I rose from behind the kitchen table and saw Noble lying on the floor to the right of the atrium. I couldn't tell how hurt he was, but his gun was lying ten feet from him. That wasn't a good sign.

I looked at the wall and saw that all the bullet holes were from the far wall. There was a room behind the atrium, and Layne had fired from there.

Was he still there?

I didn't know, but it was worth the chance.

I took about ten steps toward the atrium and then fired two shots into that wall. When no shots were returned, I quickly ran and entered the atrium.

I made my way to the right side, away from the wall I'd fired on.

I didn't hear a scream, a fall, or anything suggesting I'd hit Layne.

The loudspeaker came back on.

"Oh, you were so close, Bobby. That was good thinking, though."

The sound came from speakers throughout the house, and I couldn't locate where the voice originated.

I looked down at Nori, whose eyes were wide open. She was scared to death.

I looked down at Noble, who was staring up at me. There was blood on the floor next to him, and it looked like he'd taken a few shots. Definitely one through his shoulder. That wound was visible and looked brutal.

But he was alive.

BRIAN O'SULLIVAN

I had to keep Layne talking. Maybe I'd hear his voice before I heard the loudspeaker—and then shoot in that direction.

"I'm here, Layne. Where are you?"

"Closer than you might imagine," he said and laughed.

I was ready to fire at the first sign of him.

"Give me a hint," I yelled.

"Nice try. I've kept you in this game long enough, starting with that letter on your apartment door. You'd be nowhere without me. But truthfully, how did you find this place? That's some impressive stuff, Bobby."

I continued to only hear the loudspeaker and not the voice itself.

Just give me a chance, Layne.

Give me the slightest hint as to your location.

70

LAYNE

I was dreaming of Argentina.
No, this wasn't over, but it was about to be.
Noble had been neutralized, and Nori wasn't going anywhere.
They were the No Nos.
The first two letters of their names and the amount of help they were supplying Bobby.
I crack myself up.

ONE THING YOU CAN'T CHANGE IS INNATE TRAITS.
They are what they are.
For example, you will turn to your right if someone yells from your right.
You will look to your left if a loud explosion comes from your left.
That's why they are innate.
You have no choice in the matter.
And I was about to use that to my advantage.

I'D TURNED OFF MY MICROPHONE AND RETURNED TO THE ROOM BEHIND the atrium.

I was ten feet from Bobby. I probably could have shot and hit him, but I couldn't be sure where he was standing.

So, it was time to rely on his innate traits.

I readied myself.

It was go time.

I took the microphone and threw it in the air, toward the right side of the atrium.

At the same time, I quickly darted toward the left side.

I arrived a split second later, and sure enough, Bobby had taken the bait. He was looking in the direction of the microphone.

"Bobby," I yelled.

I wanted him to see my face before I killed him.

And I did.

He'd swiveled completely around, and our eyes caught each other's.

The last thing he saw was going to be me.

I quickly put three in his chest.

Well, technically, two in his chest, and one in his shoulder.

But it didn't really matter.

What mattered was that Bobby McGowan was dead, and I'd won.

I looked down just to make sure, and sure enough, Bobby was already bug-eyed.

He must have been dead before he hit the floor.

I looked over at Noble, who was still alive, but his weapon had ended up several feet from him.

I was bummed that Bobby wasn't going to get to see me kill Nori, but besides that, I'd accomplished what I'd wanted.

Bobby McGowan was dead.

71

BOBBY

When Noble had given me the gun earlier that day, he'd thrown something else onto the passenger seat of my car.

A bulletproof vest.

I knew I was up against it and could use any advantage possible.

It was cumbersome, and I wouldn't want to be a cop and wear it daily, but it might just save my damn life. So before I left the Hollywood Stars hotel, I put the vest on.

When I saw the microphone in the air, my eyes instinctively turned toward it.

It wasn't even my choice. It's just how my body and mind reacted.

But what I did next was all me.

As I saw the microphone flying, I knew Layne was trying to set me up, and he was going the other way, so I swirled around to face him.

I heard him yell, "Bobby," but I didn't have time to get a shot off. I just had to make sure I got my chest to face him.

Which I did.

I took two in the center of the chest and one in the shoulder.

The pain was indescribable, but I didn't scream out.

BRIAN O'SULLIVAN

I wanted him to think I was dead, before he got any ideas of a headshot.

So, I tried my damndest to make my eyes look like they were popping out of my head.

❦

THE THING ABOUT BULLETPROOF VESTS IS THAT WHEN YOU GET SHOT, they still knock the air out of you.

I realized that as I fell to the floor.

While Layne seemed to believe I was dead, my hand-eye coordination wasn't back to normal yet. It took me a few seconds.

Layne glanced in Noble's direction. I had to act now, or he was going to kill him.

The gun was lying next to my right hand. Layne was looking at Noble and couldn't see me as I gripped the gun.

As his eyes moved from Noble back to me, in one quick motion, I swiveled the gun toward Layne and fired two bullets into his chest.

He fell backward, and his gun went flying.

300

72

LAYNE

As I was looking down at Noble, something moved in my peripheral vision.

It was Bobby's eyes. They were no longer bug-eyed.

I turned in his direction with my gun drawn, but the motherfucker beat me to it and fired two bullets into my chest.

I fell backward, and my gun went airborne.

I landed with a thud, and even though it had only been a few seconds, I found breathing difficult. And I couldn't move.

There would be no reaching into my pocket and activating the knives above Nori.

As I looked up, Bobby McGowan walked over and stood above me.

My breathing had become even more labored, and I knew I was going to die.

I got one last thought in.

How the fuck had Bobby McGowan got the best of me?

And then I died.

73

BOBBY

I was in terrible pain from the gunshot to my shoulder.

And despite wearing the vest, my chest was no picnic either.

But nothing would prevent me from standing up and staring down at the monster below me.

I got up and did exactly that.

Do you know much about baseball?

Well, if a pitcher is in the middle of a perfect game, none of his teammates will talk to him. They don't want to jinx it.

That's how I felt in the moment.

I'm sure I could have said something smarmy, celebrating my victory and Layne's impending death.

But I said nothing.

Looking down at him and watching him die was my version of a perfect game.

An interruption would have spoiled it.

So, I stayed silent and watched him die.

Which he did seconds later.

THE VIDEO TAPE

※

I saw that Layne had a knife in his belt buckle.

I removed it.

He's not going to need it, I said to myself.

※

I walked over to Nori.

"I'm going to get you off of this," I said.

Tears were flowing down her face.

I looked up at the knives, which appeared stable. If for some reason, they started to fall, I'd throw myself on Nori. It would cause some nasty damage to my back, but I didn't think it would kill me.

If they landed on her face, that was a different story.

"Are you okay, Noble?"

"No, but I'll live."

I used the knife to cut the zip ties.

After I cut the last one, she got up and hugged me.

"I've got three bullet wounds and you guys are getting all lovey-dovey," Noble said.

It was obviously not the time, but we couldn't stop ourselves.

We all laughed—even Noble.

And that's when I heard the sirens.

74

BOBBY

All three of us were taken to the hospital.

Nori didn't have anything physically wrong with her—Thank God!—but they wanted to keep her for observation. I wouldn't blame her if she stayed for several days. She'd undergone a harrowing experience.

Noble had been struck three times. Once on the left flank, and twice in the left shoulder. If you're looking for a silver lining, it's better to be shot in the same place twice.

I'd been shot once, in the right shoulder. Well, technically, I'd been shot three times, but the hospital didn't count the two in my bulletproof vest.

Noble's "gift" had saved my life. There was no doubt about that.

That first day in the hospital was a long one.

We were submitted at four a.m., so it was a twenty-hour "shift."

MY FATHER ARRIVED BY NOON.

I loved him to death, but wasn't happy to see him.

Although, to his credit, he took it better than I thought he would.

THE VIDEO TAPE

Once the nurse told him that I'd be as good as new within a few months, I saw the blood return to his face.

She told him that I'd recover quicker if I got my rest. It was her way of telling him to hit the waiting room.

Which he begrudgingly did.

❧

I WAS IN AND OUT OF SLEEP MOST OF THAT FIRST DAY.

Near the end of the night, I heard some raised voices a few rooms down.

I thought I heard someone say, "We're taking you back to Missouri. No, not tomorrow. Like now."

But I was on some strong painkillers, so I couldn't be sure.

❧

I WOKE UP THE NEXT MORNING, AND A SURPRISE VISITOR WAS AT MY bedside.

Ernest's daughter, Lily.

"I've got some bad news," she said.

"Oh no."

"Ernest died last night."

"I'm so sorry."

"Don't be. He'd lived a long life and seemed almost happy to go. But I did have a question for you?"

"What is that?"

"What did you tell him when you guys had that time alone?"

"Uh, I don't remember. I'm on some powerful painkillers."

That was going to be my excuse for everything going forward.

Lily smiled. "I don't buy that for one second. Do you want to know what I think?"

"I have a feeling you'll tell me, anyway."

"I think you told my father that Layne Giles was the killer and that he was going to be arrested."

"Hmmm. That doesn't ring a bell."

Lily laughed. "Don't play coy with me."

"What did Ernest say?"

"He said stuff like 'Bobby came through' and 'I never liked Layne Giles.' Then again, my father was on some powerful meds as well."

305

BRIAN O'SULLIVAN

"That was probably it."

"And when I discovered that Layne had met his end, I told my father. Do you want to know what he said?"

"What?"

"I'm glad I outlived that fucker."

"I always knew I liked your dad."

Lily patted me on my good shoulder. "Get better, Bobby. Thanks for all you did for my father."

"He was a great guy. I'll miss him."

"Thank you. That means a lot."

⚜

AFTER LILY LEFT, I ASKED THE NURSE IF I COULD GO FOR A WALK.

"Sure. Just be careful on your feet. Those painkillers can throw off your balance a bit."

I was only five feet from my hospital room when I saw Noble approaching in a wheelchair. His left shoulder and flank were bandaged up, and he was using his left hand to navigate the wheelchair.

"I asked to walk, but they insisted I use this. What makes you so special?"

"I only got shot once. You got the trifecta."

Noble laughed. "Technically, you got shot three times as well."

"Yeah, about that. You saved my life, Noble. That vest stopped two bullets destined for my chest. I can never repay you, but I wanted to say thanks."

He shooed me away, like I was a fly. "Don't mention it. You saved your own life."

"There's one thing I haven't been able to figure out."

"What's that?"

"How did you know to go to the house in Sylmar?"

"Do you remember when I gave you the gun and the vest?"

"Of course."

"Do you know what I did next?"

I thought about it.

"You slapped the top of my car."

"I did. And when I did that, I attached a little GPS monitor to your roof."

I smiled. "You're good, Noble."

306

THE VIDEO TAPE

Noble wasn't good at accepting praise, so he changed the subject as usual.

"I'm sorry about Nori," he said.

For a moment, I feared the worst.

"What happened?"

"Nothing like that. Her mother came and checked her out. They left in the middle of the night."

I didn't know how to feel about it.

The most important thing was that she had lived through her ordeal. That mattered more than where she was going to live. I'm not even sure we would continue as a couple with all we'd been through.

I had a lot of feelings to work through with Nori, and I'd need more time.

"Part of me thought I heard that," I said. "But I assumed it was the drugs talking. How did you hear it so well?"

"Because I was in the room next to her. In fact, I was in the room between you two. It was a reverse Oreo."

I started laughing too hard, and a brutal pain shot through my shoulder.

"Fuck," I yelled too loud and saw a nurse look in our direction.

"Should I slow down with the jokes?" Noble asked.

"Yeah, not the ideal time."

"Are you getting out today?"

"I'm not sure."

"Today or tomorrow, probably. I'm sure they'll keep me a day or two longer."

"Once again, thanks, Noble."

"Shut up, or I'm going to start cracking jokes."

I almost laughed again, but was able to stop myself. "When we get out of here, I'm buying the first round."

"Now that's something I can get behind."

A nurse came walking toward us.

"Noble, I said two minutes. You've been out here for like ten minutes."

"Gotta go," he said.

I smiled as he wheeled himself away.

307

75

BOBBY
THREE MONTHS LATER

I can't believe it's been three months since that crazy night in Sylmar.

That's what Noble has resorted to calling it.

That Crazy Night In Sylmar.

He says it would make a good pop song and that the words blend perfectly.

We always laugh, but that's probably just to prevent us from talking about what actually happened.

But hey, nobody died—well, nobody worth talking about—so all is well that ends well.

I see Noble every few weeks, and he keeps pushing me to take a new case.

I'm sure I will eventually, but I've earned my current R & R.

***

Detective Heald arrived at the hospital on that second day.

I remember asking him if Sylmar was now in his jurisdiction. He took it pretty well.

I told him all I knew, which was pretty much everything.

THE VIDEO TAPE

I'm sure I'd learn a few small things when the LAPD finalized their investigation, but I was okay with not knowing every minute detail.

Plus, I didn't feel like hearing the name Layne Giles for a while.

⚜

I FINALLY MANAGED TO GET RID OF MY FATHER A FEW DAYS AFTER BEING released from the hospital.

I love the old man, but it was becoming counter-productive, so I politely told him to get his old ass back up to Santa Barbara.

Not in those exact words, but pretty close.

I head back to Santa Barbara every few weeks, and we always have a great dinner with a few glasses of wine.

I hope he meets a woman sometime soon. No one will ever replace my mother, but I would love him to have some companionship.

There was a chance Darian might have been that woman. I guess we'll never know.

⚜

SINCE MY RELEASE FROM THE HOSPITAL, I'D TALKED TO DARIAN'S daughter, Mira, Manny's daughter, Teresa, and Ernest's daughter, Lily, a few times each.

Mira and Lily are especially thankful for what I accomplished.

Lily has even forgiven me for lying to her father on his deathbed.

I still stand by that decision.

⚜

AS FOR THE BIG QUESTION, NO, I HAVEN'T TALKED TO NORI VERY often.

She sent me a text a few weeks after I got out of the hospital, thanking me for saving her life. She said she was content in Missouri and had no plans to return to Los Angeles.

It seemed very sincere, and I appreciated her reaching out.

I responded and said she didn't owe me a thanks. I'd brought her into this whole mess, and I was just happy she made it back to Missouri and seemed to be doing well.

I doubted we'd ever see each other again.

But I didn't blame Nori.

309

Everyone copes in their own way, and maybe keeping up a friendship with me wouldn't have allowed her to heal.

That would be a perfectly understandable explanation.

I was just glad she was alive and happy.

⁂

TODAY IS THURSDAY, OCTOBER 2ND, AND I'M SITTING AT AN OUTDOOR coffee shop on Wilshire Boulevard in Santa Monica.

I'm drinking an Americano and looking at stupid TikTok videos.

I know what you're thinking: I'm too old to use that app.

I don't know. Is thirty-four too old for TikTok?

I'd have to ask someone a little bit younger than me.

A pretty woman was sitting at the table next to me. We'd smiled at each other a few times, and I'm not sure why I hadn't introduced myself yet.

I didn't have an excuse anymore.

I now had an ice-breaker.

"Excuse me," I said. "Can I ask you a question?"

She turned her body to face mine. I took that as a good sign.

"Of course."

"Is thirty-four too old to be surfing TikTok?"

She smiled playfully. "First off, you don't surf TikTok. So that makes you sound old right there."

"Ouch." I gave her my best smile. "Sure am glad I asked you."

"As for the age limit on TikTok, it has to extend to at least past thirty."

"And why is that?"

"Because I turn thirty in a week and have no plans to stop going on TikTok."

"To stop surfing TikTok, you mean?"

She laughed quite loudly. "Yes. Thanks for reminding me."

"Would you like to join my table?"

"Sure. Why not," she said.

"Great."

She grabbed her laptop, set it on my table, and sat beside me.

"I'm Bobby, by the way."

"Nice to meet you. I'm Olive."

ALSO BY BRIAN O'SULLIVAN

Thank you so much for reading **THE VIDEO TAPE**!

I'd be honored if you left a review on Amazon/Goodreads, posted on Facebook, told a friend, nominated it for a book club, or anything else to help get the word out :)

I appreciate it very much!

If you are not caught up on the QUINT series, now is the time. Here's a link to all 8 novels: **QUINT SERIES.**

And here's my three standalone novels: **THE MASTERMIND, THE BARTENDER,** and **DEBUT NOVEL**.

Finally, from the bottom of my heart, I just wanted to say thanks to each and every one of you.

You make this all possible!

You're the best.

Sincerely,

Brian O'Sullivan

Printed in Dunstable, United Kingdom